ISBN: 978-1-943932-38-2

Cover Design by Chase Sanders

For Jocelyn, as she writes her first page.

THE TERROR AT
TURTLESHELL MOUNTAIN

1947

Chuck,

Enclosed, please find the latest edit of Falcon Falls. You'll note I neglected to fill in the little number marking what version this is. That, my good friend, is because maybe you know how many rounds of revisions you've asked for, but I'll be fucked if I can even make a guess.

Whatever the number is, I hope it's finally to your liking, you foghorn bastard. I can't speak for the Mexicans doing the backgrounds, but I'm waking up with feathers in my hair and it's not because I've been getting into pillow fights with Marilyn Monroe.

The picture aside, there's something to do with the park that I want to run by you. I know, I know, the theme park is your baby. But I've got an idea and I think it's a good one, so open up those barn doors you call ears and listen up.

In the park, okay? You're already going to have fruitcakes dressed up like the princes and some gams and cans stuffed into the princess dresses and that's great. No question that the kids will love it. <u>BUT</u>, your real attraction was, is, and always will be T. Turtle and the rest of them. If you really want to make money, I'm talking General Motors money, you need to sew up some Turtle, Fox, and Badger costumes and have the whole gang out there on the "streets" shaking hands and kissing babies.

I already know what you're going to say

won't work. The faces. Hand to God, right now I can picture you sitting at that big mahogany desk, shaking your head and thinking that there's no way to make cartoon faces work off of paper and in the real world.

To which I say, Jesus Christ, Chuck; since when has your audience ever been a hard sell?

They're going to want to believe. Do you get that? You're selling Santa at Christmas all year round. You get some paper-mache heads together, you literally paste the smiles on their goddamn faces, and I can guarantee that nobody is going to be complaining that their lips aren't moving. You do this and you're going to have parents with tears in their eyes saying, "Thank you, Mr. Tuttle. Thank you for bringing Timmy Turtle alive for my babies!" And then they're going to pay you five bucks for the privilege of doing it all over again.

Anyway, that's my two cents for the price of... free because we both know that the real reason you hate the Jews is because they stole all of your accounting tricks.

Get back to me on that cartoon soon, all right? I mean it, I'm starting to feel hungry when I look at bird feeders. I want this thing off my plate.

Forever Stealing Your Booze,

Mickey.

P.S.

I tipped the messenger boyo a quarter and told him to wait while you read this. I feel like a Ford man trying to pick out a Chevy, but I know you're not opposed to the occasional piece of fruitcake yourself and word is he'll occasionally put himself on the menu if the buyer's right.

P.P.S.

That's assuming you don't have any cupcake left in the fridge. Don't pretend you don't know what I'm talking about. Offered any "private tours" lately, Chuck? Don't choke, I'm not putting anything incriminating down for the record. I'm just saying that it's stuff like this that guarantees that I will never, EVER set foot in that park of yours.

The front page of that morning's Daily News is clipped to the back of the note. Beneath the ad for fast-acting-foot-itch relief, a young boy smiles up from what must be a communion photo. The boy's standing on the church lawn with a statue of Jesus looming paternally over one shoulder. His suit jacket is a little wide around the shoulders and the pants are baggy around the waist. Perhaps a hand

8

me down from an older brother. The boy's smiling at the camera, but the corners of his mouth don't quite go all the way up. Anyone who'd ever been in a similar situation could hear the boy's father as easily as if he were quoted right there in black and white- *"Do what your mother says and smile for the picture."*

Beneath this photo, there is only a single word. There's a longer story inside the paper, but that one word says the only thing that really matters:

MISSING.

1

1987

It was a mistake for Mary to come to Turtleshell Mountain all by herself.

She knew it before she even got on the plane to California, but she'd done her best to convince herself otherwise. *You love Turtleshell Mountain,* she told herself. *And you already paid for the tickets and took the vacation time. Fuck Mike, this is a perfect chance to prove to yourself that you never needed him in the first place. Go without him. Have a good time.*

For a brief moment, she thought that maybe she could. When Mary first walked through the park gates, she felt the rush of relief that came with taking a big gamble and seeing the ace come up on the river. *The Toybox Tango,* one of her all-time favorite Turtleshell songs, was playing on the speaker system and Timmy Turtle and his friends were right in the middle of Good Day To You Square, as if they were all just waiting to welcome her to the rest of her life.

Mary felt positively giddy in those first moments. Her heart beat faster. *Good* faster. As if it had been struggling to pump through channels clogged by pain and loss but one whiff of Turtleshell Mountain air had cleared all of that up, and now everything was running smooth and free.

She looked at the children all around her. They were running. Running towards Tommy Turtle and Felix Fox and a dozen others. They were laughing as they ran, laughing and screaming joyfully. Very little was spoken, but Mary heard the invitation all the same.

Run with us Mary. Your happiness is waiting right here for you to come and collect it. Run to it. Run and be happy.

Mary ran. She was thirty. She smoked. She was starting to get a little heavy. But she ran as fleetly as the nine year old that she'd once been. She bought a turtle shell hat, round and green and glistening in the warm sunlight. She jammed it on her head, not caring at all what it did to her perm. Then she treated herself to a giant turkey leg and a churro and set out to have a week full of so many perfect, wonderful memories that there wouldn't be any room left in her brain or her heart to remember Mike or any of the shit he pulled.

And she tried. Honestly, she did.

The problem was that a whole turkey leg and a churro were really too much for one person to eat all on her own. And though the Timmy Turtle costumeers would just as happily pose with a single adult as they would with a child (the giant smiles were literally sewn onto their faces), it was impossible not to notice the silent judgment in the photographer's eyes every time you posed with a bunch of children's characters all by yourself.

Worst of all was the single rider line. At first glance, it seemed like another boon: going solo meant more rides in less time. Except what it really meant was you had no one to hold hands with as the gondola cruised through the canals of the Whole Wide World ride. It meant cresting the first big hill of the Coney Island Coaster and having no one to share a final, excited glance with before the inevitable plunge.

It meant having to see the word "single" staring you in the face all day long no matter what you were doing.

By three o'clock, Mary's will to seize the day had been broken. She took off her turtle shell hat and slouched off towards the shuttle back to the hotel. *Maybe tomorrow you'll have better luck in one of the other sections of the park*, she consoled herself.

It was only by chance that Mary's dejected shuffle towards the exit took her past the Falcon Falls log flume. Mary looked up at the towering waterfall just in time to see a log full of people rocket down. Their happy screams easily reached her ears even though Mary was a hundred feet away.

The sight of her favorite ride, based off of her favorite film, rekindled a small spark of hope in her chest. *Really, it's not like it's out of my way,* she thought. And three o'clock was too late for lunch and too early for dinner. One more ride would break up the afternoon perfectly.

Those were the rational, valid reasons that her thirty-year-old mind came up with to justify staying at the park just a little bit longer.

The truthful, honest reason she wanted to stay was that Mary still believed that somewhere in this sprawling, thirty-thousand-acre resort there was a pinch of Turtle Magic reserved just for her.

Mary was far too old to believe in such narratives but, as she got onto the single rider line one more time, she couldn't help but draw the parallels between her tale of woe and the beginning of countless Turtleshell Pictures' films she'd treated as gospel throughout her childhood:

First, the beautiful girl in sour spirits. But then, inevitably, The Chance Meeting That Changed Everything. Maybe she was recruited by talking squirrels trying to save their home from logging companies, or maybe she was the less glamorous but more intelligent younger princess desperate to prove herself. However it began, the results were always the same: the handsome stranger, and then adventure, laughter, romance, and, of course, the Happy Ending.

All you had to do was believe just a little bit longer.

As the single rider line moved through the cavernous interior of Falcon Falls at its faster clip, Mary kept a closer eye on the regular line without really admitting to herself that she was doing it. She counted groups of threes and fives in hopes of seeing an odd man out with broad shoulders and deep, soulful eyes. Instead, she saw husbands with their wives and an odd number of children in tow. Or teenagers in groups of more boys fighting for the attention of fewer girls. There was the occasional flock of just men, but they were always wearing the rainbow t-shirts which told Mary not to even bother.

By the time she reached the dock where the four-person logs loaded, Mary was remembering once again that she did not live in a Turtleshell Pictures' film. She lived in shitty, shitty reality and staying for one more ride wasn't going to do anything to change that.

Then, the ride attendant held up two fingers. "We need two single riders here!"

Sudden hope soared through Mary again. Of course, the one plot twist she hadn't considered! She whirled around, ready to meet her Prince Charming.

Her Prince Charming was short. He was pudgy. He was balding. He wore glasses. He was smiling up at Mary as if he'd been harboring the exact same fantasy that she had.

Reality didn't just suck. It was actively malevolent.

A young couple wearing "Just Married" stickers took the front two seats in the log. His Turtleshell hat had a bowtie and groomsmen tails. Hers was white with a wedding veil behind it.

Mary wished syphilis on her and erectile dysfunction on him and didn't care how contradictory that was. She took the back row along with the prematurely balding little man who, as it turned out, also reeked of awful B.O.

The ride started with a small jerk. The couple in front laughed excitedly. In the back, her benchmate let out a small whoop. "Here we go," he muttered in a low, breathy voice that made Mary feel dirty. *Please don't talk to me,* she thought and pretended not to hear him.

Regardless, the feel of that voice lingered in her mind and called up unpleasant connotations as the phallic log slipped into the dark tunnel of the ride.

Falcon Falls was not just a log flume. That, Mary could have endured. One minute up, thirty screaming seconds down, then everyone goes their separate ways. But no, like most rides at Turtleshell Mountain, Falcon Falls came with a prelude. Before the drop, there was a ten-minute floating tour of animatronic displays recreating the animated tale of Fergus, a young falcon that leaves the nest before he's ready to fly, and the life lessons he learns as he tries to make his way home. The high-tech animatronics whirled and moved in display coves notched into the walls bordering the river. All the big scenes were there: Mama Falcon brandishing a dish rag at her rambunctious hatchlings; the smooth-talking crow, encouraging young Fergus to fly late one night when nobody else was looking.

The newlyweds loved it the way people who are young and in love seem to enjoy anything so long as they're doing it together. Mary was too busy avoiding her neighbor's greasy elbow to enjoy most of it.

...Except, that wasn't really fair. Truthfully, the man was fitting comfortably on his side of the log. He also must have taken off his glasses at some point, revealing eyes that were actually quite bright even in the gloom of the ride. *And he's taller than I thought. Was the floor higher where I was standing?*

He caught her looking. Mary quickly shifted her eyes as if she were only looking at the diorama behind him but she noticed him smile from the corner of her eye. It was a nice smile.

Just remember, the lights were brighter where you first saw him.

Very true, but there was still no reasoning with the warm twinge that loosened her stomach muscles at the brief glimpse of that crooked smile.

The next diorama coming up was the young falcon running from the giant tarantula slave trader. The spider had a leash of webbing dangling from one leg. The shackle swung back and forth as the mechanical spider's arm jerked up and down and the neatly hidden speaker broadcast huffing sounds and the tarantula's angry bellowing:

"YOOUUUUU COME BACK HERE!"

This was the climax of the movie and the ride. The scene where Fergus would throw himself from the cliff and discover the power to fly had been within him all along. On the ride, this same swooping exhilaration was replicated by the dizzying drop of the log flume.

But first, there was a stretch where the log floated in pure darkness, a final moment's cliffhanger and a last opportunity for the riders to psyche themselves up before the drop. Also, if you were riding with someone agreeable, it was a good excuse to cuddle close and grab each other.

When they got on, Mary would have rather leapt from the cart than even brush shoulders with her fellow single rider. Now, though, as the last of the light faded and the couple in front of them, who really were quite adorable, huddled together in anticipation, Mary wasn't so sure. She missed the warmth and shared laughter that was already coming from the darkness in front of her.

And what she missed even more was what the two of them must be doing now that the laughter had stopped and the only sound was clanking chain of the ride. *They're kissing,* Mary realized. *Two people in love, doing what they're supposed to do.*

To hell with it, she decided. Mary let out a giddy laugh and grabbed onto her benchmate's arm.

She was hoping to feel an electric connection when she touched his skin. She was hoping for something magical.

Instead, she came into contact with something hot and sticky and pulled her hand back just as quickly as she'd put it out. *Reality,* she thought. *Shitty, fucking reality.* She saw the light of the afternoon sun growing up ahead. Wonderful, now she could see what exactly was sticking to her hand. Probably just chocolate, but she'd heard stories about creeps before. *If it's jizz I'm going to throw him off this fucking ride. I swear to Christ.*

The log emerged from the tunnel. Bright, beautiful, California sun shone down on everything.

It wasn't jizz on her hands.

Logistically, amusement parks make no sense as a business endeavor. Throw as many bells and whistles around it as you want, the pitch is that consumers will spend hundreds of dollars and wait on lines upwards of an hour for an experience that takes ten minutes at most and less than five on average.

The reason that it sells is that time is elastic. When the brain is constructing memories, it blends the monotonous hour on line into an easily glossed over minute while every second of sheer joy and exhilaration felt during the ride is carefully preserved and structured so that it feels like a much longer experience.

A similar situation occurs during moments of intense terror.

In the ten seconds before the log flume plunged down the waterfall, Mary saw everything. She saw the lifeless slouch of the couple in the front row. She saw that their hats were off and she could see the pale, white bone and dirty, grey brain through the thumb-sized holes in the back of their skulls. She saw the sticky blood on her palm and she saw the couple's blood running darker and thicker down the black plastic of the seat backs. Some of it was on her sneakers.

And she saw the man beside her and the thick streaks of gore spattering his arms to the elbow. He caught her looking and smiled.

"This is the best part," he said.

Mary screamed and stood up. She knew how high she was and she didn't care. *The ledge,* she thought. She'd been on this ride two dozen times in her life and she knew that faux rock outcroppings bordered the waterfall on either side. The distance was less than two feet, a mere hop at sea level and her fear of the lunatic sitting beside her was far greater than any concern of falling to her death.

She bunched her legs to jump but his hand fell on her shoulder first and squeezed. Mary screamed, not just at the strength of his grip, which was stronger than any falcon's talon, but at the searing heat of his touch. His fingertips were like five lit cigarettes. Mary could smell her own flesh cooking. It smelled exactly like the turkey leg she'd had for lunch a thousand years ago.

"Ah, ah, ah," he admonished. "Turtleshell Mountain rule number one, keep your arms and legs in the cart at all times."

They were almost at the edge of the falls. Mary could see so many people down below them. Even from this height, they looked so happy and she desperately wanted to be one of them. That was the only reason she'd come to the park.

If the bloody thing beside her had wanted the same wish, then he had gotten it. He grinned broadly at Mary's agony.

"And Turtleshell Mountain rule number two," he said. He held up a long length of grey cable curled into a leash. "Always wear your safety restraints."

That's from the ride, she realized. *The tarantula slave driver's chain. But we went past that twenty feet back. The webbing couldn't be that long. That's just... that's just not real!"*

And then he was looping the webbing around her neck and the log was tilting downwards. Downwards, downwards, downwards, and Mary realized the webbing wasn't a leash.

It was a noose.

The log flume dropped. The bloody thing

laughed and held onto the handrail as the cart rocketed down and away from her.

Mary's drop was slower but, incredibly, she felt the same swooping sensation in her stomach as if she were still in her seat. Muscle memory had not yet caught up with the terrible conclusions of her mind. Her body still thought this was all just some ride. A fun, pulse-pounding, cheap thri-

Her neck snapped. Her body jerked like one of the simply constructed animatronic models and then hung still.

2

The entire section of the park was closed off. The reporters would be swarming soon, but they weren't going to get close enough to take pictures of anything except stern-faced security guards and sawhorses. That was plenty bad; but between showing people that and showing them three dead bodies, one of them hanging from the waterfall pictured on the front of their fucking brochure, Raylene would take it.

But that wouldn't keep the presshounds fed for long. Eventually, the newspapers would turn their forks and knives on her and, two hours after the last details had come in, Raylene was still no closer to drafting a press release that would convince them to try and carve chunks out of a juicier meal somewhere else.

She had a brand-new word processor. State of the art. Each one cost as much as a month's salary and was supposed to make the whole department more efficient. But so far, the only difference Raylene noticed was that she was more efficiently putting out copy that she wouldn't stick underneath Pedro Parrot's ass.

She knew exactly what had happened. Three people had gone into *Falcon Falls* together. Two of them had reached the bottom with holes punched in the back of their heads and the one who'd done the hole punching had hung herself from the top of the waterfall with a scarf. All the pieces were there, the problem was that there was no way to put them together in a way that wouldn't bury the tallest peak of Turtleshell Mountain underneath an avalanche of shit.

Raylene started again.

`Turtleshell Mountain takes every precaution to ensure the safety of our guests. That being said`

…What? "That being said," what?.

`That being said .fbskhfoih`

She smashed both fists against the keyboard as hard as she could. These new keys didn't even make satisfying sounds when you hit them.

Fucking single riders. That should have been all the explanation she really needed to say. No matter what the problem was, the explanation almost always had something to do with a fat, delusional, mother-fucking single rider.

`That being said, let me assure you all that, effective immediately, Turtleshell Mountain has instituted a new policy: weirdo, middle-aged fat women will no longer be permitted on any Turtleshell Properties unless they're accompanied by an actual, real life, fucking child.`

There. Problem solved.

Except not really. She bent back over the keyboard and started typing again, wishing all the while that she had the authority to round up every

single rider in the park and have them gassed like
stray dogs.

3
2014

It was a wonderful January day. An easy eighty degrees and not a single cloud to be seen.

It was the kind of day that always made Erin, originally a child of North Dakota, smile. Especially when it came on a rare three-day weekend when her boyfriend and her best friends were all off duty and free to enjoy it together. Even if the group time off had been granted for reasons that were... bittersweet, Erin was determined to take full advantage of it.

Jack was bringing her bags out to the SUV. Erin could have carried them out herself but Jack, ever the gentleman, had insisted. Not that Erin was complaining. The bags were just weighty enough that Jack had to flex to lift them, and she could have watched his arm muscles bulge beneath that tight black t-shirt all day.

The wind blew again, hard enough to shift her hair. Erin bent down to check her reflection in the Explorer's side view mirror. She fixed her bangs with a few quick swipes, and since she was already there she decided to give herself a quick once over.

Erin was a CSI technician. She spent so much time in a baggy, blue jumpsuit that she made it a point to always look her best when she wasn't. Right now, she liked what she saw, a compact woman with dark hair and dark eyes to match. Her makeup looked good and, bent over as she was, she saw that her cleavage was as inviting as ever. Strictly a B in size but an A+ for shape and definition. She couldn't check out her own ass but, if she wanted an evaluation, she got one when she heard the wolf whistle from behind her.

"Objects in mirror are closer than they appear, right? What do I have to do to get that ass in a mirror?"

Erin could see him without having to turn around. Scott was reflected in the corner of the mirror, scruffy and leering and perpetually amused, but she whipped around anyway because sometimes Scott needed to be glared at, and a reflection just wouldn't do the trick.

Scott just shrugged. "What? I just asked a question. Was it the whistle?" He pointed to the Willie Wolf t-shirt he was wearing. "I'm just trying to get into character."

Erin was not amused. "I don't know. Jack, do you think it was the whistle?"

Scott didn't have the benefit of a mirror. He had to turn around. When he did, he came face to chest with six and a half feet of very not amused Jack.

Jack slugged Scott in the shoulder. He put much more muscle into it than he put into carrying Erin's bags.

"Ah!" Scott recoiled, clutching his arm, but he seethed back into Jack's personal space just as quickly. "Learn to take a joke, Captain America!"

"Learn to mind your manners, traffic cop." The last word came out like it was a slur.

25

Erin got between them. She was the smallest but she pushed against them both and they moved back when she did. "We're not in uniform," she snarled at them. "Nobody outranks anyone here, so quit that crap right now."

Scott and Jack had never really been close. They were usually cordial because of their shared friends, but once Erin and Jack had started dating, Jack had become more protective of her and less tolerant of what he called Scott's "frat boy crap."

Part of it was her fault for egging them on and she knew that. She'd been worried for a while that one of these times she wouldn't be able to separate them, and the way that Jack was straining against her hand made her terrified that time was going to be right now.

Not today. Please, God. Not today.

The men stared each other down from across the length of Erin's wing span. She waited for Scott to say something that was still obnoxious but at least semi-conciliatory enough to cool Jack off. Instead, he was smirking at Jack with his scrunched up weasel eyes. Eyes that Jack had already told Erin he'd love to close permanently.

"I don't know," he said. "Like you said, Erin, we're off duty. That means I don't need to listen to any bitch who's telling me what to do."

Jack stopped pretending that Erin could hold him back if he really didn't want to be held back. Her elbow swung inwards like a door on a hinge as Jack pushed forward. She saw his hand ball into a fist again. *No, no, no.*

The honk of a horn was her salvation. There

was a neat little four-door pulling up in front of the apartment building. *Aaron and Tess, thank God.* Jack had already unclenched his fist, but she pushed hard on both of them anyway.

"That's them. Knock it the fuck off, both of you." The thought of Tess did what Erin could not. Jack stepped back and Scott didn't say anything to make him come forward again.

Aaron shifted into park. He and Tess could obviously see the three of them but it didn't look like either of them thought anything was wrong. *Please,* Erin thought. *Please don't let her see anything to make her upset.*

She watched Aaron get out first. Conscientious, devoted, totally should be getting laid but wasn't, Aaron. He ran over to her side of the car, but Tess had already opened the door on her own. She was standing up by herself, which was good, but she was still so pale and thin. Her t-shirt hung off the rickety wireframe of her shoulders, and Tess' sunken face was nearly lost in the curtains of her dark red hair.

The first thing Tess did was look critically at Erin's skirt. "You're wearing red too?" she said. "Oh, this won't do at all." She plucked the wig of red hair off of her head and reached back into the car. When Tess reemerged, she had a scalp of short, shaggy blonde locks dangling from one hand. She set it carefully on her head and tucked the loose strands of hair behind her ears.

"There. Much better."

It was meant to be a joke. And the slopes of Tess' bald head were only visible for a moment while she changed wigs. But that short glimpse was all it took for Erin to start crying just like she promised herself that she wouldn't.

"I'm sorry," Erin sobbed. She tried to smile through watery eyes but that hair, the blonde lie of it, wouldn't allow her to.

Her hair's supposed to be brown. Plain brown. Boring brown, really. She thought of all the years that she'd *begged* Tess to let her dye it, *"Strawberry blonde, Tess, it would look so good on you!"* and just cried harder.

"Now who's ruining things?" Scott whispered as Erin kept crying. Jack shot an elbow into his side and didn't care who saw it.

Tess didn't even hear them. She pointed a stern finger at Erin and spoke in a tone not unlike the one Erin had used on Jack and Scott. "You've got five seconds, Erin. Cry what you've got to cry because if you so much as whimper again I swear to God I'll leave you in the car. We're going to the Most Joyous Place on Earth and we're going to keep it that way. If my wig comes flying off on Falcon Falls, you just smile and treat me to a turtle shell hat. Got it?"

Sniffling, Erin nodded. Tess went over and gave her best friend a hug. The warmth that came with it should have been more than her bone-thin arms had to offer, but it was there all the same.

Deprived of his door opening duties, Aaron had brought their bags to the open truck. While the girls were still hugging, Jack and Scott sidled up beside him. "Did she tell you anything?" Jack asked. He spoke with the same short, clipped tone he'd use in an interrogation.

Aaron shrugged. "Yeah. She said she wants to ride the Coney Island Coaster until she doesn't know which direction is up anymore. She also thinks that we should go to the Brontosaurus BBQ for lunch."

"But what about her?" Scott asked.

"I don't know."

He picked up their suitcases and placed them in the trunk, first Tess' and then his. He did this with as much careful diligence and focus as such a simple task could be done. Aaron had large, expressive eyes and the rubbery, dexterous features of an actor. It was not hard to tell if he was happy, sad, or about to beat you in poker. Right now, the fixed set of his features said, *Man hard at work. So sorry, but no time to answer questions here.*

Scott ignored the hint. "Aaron, she stops telling us how treatment's going, you included. She decides at the last minute she wants us all to go on this trip together. The evidence is kind of piling up here. Is she...." He made a see-saw gesture with his hand that they all understood to be balanced on the fulcrum of life and death.

Aaron slammed the trunk down. "I don't know," he hissed at them. If he hadn't caught himself at the last minute, he would have screamed it. The only reason he didn't was because Tess would have heard him. It wasn't fair to lash out at them for asking the same questions he himself wanted to ask, but he couldn't help it. Aaron was afraid. Beneath his fear was anger. Both emotions demanded answers and there were times, like now, where that demand was so great it threatened to explode out through whatever valve it could find.

"Everything all right over there?" Tess called out.

Aaron turned around at the sound of her voice. Beneath whatever else he felt, first and foremost was always love for her. He quickly wiped all of the fear, anger, and frustration from his face before saying, "We've got a two-hour drive, and you're sitting here getting all touchy feely while the lines at Turtleshell Mountain are getting longer and longer. So, no, it's not all right."

Tess waved him off with a smile. "We'll tell them I'm dying. Somebody will let us cut."

Aaron and the others laughed, but only because they felt like they had to.

It very well could have been Tess' way of telling them that she actually was dying.

"I still need to get my purse," Tess said. She went back towards the car, and Aaron couldn't help but feel a small flare of hope. She looked very light footed on her way back towards the car.

Stop that, another part of him insisted. *Spend the whole day keeping a tally of when she looks good and when she doesn't and you're going to make yourself crazy. You'd also probably find yourself on the losing side of the scoreboard.*

That was the truth. He knew that. But it was hard to listen as he watched Tess move so easily that you'd think there was nothing wrong with her that an extra-large milkshake couldn't fix.

And then she stopped and had to lean against the car to catch her breath, and the truth was all there was. Even when she walked back with her purse without a single misstep, he knew that there was plenty wrong with her.

"I'll take that, Tess," Jack said.

"Is the trunk unlocked?" she asked, as if she hadn't heard him at all. "I'll just throw it back there."

"I'll put it up front with me," Erin said quickly. A coded look passed between her and Jack.

"Along with that laundry sack you call a purse? Please." She reached for the hatch and opened it before anyone could stop her.

Tess looked at what was inside for a long time.

"….What the hell is this?" she asked.

Jack finally spoke. "I just thought it wouldn't hurt to have one handy. I'm not saying you need it. I just mean there's a lot of walking at Turtleshell Mountain and….. I don't know," he faltered. "Just in case you get tired is all."

He braced himself for an outburst, but Tess just reached into the trunk and slid the folded wheelchair out from between the bags. She opened it up and pushed it back and forth a few times.

"This rolls nice," she said. She reached down and pressed her hand into the cradle of the seat. "And firm. You ever sit in one of those hospital wheelchairs? Ass grooves like they're moving around watermelons in those things."

Jack laughed, mostly from relief that she wasn't mad. "And I was looking at the rules. If your party has someone in a wheelchair, you get to cut the lines."

"Come on, the lines are part of the experience

31

just like everything else," she said.

Jack shrugged, not wanting to argue. "At least you can wait in style."

Tess laughed. "Style for sure. This thing's a Cadillac for cripples" Still smiling, she gave the chair a hard push. It rolled down the driveway, across the street, and came to a rest when it bumped against the curb on the far side of the street.

"And I'm sure somebody who needs it will really appreciate it."

In the silence that followed, Tess clapped her hands. "Let's get rolling. I'm not sure how far ahead 'I'm dying' will actually get us on the heavy hitters like Falcon Falls, so I hope nobody has to use the bathroom on the way."

She started towards the car, but she stopped when she saw the crestfallen look on Jack's face. She briefly touched his arm. "If I do get tired, I'm sure Erin won't mind if you carry me around for a little while. I promise I'm not too heavy." She stretched up and kissed his cheek.

She got into the back seat and the others were all smiles as they followed. Even Aaron. Even as some small part of him insisted on noting:

Not too heavy. No, not too heavy at all.

4

Death is all around you at an amusement park.

Safety precautions abound, but there's nothing that can change the fact that you're paying for the privilege of getting strapped into a bullet and fired higher than a building at speeds of better than fifty miles an hour. After that, you can get whipped around like a rock in a sling with nothing but a thin chain to keep you from being flung all the way out to the parking lot. Then, if you're hungry, you can choose from a dozen different restaurants, so long as you like your food fried in trans-fat, loaded with preservatives, and smothered with powdered sugar.

Nobody questions any of this because amusement parks are full of flashing lights, cheerful cartoon characters brought to life, and the illusion of security. The guests who aren't already children become children in their minds. And children are never smart enough to be afraid of death.

That's why nobody sensed anything wrong as the Single Rider sat there and enjoyed his candy apple. They walked right past him, walked right on by like rabbits strolling past the wolf, and none of them so much as twitched a whisker. All they saw was an attractive redhead enjoying the afternoon sun with his legs stretched out. The fear of the predator, the one honed by a hundred generations of prey to go off at even the slightest threat, wasn't just lulled into ineffectiveness, it was willfully switched off.

He took another bite of the candy apple. The hard, red shell cracked between his teeth like baby's bones as he watched the Comet Drop haul another fragile cargo of organs and tissue higher and higher until they were nothing but dots against the cloudless blue sky. At least they were dots for now. In a moment they would start getting bigger and bigger again, like falling china ornaments that God had placed too close to the edge of a shelf in Heaven.

They would be caught before they could shatter, of course. Slowed and gently lowered as if by the same invisible hand of God.

This time anyway.

The Single Rider swallowed the morsel of apple and cavities. He savored the flavor as it worked its way down his digestive tract.

He enjoyed it all the more because he knew that there was something sweeter on the way.

The Single Rider felt it coming as surely as he saw the Comet fall to earth.

5

He was going to be sick.

Eddie felt it coming up as surely as he felt the Comet Drop going down.

Eddie closed his eyes, finding stillness even as the rush of air hit him like a continuous uppercut. He found tranquility even as thirty people and 60-mile-an-hour winds screamed directly into his ears. He found his voice even as his lips were clamped shut in a desperate bid to keep from throwing up everywhere.

God, the Youth Minister prayed. *This is your humble servant, Eddie. I understand if you're busy somewhere else, but I'd like to remind you that I'm very much on the clock right now with the humility and the service. I also gave my extra clean shirt to Luis after he spilled chocolate ice cream all over his. With all of that in mind, I would really appreciate it if you'd help me not to blow chunks all over myself.*

That might have been a tall order, even for the Almighty, because the Comet Drop did not just go up and down once. It rocketed up and then it plummeted back down and then it rose halfway up and dropped a quarter of the way down, and then it kept dropping in herky-jerky spasms that left Eddie feeling as ready to explode as a thoroughly shaken soda can.

But, however condemned to regurgitation he

felt, the Lord had seen fit to provide and Eddie's insides remained inside rather than all over his shirt and lap.

Not that Eddie would have had any hard feelings even if the Lord God had decided to turn a deaf ear to that particular entreaty. Mysterious ways and all that.

Mysterious ways like why God had seen fit to send Eddie to Turtleshell Mountain even though he hated rides and amusement parks with a burning passion.

A small hand grabbed his as they were getting off the ride. Gabrielle, whose father's tour in the Middle East had been extended while everyone else's was getting scaled back. It was Gabrielle's turn to pick the next ride, and the excitement beamed out of her like sunshine itself. "The Rhinos," she exclaimed. "I want to go on the Rhinos!"

Oh, right. Not so mysterious after all.

Eddie let Gabrielle lead him by the hand. The other fourteen children raced ahead, but that was fine. They knew not to race too far along, and he could keep an eye on all of them if he was last in line.

His eyes were on the children, but his mind still lingered on the idea of mysterious ways. It was a sermon he'd made once before, and it had been a particularly well received one. Perhaps enough time had gone by that he could revisit the concept.

The nausea took him then, and it took him without warning. One moment, Ed was idly considering the beautifully unreadable machinations of the Lord God. The next, his legs tangled together and he had to grab the railing to keep from falling on his face. Cold sweat broke out on his brow, but was it running down his face or up? Ed didn't know. The world spun round him in a blur of colors, the only fixed point Ed had was the metal rail and he clung to it with both hands.

If I let go of this handrail, I'm going to fly off the face of the Earth. I swear to God I will.

But then the nausea passed as abruptly as it came. Eddie's gorge receded and the foul taste in the back of his throat went with it. The spinning earth slowly steadied around him. Experimentally, he let go of the railing. His feet stayed on the ground.

But the confusion remained. This wasn't the ride, he was sure of it. No, what had happened was more like opening an old storage space and getting blindsided by the stench of something dead and rotting.

Except there was no smell. There was only a surety that felt like something was rotting in the center of his brain.

Maybe it was the ride. Your inner ear wasn't as settled as you thought. Your inner ear or your inner gut. Or maybe your outer gut. You need to do less fish and loaf multiplying and more fasting and you know it.

Gabrielle tugged at his hand again. "Minsta Ed? Are you ok, Minsta Ed?"

He forced himself to smile. "I'm not a talking horse, Gabs. Say your ee-s and ar-s like your speech therapist taught you," he gently chastised.

"And I'm all right, thank you very much for asking." He looked at the other kids and realized they had all lingered beside him. He saw varying degrees of concern on their faces and forced his smile a little wider. "Come on," he told them. "This is The Most Joyous Place on Earth, keep frowning like that and you'll get us forcibly ejected."

Assured that their chaperone was not in mortal danger, the march to the Flying Rhinos resumed, and Eddie followed with Gabrielle's hand squeezed reassuringly in his own.

He spared one more look around. Perhaps there was an overflowing trashcan or something else noxious that he had missed.

There wasn't. The only thing worth looking at twice was a truly breathtaking redheaded woman enjoying a candy apple. Eddie sincerely doubted that she was responsible for anything even remotely nauseating, but it didn't hurt to make sure.

It would hurt to do anything more than that, though.

That was his own better judgment speaking, not God's except for in the sense that all things came from God. He knew that, for one, his kids would be all too happy to tell their parents about Minister Ed's nice new friend with the long red hair and longer, creamy white legs. Protestant clergy may be allowed to marry, but they were somehow supposed to do it without ever courting an attractive young woman whom they weren't already married to.

For two, a woman that beautiful had to be waiting for a boyfriend to come back with cotton candy and a funnel cake. Maybe even a girlfriend. Minister Ed kept his opinion on such matters carefully neutral. Even if God said that homosexuality was a sin, the Bible sitting in Edward Harrison's office made it perfectly clear where people with sins of their own stood in the line of stone throwers. Eddie may have been a Man of God, but he was more specifically a twenty-five-year-old Man of God who needed to ask forgiveness for certain kinds of sinful thoughts more often than others.

Either way, he thought as he spared her one last glance, *no matter what kind of company she keeps, there's no way a woman that incredible looking doesn't have somebody waiting for her.*

The beautiful redhead stayed where she was, relaxing on a bench with her long legs stretched out in front of her, and finished her candy apple. And Edward Harrison turned his focus back towards his children.

6

There was some debate between Erin and Tess as to where they should park.

"Lily White Lot!"

"Prince Warren Lot!"

"Itchy Lot!" Scott piped in.

"That's the wrong theme park."

Jack suddenly cranked the wheel to the right. "We're parking in the Lavender Twist lot," he announced.

"The who lot?" Aaron asked.

Erin rolled her eyes. "Don't ask."

"I'll ask," Scott said. "Who and why?"

"I kind of remember it," Tess said. "It's the one with the garden, right?"

"It's a nursery," Jack said. "You know, a plant nursery. My grandma had the tape. I always used to watch it when I slept over there"

"And..." Erin prompted.

Jack sighed. "And I had a crush on Lavender when I was a kid."

"Aww," Aaron crooned.

Scott would have gotten a scowl. Coming from Aaron, Jack didn't mind chuckling.

"I was eight," he said in his own defense. He parked the car directly under the signpost for Lavender Twist 3B. Lavender herself, some kind of leggy wood nymph with white flowers for hair, hovered over them with her arms perched sassily on her hips.

They got out of the car. "I guess I had a thing for Dustimona," Aaron said. "There's no beating the classics."

"Or those ultra-classy glass high heels," Tess said. "That's a fetish just waiting to mature."

"The Princess and the Pauper were my cartoon crushes," Scott weighed in. "I wanted both of them at the same time before I even knew what that meant. I figured we'd just all get ice cream."

Scott turned to the girls. "Fess up, ladies. Who put the shine on your Turtleshells? It wasn't Donnie Donkey, was it? That would raise some awkward questions."

Erin grabbed Jack's bicep and kissed his cheek. "Brave Sir Gallant for me."

Tess just smiled. In that moment, she remembered the little girl who was babysat by Timmy Turtle and a dozen other characters while her single mother worked double shifts six days a week. Turtleshell videotapes were the one luxury that little girl got. Her daily ration of a world where if you were a good person and you never gave up hope, then things always somehow worked out in the end.

Tess adjusted her wig before she spoke. "I always liked Quabol."

"Quabol?" Scott asked. "Bumpy head, bumpier back, *Hunchback of Saint Patrick's* Quabol?" He knocked on her skull. "What have those doctors been spraying you with?"

She shrugged one shoulder. "All of the other princesses had to jump through hoops before their princes fell in love with them. They were all either giving up their voices or pretending to be men or getting poisoned by witches. Quabol didn't make Ruby do anything. He just loved her."

She went to help Jack and Erin get the bags out. Lingering behind, Scott nudged Aaron with an elbow. "She likes guys who are low maintenance and doesn't care how ugly they are. You're clear for landing."

Aaron wasn't a tween just entering puberty. He was too old to blush because somebody teased him about a girl he liked. That being said, you're never too old to pretend not to hear something you don't want to talk about.

Scott might have forced his hand anyway, he had a way of keeping after something once he smelled blood, but a distraction from the trunk caught his attention first.

"What are these?"

Aaron turned and saw Jack holding up four printed out computer pages. Aaron was too far away to read what they said, but he could easily see the Turtleshell logo emblazoned boldly across each one.

"Oh man, were those sticking out of my bag?" Scott asked with feigned innocence. "Those were the unlimited Quik-Trik passes I bought for the OTHER friends that I'm meeting here."

Tess' eyes widened. "The Harry Hare passes? Scott, those cost-"

"A lot? Each? Let's just say I won't be making Adult-con OR Adult-expo this year. I hope you're happy."

And then Tess was hugging him. "You are a sweet, sweet, sick, perverted man," she said into his shoulder.

"Yeah, yeah, just call me Saint Scum," he said. He was trying to hide how pleased he was at Tess' happiness, but he was doing a lousy job of it.

It wasn't the kind of pleased that would make Aaron automatically jealous either. It was the kind that showed just how easily Tess encouraged the best in everyone she came across.

Jack didn't say anything as he folded his pass and tucked it into his pocket, but there was a slight smile on his face. His mouth was like a rigid plank of wood bowing in the middle underneath a tremendous amount of pressure applied at just the right point. He pushed Scott's bag into his chest, but there was no malice to it and Scott only had to take a single step backwards.

"Thanks, creep," Erin said kindly.

Tess and Aaron got their bags, Aaron insisted on carrying Tess' for her, and they joined the procession heading towards the Monorail leading into the park.

"Don't worry, Quabol," Scott whispered to Aaron. "I'm just your good-natured, talking Gargoyle wingman. They didn't even draw me with a prick."

"Wouldn't do you any good if they had," Aaron muttered back, happy not to pretend that he couldn't hear Scott.

- - -

43

The Monorail was waiting for them at the station. The elevated track was at the end of a long stairwell with side panels painted with the likeness of Turtleshell Pictures characters. Timmy Turtle, Felix Fox, Donnie Donkey, and a dozen others. All of them racing excitedly up to the platform where their carriage awaited. The Monorail itself was adorned with large cartoon eyes and a broad, toothy grin. A little cross-promotional work for the upcoming *Train-ing Day* animated feature.

Everyone boarded the monorail like a kid, no matter how old they were. The urge to run up the stairs and race inside and fight for a window seat was impossible to resist. Excitement may be anticipation but when you're so close that you can smell the giant turkey legs wafting in on the breeze, you don't want to wait anymore. By the time you reach the monorail, you've already sat on a plane or you've driven for hours on end. You've plotted which rides you want to go on first, which characters you want to see, and where you want to eat. By the time you're in your seat, anticipation has peeled back years of maturity like layers of onion skin and no matter what your driver's license says, it's wrong. At that moment, all you are is a child who's tired of waiting and just wants to get to the park.

Tess and the people she loved most were no exception. The five of them moved towards a long bench at the back of the lead car, each one already thinking of what they wanted to do first. Erin wanted to get her hair done at Melisande's Magic Mirror Salon. Scott and Jack, for all their differences, were excited for the thrill rides. Drops and loops and the wind whipping through their hair.

Aaron simply wanted to give Tess whatever she wanted. All weekend, there would not be a single suggestion she had that would not sound like the best idea in the world to him.

Tess wanted pictures and souvenirs. She looked at her friends: Erin and Jack holding hands; Scott sipping vodka from his Felix Fox water bottle; Aaron laughing and teasing Scott about his "water" but still keeping her in the corner of his vision, just to make sure she was ok. She felt so much love just seeing them all there. And she wanted to come home with every tangible emblem of that love that she could get her hands on.

Most of all, as they took up the long bench at the back of the lead car (Tess was seated in the middle. Not by accident), what they all wanted was to feel the sensation of the monorail moving forward under their feet.

Whatever forces of the universe there were, God or Ka or maybe just good old-fashioned Turtleshell Magic. They all heard the low hum of the electric motor starting, but only for a moment before several loud cheers and yells from the passengers drowned it out completely.

The wait was over.

Turtleshell Mountain was laid out like concentric circles. The inner rings housed the eight different hotels on the property, accommodations for every price point, along with various restaurants and gift shops.

The outer ring was what people immediately thought of when someone said, "Turtleshell Mountain." Outside of the hotels were the rides.

The children gasped and crowded at the windows as the Monorail crossed over the border of the parking lot and into the park, offering them a bird's eye view of games and rides and streets crowded with balloons, snack carts, and the characters from seventy-five years of Turtleshell Pictures iconography brought to life.

The chatter began immediately.

"Dad, can we go on the Coney Island Coaster first?"

"Mommy, I see Princess Francesca's Castle!"

"Look, baby. Wave to Bella Badger!"

"Well, we have to go down Falcon Falls first. It's a tradition."

"Yo, you know what I heard happened on that ride...."

Aaron, Erin, Tess, Jack, and Scott were crowded right there along with everyone else. And, just like them, the sight that inspired the most joy and excitement wasn't any particular ride.

It was the statue.

It was positioned far closer to the hotels than the edge of the parks. That was because, when it was first erected, it *had* been the entrance of the park. Turtleshell Mountain had grown tremendously in the last 64 years, but that statue had stayed right where it was put in 1950. It had never been replicated anywhere else or reproduced in miniature for the souvenir shops. When you saw that statue, it meant that you were only in one

46

place in the whole, entire world.

You were at Turtleshell Mountain!

The statue was a bronze, fifty-foot-tall casting of a skinny, stooped figure with receding hair, a thin mustache, and a pencil tucked behind his ears. His was not the kind of physique you expected to see immortalized in bronze like a Greek God's.

But this was Charles Tuttle, the man with an imagination mightier than any muscle. And sitting atop his shoulders was Timmy Turtle, the most beloved of all the characters that had sprung forth from the forehead of Charles Tuttle.

The Monorail had been designed so that the tram traveled at exactly eye-level with Timmy. The engineer slowed down just enough so that everyone could get a good look at him as they passed. The Turtle's expertly crafted, chubby face seemed to be alive with genuine excitement at the sight of every new guest's arrival, and it was a tradition for children to wave at him as they passed.

"Hi, Timmy!"

"I love you, Timmy!"

"Timmy, dad! Dad, look! It's Timmy!"

Erin blew him kisses.

"Lookin' shiny, Timmy!" Scott shouted. "New turtle wax?!"

Aaron waved. Jack sketched a salute. Neither one felt as silly as they expected they would.

Tess waved as well. But not with the same exuberant, windshield wiping motion as everybody else. It was a slow sweep from the elbow, like a pendulum slowing to a stop. None of the others noticed.

Aaron did.

The Monorail pulled into their hotel, the stately Kubla Khan. Like all of the hotels, the monorail passed right through the lobby. Unlike most of the other hotels, the Kubla Khan was preserved with its original 1950s décor and the reception area was decorated with genuine Turtleshell memorabilia from that era.

Erin practically bounded out of the Monorail. "We're here!" she sang. "We're heeerreee!" Jack picked her up and swung her around.

The two young women behind the check-in desk just smiled and shook their heads. It was nothing they hadn't seen before and it was nothing to discourage.

"Tess Cameron!" Aaron boomed. "You've just made it to Turtleshell Mountain! What are you going to do now!?"

Tess threw her fist up in the air. "I'm going to..." Her fist sagged comically. Her shoulders followed suit.

"Oh," she said. "Crap."

And then she jumped in the air and kicked her heels together.

"WOOOO! TURTLESHELL MOUNTAIN!"

She held her hand up for a high five and Scott obliged. The others cheered with Tess just as loudly, Aaron included.

But, in the back of his mind, he could not get Tess' wave out of his mind.

It looked too much like a goodbye.

48

7

They stopped in their rooms first to unpack.

Erin and Jack had a room together. Aaron would have been fine bunking up, but Scott had insisted on getting his own room. *Probably convinced that one of the Princesses is just dying for an opportunity to come back with him and make a XXX parody of a Turtleshell movie. Maybe he's even hoping to finally cross the Princess and the Pauper off his list.* He threw his suitcase on the bed and chuckled to himself. Jack was his best friend. That probably meant some statute of guy code required him to dislike Scott too. But he couldn't help it. He liked Scott, even though sometimes it took some effort. That didn't make his "game" any less pathetic.

He was still smiling and shaking his head as he opened his suitcase. But his smirk shattered and his head froze in mid-pendulum swing when he saw the Hawaiian shirt folded neatly on top of his other clothes.

It was actually a very nice shirt. The lack of details in the beach scene stitched across the front of it made the shirt subtle and aesthetically clean instead of just tacky. The sandy shoreline started by one hip and slanted across to the opposite side of the rib cage and clear, blue water lapped horizontally across the stomach. Right over the heart, a bright, yellow sun cast a layer of warmth over the whole scene.

The warmth didn't touch Aaron at all. He looked at the shirt and felt very, very cold.

The last time he'd worn it had been a year ago. He had been in a hotel then too. A basic, inexpensive chain hotel in Santa Monica. The kind meant for tourists who spent most of their money just getting out to California from the middle of the country. Hence, the Hawaiian shirts and Texas accents they used when they checked in. Aaron had thought the accents were a little much, but Tess had thought it would be good fun so he went along with it and just let her do most of the talking.

She kept it up even after they were past the check-in desk and into the room. "Jed," she marveled as she planted a tiny microphone behind the TV where it could catch acoustics off the wall. "What do you suppose 'HDMI' means?"

Standing on the bed so he could drill a pinprick hole into the ceiling, Aaron shrugged. "I don't know, Lulubelle. Maybe it means 'Hidmy.'"

"Well, then what does 'Hidmy' mean?"

"I haven't the foggiest idea, Lulu. I reckon it's just more of Obama's ghetto terrorist talk."

Tess poked her head out from behind the TV. "Dude," she said. She was speaking normally now. "Not cool."

"These characters were your idea." He went back to the suitcase that was covered with stickers from Arizona and New Mexico and selected a camera the size of a sewing needle from the surveillance kit inside.

"Yeah," Tess went on. "But they're not *racists*.

I've got a black half-sister and you own a diner with a very loyal African-American customer base."

Aaron slid the pinprick camera into the small hole he'd made and tried to envision the angle in his mind. Yes, this one should catch the doorway and give them a good head-on look at all of the nice people coming in to buy illegal automatic weapons. He wanted one more facing the table and then one in the bathroom too. They wouldn't be able to pick their noses without it going in an evidence locker.

He hopped off the bed with the drill and took it into the bathroom. "So, what's Jed and Lulubelle's relationship status?" he called out into the bedroom. He asked this calmly, as if he were really talking about somebody else and his heart wasn't pounding in his chest like a drum solo.

"What do you mean?"

He stayed in the bathroom. It was easier to talk without looking at Tess. He also sweated less.

"I mean, they're taking a trip together. Are they related? Are they friends?" he swallowed. "Do they have anything Facebook official? What does she think about him?"

"...I don't think they're related," she said. Aaron still couldn't see her, but he could hear the delicate care in her voice. He also heard a low clunk as she set down whatever piece of equipment she was using. Probably the audio calibrator.

"So, what are they? Good friends?"

"Well," Tess' voice said. "That's what Jed says, but sometimes Lulubelle wonders if she's missing out. I mean, she shares a lot of things with Jed that she wouldn't feel right telling anybody else about. Sometimes she even gets her assignments switched so she can work with him because they always grab crappy food together after they get off shift and that beats the hell out of anything else she could do after work."

"I thought Jed ran a diner." Which was fine because Aaron could talk about Jed and Lulubelle. The idea of talking about anybody else was goddamn terrifying.

"He does. He also moonlights as a surveillance technician for the Santa Monica PD."

"Oh. He sounds busy."

"He is. But he's also very sweet. And he gives good advice and he doesn't hog the radio in the van and he would be a very wonderful person to be more than friends with."

"Then… then maybe Lulubelle ought to think about going out with him some time for food that *isn't* crap."

"She'd definitely consider it. That's why it's too bad it will never happen."

"Why not?"

"Jed says they're just friends."

Well, Jed's a fucking moron. Aaron made a decision and turned around. "Tess."

She'd slipped into the bathroom while he'd been too focused on stringing words together to notice literally anything else. She was right there in the doorway. So close he could reach out and feel the cushion of her cheek against his palm if he wanted to. Their eyes met, and it was *their* eyes.

Aaron and Tess', not Jed and Lulubelle's. She wasn't pretending to be anything- not somebody else, and not somebody who just wanted to be friends. In that instant, there was not a single lie in her eyes.

But there was blood.

Tess' left eye was full of it. The blue of her iris floated in that red sea like a gruesome inner tube.

And still she smiled, completely oblivious as a stream of blood ran from her left nostril.

"I'm impressed, Aaron. You haven't even kissed me and I'm already feeling light headed."

That was the last thing she said before she collapsed.

And that was the last time I wore that shirt. I got home from the hospital at six in the morning, and I stuffed it into a trashcan. It was spotless, but I couldn't stop thinking that it smelled like her blood.

And yet here it was, neatly tucked in next to the Baron Chill t-shirt that proclaimed the wearer "One Cool Dude."

Three knocks came at his door. They sounded like accusations.

"Aaron!" Tess shouted through the door. "Are you in there?"

If Aaron hadn't been rushed, he might have spoken to one of the others. Not Tess, never in a thousand years, but Jack or maybe Erin. They wouldn't have been able to explain how the shirt had gotten there either, but at least that would have been another mind aware that something wasn't right. If he had, perhaps someone might have noticed more forewarnings. Maybe they would have been better prepared when everything went to hell.

Instead, he heard Tess coming and the single burning imperative in his mind was that she could not see that shirt. Not when she was either in good spirits or desperately pretending to be for the sake of everyone else. "One second!" he shouted back, praying his voice sounded normal. "I'm not decent!"

"Says who?! Don't listen to them, I think you're great!"

He dropped the shirt and kicked it under the bed. *No,* he thought. *You think I'm wonderful.* Not that Tess had any memory of her collapse or anything else that had happened in the bathroom. And Aaron would never bring it up. He didn't know if he was decent or not, but that day was something he would never take advantage of.

He opened the door. Tess was there in a Tina Turtle t-shirt and the wraparound sunglasses that future Annabelle wore in *My Sweet Thirty-16.* Tess had set down a strict mandate of Turtleshell films apparel only and she was obviously leading by example.

"Nice look," he said.

"I wish I could say the same. You're not even changed." She pushed her sunglasses up on her forehead. Her eyes were wide, shocked and mischievous. "Oh. When you said you weren't decent..."

Aaron's eyes got even wider. "What? No!"

Tess smirked. "It's all right, I owe you a little

indiscretion."

He grew serious. "You don't owe me anything, Tess."

"You would say that."

"What would you want me to say?"

She smiled, small and tilted towards one side. "That I was terrified of facing all of this alone. That I was afraid I was going to wake up vomiting and there wouldn't be anyone to help me change my sheets. That there were a million things that needed to get taken care of and I was certain I'd forget at least half of them."

He'd known none of that. From diagnosis to now, relatively healthy or hospitalized with complications, Tess had never been anything but Tess. Unsinkable, unshakeable, never-say-die Tess.

Aaron tried to shrug but his shoulder didn't want to cooperate. "We all helped."

"That's not what I want you to say," she told him. "I want you to say that you were the one who forgot everything else. That more than anyone in this world, it was you who made sure that I never, ever, felt like I didn't have a chance."

"You still have a chance," he said harshly.

Tess just smiled and brushed a strand of someone else's hair behind her ear. "Semantics. There's a character brunch down in the lobby. No one else is ready, but I just wanted to see if you wanted to come down with me. But if you haven't unpacked-"

"Bottomless mimosas with Molly Manatee? Give me two seconds." *And please stop doing things to make me think that you've got some bad news you haven't told us.*

"Great." She put her sunglasses back on and turned to go.

Then she stopped and turned back around.

"One more thing."

She stood on her tiptoes so her lips were almost at his ear. "If you ever do want to say those things, I'll be sure to say thank you," she whispered.

And then she was walking back to her room. Cotton pale. Curves worn away by radiation.

The most beautiful woman he'd ever seen.

Jesus Fucking Christ.

He went back to his suitcase. What the hell, he grabbed the Baron Chill tee.

The Hawaiian shirt, for better or worse, stayed under the bed where it would soon be forgotten.

A corner of it was draped over the face of the dead woman stuffed under the bed.

She'd been a cleaning woman and mother of two in life. But now, she was just a corpse with its eyes frozen in a final wide stare of terror and its mouth packed full of cotton candy.

In the chaos that was to follow, she too would be forgotten.

8

Scott was changed and unpacked when the knock came at his door.

"One second," he called out.

He hadn't been lying when Tess swung by and he told her that he wasn't ready to go yet. Yes, he was dressed. Yes, his things were put away. But there was one more thing he needed to do before he left for the day.

And here it was now.

He opened the door. Erin was there.

"Good, you can play tie breaker," he said. Scott held up two tin-foil wrapped condoms. One was red and the other was neon blue. "You want to stick with the cherry-flavored or do you want to try this hot/cold thing?"

"I forgot my phone charger," Erin said. She glared at him, daring him to suggest otherwise.

"And Jack bought that?" He shook his head. "I hope he's not thinking of going out for detective."

"Fuck yourself. Do you have yours or not?"

"Never leave home without it."

He went back inside. He didn't have to ask Erin to follow him. He knew that she would.

Just like he knew that she'd lock the door behind her.

The charger was coiled up on the dresser. He grabbed it and turned around. As Scott expected, Erin was right behind him.

He held the charger out for her to take.

Erin didn't take it. She stood where she was and stared blades at him. He could see a dozen curses snarling to break free from the cage of her clenched teeth.

Scott took the hand that wasn't holding the charger and pressed it firmly into the small of Erin's back. He pulled her tight against him. Her hands hit his chest as clenched fist but they unknotted and hooked into his chest like claws.

They kissed.

Scott initiated it, but it would be unfair to say that he kissed her. Their lips met with equal intensity, and she was groaning into his mouth like something long tense and knotted was being massaged loose into blissful satisfaction. She wrapped one leg high over his hip. He grabbed her ass with both hands and held her there while his lips went to her neck and traced a long, decadent path down her throat. Erin threw her head back and had to bite her tongue to keep from screaming. Scott's kisses took her higher... *higher*...

And then she nearly fell as the warm hands released her. His lips untethered from her neck and something small and hard was wormed into her hand.

The phone charger.

There was a click. She looked up and Scott was unlocking the door. He swung it open and then stepped aside so Erin had a clear path out to the hallway.

"Glad I had what you were looking for," he said. "If you need anything else, all you have to do is ask for it."

Erin was almost running as she left the hotel room.

9

Nothing good ever just drops out of the sky simply because somebody deserves it.

That's what teachers say. That's what parents say. That's what bosses and motivational speakers say. Work hard, because nothing you want in life is ever going to just appear in front of you.

Raylene would have dearly liked to take one of those people by the hand and lead them back in time to the year 1987. She would take them through Good Day To You Square, down Main Street, past the Whole Wide World ride, past the gift shops and concession stands with their 1930s facades, and bring them to a stop right at the base of Falcon Falls.

Then, she would invite them to crane their heads up. Way up! They may have to squint against the sun to see it, but Raylene would show them the woman dangling from her broken neck at the top of the falls. She would wait for them to get a good look at that body hanging way back in the same year they invented Prozac and then suggest that maybe the problem wasn't that good things didn't just drop out of the sky. Maybe, it was just that most people didn't have the reflexes to catch them when they did.

Not that she EVER spoke of that day as anything but a senseless tragedy, but the truth was that Raylene had been a brand-new junior PR rep back then. She wasn't even the low man on the totem pole, she was the dirt the totem pole was built on. The only reason she was in the office that Saturday (the ONLY one in the office that Saturday) was because Barry Fucking Harvack had dropped twelve pounds of brochure proofs in her lap on Friday afternoon and Hey, Raylene, could you proofread all of these for Monday morning? Thanks, sweetheart.

But then the call had come in from security. No real details at that point, only frantic babbling about blood and police and bodies and, Oh, God, what do we do? The marketing office was on the Turtleshell campus along with every other department. By the time the guard was finished talking, Raylene could already hear the screams that were starting to bubble and boil out from the park.

In those prehistoric days before cellphones, anyone above her pay grade was too busy fucking on their boats or touring the vineyards in Napa to answer her call for help. So, without input from anyone, she had security widen the barricades to keep the press out of photo-taking range and she took the initiative to offer lifetime park passes and free accommodations to any guest who came forward with the original negatives for any photographs of the victims or the crime scene. The terms were tempting enough that, to this day, not a single photo of the victims had ever appeared in print.

She gave the press statement herself as well, outlining what had happened in non-sensationalist terms, praising the security standards at Turtle Shell Mountain and reminding the press that, compared to the pristine fabric of Turtle Shell Mountain history, really, what was one tiny, miniscule little fray?

Hours later, once the bodies had been taken down and the reporters were content to leave with nothing more than the official summation of events, then and only then did her superiors show up in a frantic, red-faced craze. But, by that point, all that was left to do was tell Raylene what an excellent job she'd done, and she made sure each and every one of those day late and dollar short cocksuckers, especially Barry Fucking Harvack, did just that. If that lunatic hanging from her neck was a piñata, then Raylene had beaten her to pieces all by herself. And when the candy of praise started falling out, Raylene would be goddamned if she was going to share it with anyone else.

Twenty-seven years later, Raylene was the Queen of Turtle Shell Mountain. She was Director of Marketing and Public Relations, she had a seat in the boardroom, and now she was the one with a Porsche and a timeshare in the Caribbean and she never, EVER came in to work on a weekend.

The exception was one Saturday a year. The anniversary of the *Falcon Falls* double murder suicide. It had gotten so she no longer even had to tell the other staffers to take the day off. Those that had been working there longer just passed the word on to the new hires. *If you're thinking of getting some extra work done the third Saturday in June, don't bother.* No one knew why, they just knew that Ms. Adams didn't want anyone else in the office that day.

Raylene stepped off the elevator that morning, Versace sunglasses over her eyes and venti iced coffee in hand, and the silence told her that her reputation had once again done its job. She was alone. She walked through the reception area, crossing the stone tiles and listening to her heels tap out the same mantra they'd tapped every day for the last twenty-seven years.

Victory.

Victory.

Victory.

She came to a stop with an east-facing window at her back and the morning sun shining over the cubicles and conference rooms before her. Bathed in that Saturday morning light, Raylene once again looked more beautiful than she did the year before. And it had nothing to do with the facelifts, designer clothes, or her salon-crafted, tastefully androgynous, black hair. It was all about the look of supreme, perfect satisfaction on her face as she surveyed the office space before her and gleefully whispered a line from *Jungle Tails,* "Everything the light touches is your kingdom."

The rush that ran through her was more amazing than sex.

She sat at her old cubicle and took a single pen just because she could. Then she took it back to her desk, her desk that was a one-of-a-kind Italian original, and used that twenty-five cent pen to sign the approval slip on a brochure that would be reprinted around the globe in a hundred different languages. Then, she took out the folder of incoming interns and contemplated which one she was going to make into her sex servant for the summer.

A knock at the door interrupted her silent revelry but, truthfully, Raylene wasn't that bothered. She appreciated the opportunity to relish her Kingdom in solitude, but one should never be too busy to receive tribute from ones' subjects.

"Come in," she said. She didn't bother to close the intern folder, but she did sit up straighter in her throne.

The man coming through her door was really just a kid. Ten years ago he probably hadn't been tall enough to go on any of the big boy rides. The blue coveralls said mechanic. The anxious way he kept wringing the oily rag between his hands said that he was nervous.

Good.

"Yes?" she asked him.

He didn't come any farther into the room, obviously mindful of the filth on his boots and the expensive carpet. "We've got a mechanical error, ma'am."

"And I look like ride maintenance to you?"

Sweat glistened on his already greasy forehead. "No, ma'am. We only figured you ought to know because you have to-" He realized that sounded too much like he was giving her an order and hastily back pedaled. "What I mean is, if you think it's a problem. I only thought that-"

"You have five seconds, gnome," she said. That was Raylene's not-so-private nickname for the grounds workers. Word had gotten around that if she said it to your face, it meant you'd better shape up quick and then disappear from her sight if you wanted to hold onto your job.

"It's the Sinbad-bot, ma'am!" he blurted.

Raylene sighed. Now she understood why he'd come to her. Sinbad was the main character of the still hugely popular '90s animated film chronicling, you guessed it, Sinbad and his talking camel's adventures in medieval Arabia. It was also the theme of the newest park area opening up next month. Most of the rides were up and running, the concession areas were set up, struggling actors had been hired to be the costumeers of dashing Sinbad and beautiful Scheraze, and they were fully expecting to meet their projected opening date in three weeks. That was why there was a large, animatronic Sinbad installed over the entranceway to the park area, reminding the flocks of guests that there would be a whole new slope opening at Turtleshell Mountain and, hey, kids! Encourage your parents to buy a season pass today so you can hurry back soon!

Except, if this gnome was here, then obviously the robot had broken down and that message wasn't getting out to the masses and every second it wasn't was money pissed down the drain.

The mechanic gnome was still talking. "That's why I came to see you. I don't know if maybe you want to put out a tweet or-"

"I want everyone you have getting that piece of shit running again. Until you do, have someone print up a sign announcing the park opening. On

65

second thought, wait for me to e-mail you the copy and then follow it to the letter."

"But that's the strange part, Ms. Adams." The mechanic knew he should have left with his head still attached, but sometimes the inexplicable just demanded to be spread. "The audio's still working."

"What do you mean?"

"I mean it's still waving and talking, it's just not saying the right things."

"Well, it didn't just decide to go off script by itself." The animatronic was a glorified tin can. It couldn't say anything except what was already programmed on the tape. She supposed it was an mp3 by now, but the principal remained the same.

The mechanic heard the anger simmering in her voice. He wished he'd just left when he'd had the chance. "We'll fix it," he said quickly. "We have the original audio file, and one of the tech guys can just re-upload it."

"Re-upload it and replace *what*?" Raylene demanded. If some asshole had thought it would be cute to switch the tape with something dirty, she would find out who it was and turn him inside out. "What's it saying?"

"Tonight," the Mechanic said. "The robot's saying that the new park opens tonight."

<u>10</u>

Tess' wig did not come off on Falcon Falls.

The moment they handed their tickets over and pushed through the turnstile into the park, health scares, guilt over infidelities, and confusion over the paranormal were all left behind along with all of the other myriad anxieties and burdens that make someone an adult. Turtleshell Mountain sprawled out before them in all of its promise and innocence, and they threw themselves into its comforts with reckless abandon.

They hit the thrill rides, of course. The roller coasters and death defying drops. Chef Graham's Spinning Egg Scramblers and The Crimson Oyster Swinging Pirate Ship. But, even with the Turtleshell flavorings, those were the kinds of rides you could find at any amusement park in the country. You went to Turtleshell Mountain for magic. And Tess, Aaron, Jack, Erin, and Scott all binged on as much of it as they could get their hands on.

They went on all of the rides that were nothing more than slow-moving tours of poorly animated dioramas and loved every one of them. They waited in line behind seven year olds to pose for pictures with princesses and talking animals and didn't feel the least bit silly as they did.

Erin insisted on posing with Jack at every one of the "Movie Moment" photo-ops. She kissed him on the cheek on the steps of the castle from *The Sister Princesses*. She leapt into his arms in the Louisiana chapel from *Monsieur Rabbit's American Vacation*. Tess loved it every time they did this, and Aaron couldn't help but smile every time the two of them pressed foreheads and Jack cradled her so gently in those hands that were as large and formidable as cinderblocks. Even Scott seemed to enjoy it; but, there was a crooked quality to his grins that Aaron couldn't quite get comfortable with. It was as if the smile started at the side of Scott's mouth and then continued under the skin where nobody could see the rest of it.

Diets were forgotten. As were old knee injuries and how badly Erin's borderline lactose intolerance flared up when she ate too much ice cream. They were enjoying every moment to the fullest.

"Let's get a picture," Tess said to Aaron after they got off of The Whole Wide World ride for the second time.

"With who?" Aaron asked. He looked around to see which character was nearby.

"Just us," Tess said. She grabbed his hand and his whole body jumped like an electric current had run through it, but then Tess took Erin's hand as well and his body voltage dropped to the same low thrumming it always was when he was near Tess. *Of course. She means all of us.*

Tess flagged a passing tourist down and got him to agree to take the picture. The five of them grouped together into a mass of grins and one-armed side hugs. Like on the monorail, it was only natural that Tess would be in the center of the photo. They were all friends, but if you asked who each of them felt closest with, the answer would invariably be Tess. They always put her in the middle because she was the adhesive that kept them together when their bonds were strained by Jack and Scott's antagonism or Erin's secret opinion that Aaron could be kind of boring.

Tess was also fragile and chipped and, if they kept her in the middle, they could imagine that they were protecting her against something none of them could actually fight.

The tourist, older and possibly not a native English-speaker took a moment to puzzle out the camera functionality of Tess' phone. Finally, he held it horizontally and beamed at them because at Turtle Shell Mountain, being waylaid to take a picture for strangers was not an inconvenience, it was an opportunity to share in somebody else's joy. "Ready!" he finally announced.

Tess pulled Aaron and Erin closer to her. Their idling half-smiles throttled up to the fully unleashed, wide grins of people who undoubtedly could not be happier.

A moment before the camera flash, Tess said, "All right, everyone say, 'I'm in remission!'"

The flash went off.

In the days that followed, there would be many attempts to count the costs of whatever transpired in that final, horrific night at Turtleshell Mountain. Politicians and pundits would try to quantify the lives and profits that were lost. They would try to count the wounds slashed into the psyche of the world. Inevitably, they would have to settle for estimates in the face of losses that were simply too large to comprehend.

Adrift in that ocean of woe, nobody would spare a tear for the photo of Tess Cameron and her friends that never made it online.

But that was only because they didn't know what they were missing. Under normal circumstances, it was the kind of photograph that would have been reposted and shared all over the internet underneath headlines like: *This girl had some good news to give her friends. This is how they reacted.*

And, for once, that kind of curiosity-bait would be justified. The picture was taken exactly as Aaron and the others realized what Tess had told them. And no photo would ever again so perfectly capture surprise, euphoria, or the thin line that separated the two.

11

Aaron took the camera back and shook the photographer's hand without even thinking about it. If he had cash on him, he might have tipped him twenty dollars with the same lack of thought.

When he turned back around, the others were still raving wildly.

"Oh my God, Tess!"

"What?! Fucking *WHAT!?*"

"Did you just find out!?"

All of them were excited, but none of them had truly processed the news yet, so they were all relying on volume to express their feelings while they waited for reason to catch up.

Rather than the future, Aaron was surprised to find himself thinking of the past.

She'd woken up in a hospital bed, and her first question had been about the surveillance, he remembered. *"Did you clear out our equipment? Who cycled in to finish installing the rig?"*

Aaron leaned forward in the chair he'd been sitting in for the last five hours. He took her hand in his and tried to sound calm. "Chris and Taylor got in to wire the last of the cameras." He didn't know if that were true or not and he didn't care. All he cared about was that the doctors had obviously drained the blood from her eye but Tess' cornea was still tinted a rosy pink that was anything but romantic. It made him sick just looking at it. Not

71

*because it was revolting. Even like this, there was
nothing revolting about her. The tinted eye made
him sick because it was a constant reminder that
there had been something very wrong with Tess.*

*"Don't worry about that," he said. He carefully
looked at the bridge of her nose so it would seem
like he was looking her in the eye and he could still
talk as if there were nothing really wrong. "What
about you? Are you feeling all right?"*

*"I'm sitting here laid up like someone's sick
grandma. How do you think I feel?"*

"Would some jello help?"

*"I'd say you're lucky we're in a hospital, but
I'm not sure how handy forceps are for removing
gelatinized sugar snacks from someone's rectum."*

*"We can get another opinion when the doctor
gets here, but I think a vacuum cleaner might work
better."*

*Then they were both laughing and, for a brief
moment, they forgot how they had gotten in that
hospital room.*

But then the doctor had actually come in, and
there was no talk about jello or vacuums. There
was only the news that Tess had a tumor the size of
a prune in her frontal lobe. Inoperable but they
were going to start chemotherapy immediately.

*Except they put her through round after round
of chemotherapy, and after each treatment the
doctor would deliver the same toxic combination
of grim results and hollow promises that next time
might be better. And every time he did, Tess would
just nod and say, "See you next week, Doctor."
And each time, Aaron was terrified that next week*

*would never come, that either Tess would finally
just slip away or, worse, that the doctor would say
that there would be no point in coming back next
week.*

But none of that mattered now. Now, there was
only Jack lifting Tess off her feet and squeezing
her so tightly that Aaron almost wanted to warn
him to be careful of her bones. He refrained
because it was obvious by the look on Jack's face
that even in his enthusiasm he would do nothing to
hurt her. Erin was crying too hard to say anything,
but Scott was jumping and red-faced and
screaming that they needed to get to the World's
Fair park area because they served alcohol there
and they needed to go someplace where they could
celebrate properly.

Aaron watched all of this from where he had
taken the camera.

He watched everything he'd been desperately
hoping and praying for actually come true, and he
watched the people he cared for most share in that
joy.

He watched and wondered why he wasn't
happier.

12

The Single Rider was waiting in line.

He didn't have to, of course. If he wanted to, he could be on any ride at any time.

He could be sitting in the back car of the Storytown Train when it broke down in a long tunnel on the hottest day of the year. He could be there smiling while frightened children swore that something touched them in the dark and sweating, irritable parents snapped at them to stop being silly, there was nothing there.

A person looking at a screen of souvenir photos taken mid-ride could see him in a half-dozen pictures at any given time. The Single Rider's appearance was always different, but the faces in the frame with him were always the same. Their eyes were always wider. Their faces were paler and their mouths were twisted into distorted, funhouse mirror screams that spoke of more genuine terror than any cheap thrill of speed and steel.

The Turtle may have been on all of the merchandise, but it was the Single Rider that truly lurked inside of the park's shell. He was in every dead mouse caught in a trap hidden discreetly from the eyes of passing guests. He bared the teeth of the grimace inside the smiling character head of every costumeer who put his hands on a child's shoulders and wondered, just for a second, what it would be like to tighten his large, gloved hands around a shrieking, demanding little throat. The smell of his warm breath lingered on the food that was a hair past its expiration date but served anyway for the sake of the bottom line.

Turtleshell Mountain was his kingdom. And Kings did not wait in lines.

Actually, that's not quite true, he reminded himself. *Kings do whatever they want*. And, right now, the Single Rider wanted to wait in line. He'd been on rides all morning. He went on Chef Graham's Egg Scramblers with the oldest daughter of a family of five. When the ride was over, the girl ran to her parents and brother, who'd been together in another scrambler. Blushing, the girl stood on her tip-toes and whispered into her mother's ear that she'd gotten her first period.

He and a seventh wheel from a group of accounting clerks went on the Coney Island Coaster together. When the ride came to a stop, he left the accountant clutching his left arm and complaining about chest cramps.

He was in the front row of the 4-D movie featuring a brand-new adventure with all of your favorite misfits from *Grammar School Ghouls* and oh, the Single Rider laughed until some of the people around him started bleeding from their ears.

He did all of this and a dozen other things and, still, the Single Rider felt like he was doing nothing but killing time for something else.

So, rather than fight it, the Single Rider was waiting in line. When he reached the front of this one, he would simply move to the back of another.

He would do this until he reached the front of whatever line he was truly waiting on. The Single Rider didn't know exactly what that was, but he knew he was getting closer.

And he knew that the longer the line, the better the ride.

<u>13</u>

They went on The Mariner's Maiden Voyage next. An old ride based on the classic Turtleshell animated film about a bumbling, inexperienced mariner who falls in love with a beautiful maiden on, you guessed it, his maiden voyage.

The ride was not exactly thrilling. It was another guided tour of crudely constructed animatronics acting out key scenes from the film. It was also on the opposite end of the park from the beer tap where they'd posted up and toasted "To health!" until all of them were starting to feel distinctly unhealthy. They were going to walk past, literally, a dozen better rides to get there, and Aaron knew that there was only one reason for Erin to insist that they go on that particular ride next. It was the same reason why Scott and Jack would both so eagerly agree that The Mariner was the place to be.

If Aaron's suspicions weren't already raised, they would have gone up to half mast at the subtle maneuverings on the line so that Aaron and Tess had the first of the high-backed, seashell shaped carts all to themselves.

And then there was the way Jack and Scott looked at him as he helped Tess into the cart. He didn't need to be on the lookout for signals to read their body language.

Jack: *You went with Tess to chemo twice as*

77

often as any of us. You practically lived on her couch from the moment she was diagnosed. You never said anything before now and we all know why. But this is how it's supposed to happen, Aaron. This is the happy ending both of you deserve.

And Scott: *Dude, under the shirt, over the bra. At least.*

Inside the ride, it was cool and intimate. The darkness between animatronic displays and the high-backed carts made it so they couldn't see anyone else around them, and it gave the whole scene an undeniable sense of privacy.

He and Tess sat together while talking sea lions and jerkily animated slapstick reigned supreme around them. There was no pressure. There was only the comfortable sense of completeness that came whenever he was with Tess.

Then their elbows brushed against each other, and there was suddenly something else there with them in the dark.

Desire.

Aaron looked into her eyes, and there was no red there now. Only a blue so vibrant that they glowed even in the dark coves of the ride. Tess leaned forward. Not close enough, but there was no mistaking her intentions. Aaron matched the movement. He too was not quite close enough, but his intentions were just as clear. They inched towards each other the way they always had, rigidly and hesitantly, when they should have come together with the fluid ease of a river rushing into the ocean. There was nothing between them now, though. No sickness, no confusion over who wanted what; there was only the perfection of the moment.

"I wasn't trying to work an angle," Aaron whispered.

"What do you mean?" Tess said.

"I mean," Aaron said. They were close enough to kiss now, but he couldn't bring himself to close the last inch between them. "I didn't plan this like some nerd with a 4.0 tutoring the hot cheerleader so he could get into her pants. I wasn't sleeping on your couch and holding your hand while you threw up on the off chance that you were going to get better." Whispered tenderly, his words might have been a declaration of love. Hissed out like a poison gas leak, they were anything but.

"I know that, Aaron." She tried to grab his hand, but he yanked it away.

"Then why now? Why not last week? Or last month?" He was overreacting, he knew that. But the possibility that everything he'd done for her had been meticulously counted and catalogued as some debt to be repaid made him feel like one of the prostitutes he saw waiting to be processed at the station house.

"Aaron, it doesn't matter," Tess begged.

"It matters to me. I want to know why all of a sudden I'm a prospect."

"You're not the prospect, asshole!" The blue of her eyes was truly an ocean now. Her barely checked tears gave them the shimmering quality they'd been missing. "I was DYING," she screamed. "Our first date would have been plain chicken broth after chemotherapy. You might have buried me on our six-month anniversary." She hit him in the shoulder but struck him square in the soul. "Why would I do that to you!?"

"It wasn't your decision!"

"It was if I loved you!"

The silence that followed was complete. Her final proclamation was delivered in the emptiness after the ride ended but before they came back out into the constant sound of the park at large.

Then, they were in the sun again, and he wondered how loud they had been. He got his answer in the way everyone refused to look at them. Not just Erin, Jack, and Scott. Total strangers too.

They got out of the cart. Tess wouldn't look at him, but she didn't run either. Aaron wished she would. Seeing her run from him would hurt, but not nearly as terribly as seeing her stay no matter how badly he'd hurt her.

"…I'm feeling tired," Tess whispered. "I want to go back to my room."

<u>14</u>

The Single Rider did not know why he was.

There had been no explanation waiting for him when he opened his eyes again for the first time. He possessed no memories of who he'd been before he was who he was. In many ways, he was much like a tumor himself. An independent knot of tissue that had suddenly sprung into being inside of a larger body; feeding and growing in the darkness.

But he was a tumor with a purpose. The Single Rider knew that much. He knew that there was a reason he was growing fat in the shadows of the Brightest Place on Earth. He knew there was a reason why he felt stronger with every passing year,

Just like he knew that there was some great feast coming towards him very soon.

The Single Rider felt it coming. The aroma of it was thick and cloying in the back of his throat, like the stench of vomit rising when you knew there was no way to stop it.

The line in front of him moved.

The Single Rider moved with it.

<u>15</u>

Eddie's spirit was flagging.

His feet hurt. His calves ached. The inexhaustible power of the Raging Fire of God's Strength, as it was sometimes wont to do, was departing him. Perhaps there was somebody out there who needed it more right now. Minister Ed was fine with that. But, if he could have made a request, he would have liked to have held onto it until his kids were no longer filled with the power of sixteen pixie sticks apiece.

They were at the arcade now. The five dollars each he'd given them had not been part of the original budget, but it was the closest thing he could get to a break. The arcade had only one door. Ed could plant himself by it with a bottle of water and catch his breath while he watched the kids play skeeball or mow down an army of invading aliens.

That one does seem a bit violent, he thought. He almost got up to tell the Davis brothers to play something without so much shooting but, in the end, he decided against it. Simon and his brother Mike were two of the sweetest kids in his ministry. He doubted a few minutes of blasting computer-generated aliens into goo would change that. And if he was being completely honest, he doubted this was the first time either boy had played extraterrestrial exterminator either.

"Is there anything I can help you with, Father?"

Ed looked up at saw a Turtleshell Mountain attendant at his side. The man was smiling solicitously, but Ed could see the hint of something less courteous lurking behind that smile.

The grin Ed gave back was completely sincere. "I'm a minister, actually, but personally I've never thought much of the distinction. Either way, I'm fine. Thank you for asking." He pointed to some of his kids. Ellie Turner saw him pointing and waved back. "Just keeping an eye on my little turtles. Youth group trip."

The attendant kept smiling. He was paid to smile. The hostility behind it never quite went away, though. "Well, glad to see they're having a good time. If you do need anything, just let one of us know."

He went back behind the display case where he was stocking prizes, but Ed saw that he kept sneaking the occasional glance at the man wearing a roman collar as he sat all by himself in a children's
theme park.

Ed understood. Truly, he did. If you were going to share in the glow of the best of your Brothers in Christ, you also had to accept the tarnish of those who had no business putting on a collar.

Nothing negative was insurmountable. That was God's Gospel and Ed's Gospel. He had eighteen boys and girls with him from thirteen mothers and thirteen fathers who all knew and trusted him implicitly. The knowledge that the trust had to be earned instead of just assumed made it all the more valuable, and the suspicious glances from the attendant just made him treasure it more.

He was so lost in his meditations that he didn't immediately notice the change as the melody of beeps and sirens around him had taken on a more ominous tone.

But then one of his kids was tugging at his arm and that was something he could never ignore.

"I wasn't dying!" Lily Crenshaw protested.

He smiled. "I should hope not. I don't think your parents would be too happy if they're waiting for the bus tonight and you're not on it."

Lily was not amused. She pointed at the game she'd been playing, a 16-bit antique from his own arcade golden years. "I wasn't dying!" she repeated. "I had three lives left but the game said I was DEAD!"

Ed followed the line of her finger and saw the words "GAME OVER" printed across the screen.

His first suspicion was that Lily had used up her last token and was bearing a little false witness against the arcade machine in order to pry a few more coins from the Minister. But, as Ed looked around the arcade, he saw "GAME OVER" glaring back at him from every screen. Ominous, end of the world, funeral dirges for a dozen different fallen digital heroes bled together into an indistinguishable cacophony of doom. It tolled around them, louder and louder until it drowned out almost everything else.

GAME OVER.

GAME OVER.

"I don't know, Lil," Ed said. "It looks like none

of the games are working right."

Lily's eyes got big and excited. "We should sue!" she proclaimed.

Lily's parents were lawyers. Ed smiled and ruffled her hair. "How about we get some lunch first? Help me find everybody else, okay?"

Already, Ed could see that Lily wasn't the only one upset by the abrupt end of their game. Some of them were using decidedly un-Christian language to express their displeasure.

That was all right. They had another four hours in the Most Joyous Place on Earth. One video game misadventure wouldn't be enough to ruin that.

Ed would make sure of it.

<u>16</u>

Aaron lay in his bed and looked up at the stucco ceiling. He was counting all of the different things he could have done to change the course of the afternoon and, possibly, the entire rest of his life.

So far, he was up to twelve.

In her own room, Tess had made it up to nine.

Jack was watching football in the room he shared with Erin. It was a good game, Oklahoma versus Texas Tech, but Jack dearly wished that he was watching it tomorrow on DVR like he originally planned. Seeing the game later but with his friends happier would have been much better than watching it live and knowing that people he thought of as family were aching.

Erin stepped out of the bathroom. She'd showered and was still toweling off her hair as she came out.

"Anyone call?" she asked.

He shook his head. "Total radio silence."

Erin huffed out a breath that blew wet strands of hair away from her hair. "God, what a disaster."

Jack only shrugged. "It could have gone better."

"Better?! It was right there in front of them," Erin lamented. "If one of your football teams tanked it on the one-yard line like that you'd scream yourself into a stroke."

86

Speaking of football, she realized she was standing between Jack and the TV and hurriedly stepped aside. "Sorry! I didn't know you were watching the game."

He smiled at Erin. "I've had worse views." He patted the bed beside her. "Want me to put something else on? Bet I can find a *Criminal Minds* rerun on somewhere" Erin came over to him but didn't get on the bed. She kissed his temple, just over his eye. Jack tried not to shiver. "Watch your game." She said. She quickly threw on shorts and a t-shirt. "I need some aspirin, I'm going to go check the hotel store. I'll be back in ten minutes."

Jack sat up. "Are you okay?" he asked her.

Erin shrugged. "Yeah," she said. "Just a little headache. I'll get something to knock it down." She waved her fingers at him. "I'll be back soon, baby."

She left. Jack stayed where he was and watched Texas Tech line up for a punt. They were down by three touchdowns in the third quarter, and it looked like Oklahoma was going to take this one. He tried to think about what that meant for the Bowl game standings and found that he couldn't focus enough to sort out the rankings. Probably for the same reason that Erin had complained of a "Headache."

Headaches. Heartache was what it was, and in the quiet of his own heart he was suffering from a little bit of it himself. A steady current of romanticism ran beneath Jack's three years as a Division 1 defensive end, daily 5 a.m. workouts, and department-leading arrest record. It was down deep but it was there nonetheless, and Tess and Aaron's fight on the Mariner ride had left him deeply troubled. They obviously loved each other. That love had been at the crux of their conflict, and every argument Jack had overheard only underlined how deeply they cared for each other.

In Jack's mind, that love should have rendered everything else as a wash.

He raised the volume of the TV to block out his thoughts. Not that it did much good. The moroseness clung to everything in his head, tinging even the purity of NCAA ball with its melancholy.

But then he thought about Erin dropping her towel and shimmying into a skirt and a t-shirt without bothering with a bra because she'd be back in a few minutes. As always, Jack thought of her and smiled. He smiled all the more because seeing two people who loved each other fight was a lot like passing an autowreck on the freeway. It really made you appreciative of what was undamaged in your own life.

Aspirin, she'd said. Not a long trip at all. Elevator down, hotel store, elevator up, and then back into bed alongside him. Maybe they would get room service. And if Tess texted Erin to say that things were better and she wanted to go to dinner with all of them? Well, Jack would be happy for her and Aaron, but he also didn't think they would be joining them.

- - -

Erin knocked on Scott's door.

She didn't have to wait long. Scott opened the door, but he didn't invite her in. He didn't even say a word. He just stood slightly left of the center of the doorway, giving Erin a clear path inside. If she wanted it.

For now, they just looked at each other. Scott, politely interested, as if she'd shown up at his door with tracts about the Watchtower. Erin, breathing heavily through her nose, knowing that she wanted to run but not knowing in which direction.

Why was she here? Scott was inconsiderate. He had the sense of humor of a mean-spirited middle schooler. Objectively, he wasn't even all that handsome.

Jack kept all of her shows recorded on his DVR, just in case she was waiting around his apartment while he was still on shift. He was protective without making her feel like she couldn't take care of herself. Sometimes he talked in his sleep with his blonde hair tussled over his eyes, and it never failed to strike her as the most perfectly adorable thing ever. When they made love, his large arms enveloped her and made her feel like she never wanted to be any place else.

So why was she here?

"What's the matter?" Scott asked conversationally, "Need another charge?"

Yes, that was why she was there.

Erin ran into him. She didn't stop until she was straddling him on the bed and kissing Scott like she was underwater and his mouth was the only way she could get oxygen.

Scott's taste always reminded her of different things. Cigarettes stolen from her grandmother's nightstand. Whiskey smuggled into the bathroom at junior prom. Ecstasy, salty with a stranger's sweat at a club.

Erin had loved her grandmother very deeply. She was an honor student and senior valedictorian. In college she volunteered for a program that went around talking to high school kids about making drug free choices.

But there was that other side of her always underneath it. Like roots underneath a rose. The side that craved the dirt no matter how beautifully she bloomed.

She bit his lip. Scott gasped, but not in pain. Then he chuckled. "Mmm, you're hungry. Jacky Boy must not be feeding you enough."

Erin dug her nails into his shoulders. "Shut up," she hissed. Even as she ground her hips faster against him. "I love him. I fucking hate you."

Scott surged up beneath her. His surprisingly strong, wiry body lifted Erin and twisted her so now he was the one on top. He planted burning kisses on her neck and the tops of her breasts. "That's fine," he said. "Just so long as you don't hate fucking me."

She didn't. God help her, she didn't. Her hands were already fumbling for his belt and his rough, oily fingers were underneath her skirt, pulling at her underwear in anticipation of what was coming next.

"That's one hell of a wrong turn you took there, Erin."

Scott and Erin flew apart as if the fire between them had become literal. They took refuge on separate sides of the bed, as if the empty stretch of comforter between them was proof positive of their innocence.

I locked that door. Scott thought. *I know I did. I heard it click.*

And yet Jack was there. He was leaning in the vestibule, blocking the path to the door with his exceedingly muscular arms folded across his chest. "Or is this what you meant when you said you needed something for your headache?" he asked. Jack turned his eyes towards Scott.

Green eyes.

All street cops, even traffic cops, were supposed to be caught up on the constantly changing world of gang signs, but it was something Scott had always struggled with. Other than red Bloods and baby blue Crips, he could never remember who wore purple or what a hat cocked 45 degrees to the left meant.

Jack didn't seem angry. He was standing there as if he'd walked in on Scott and Erin doing nothing more illicit than wrapping Christmas presents. But Scott looked into those green eyes and understood what they meant just fine.

They meant death.

"Well?" Jack prodded. "Scott, I don't suppose that's an aspirin bottle I see down there?"

It wasn't. It wasn't anything anymore. Scott's erection was going, going, gone because he was mortally terrified that he was about to be beaten literally to death. If Jack had come in red-faced and raging, Scott would have expected to be punched. He would have braced himself for a black eye or maybe even a broken jaw and then considered them even.

This quiet said something else. The quiet said that Jack was going to slowly and methodically pound blood, breath, and life out of Scott until there was absolutely nothing left inside of him.

Scott started to inch slowly backwards. It looked like he was just trying to put some distance between himself and Jack, and that wasn't exactly suspicious, but it also moved him closer towards the nightstand.

Erin found her voice. Or rather, she found a voice. Who this shaky, terrified voice belonged to, she had no idea, but it certainly couldn't be hers. "Jack, before you do anything. Will you let me say one thing?"

"Shut the fuck up, bitch," he said casually. "I'll get to you in a second." He took a step forward and inward, putting the brick wall of his body more firmly between the bed and the door. "If it's all right, I'd like to talk to Scott right now."

Not trusting himself to speak, Scott nodded. He also moved another half-inch closer to the nightstand.

"Now. It's obvious there was something…" his lip curled back like a dog bearing its fangs, "sexual going on here. And obviously I have… feelings about that."

He clapped his hands together. Erin and Scott both jumped.

"But! I am still a cop. So rather than do

something I might regret later, I'm going to carefully gather all of the facts and make sure I understand exactly what it is I'm looking at here." His hands were still pressed palm to palm, and then his fingers interlocked and turned his hands into a single fist the size of a tea kettle.

"Scott," he began. "Would it be accurate to say that this was the first time you and my girlfriend have ever been intimate?"

Scott nodded. "Never even crossed my mind before today. She came in looking for aspirin and it just sort of happened." Jack didn't believe him and Scott didn't care. This was all about buying time. Another few inches and he could grab the lamp off of the nightstand. Then, he'd wing it at Jack's face as hard as he could and run all the way to Turtleshell Peak in Florida if he could make it. If Erin was smart, she would be right behind him. If she wasn't... well, he would shout like hell for hotel security and 911 while he was running.

"All right," Jack said evenly. "Next question. Would you characterize this sexual activity as consensual?"

"No," Scott said. Again, an obvious lie. But the truth was very much a straight line proposition. He answered. Jack murdered him. A lie was a detour. Detours meant time, and all Scott needed was just a few more miserable inches.

Jack was nodding. "Non-consensual," he remarked in the same tone of voice he would use while jotting something down in a notepad. "So it was rape then."

And then Jack's hand was suddenly full. Which

was impossible because he'd clapped his hands and Scott and Erin had both seen that they were empty. It was like the set up to a magic trick. Watch closely, nothing up my sleeve, and then-

Gun. Oh shit gun. Gun. Shit. SHIT. Scott froze and forgot about the lamp completely. Erin saw this new, nightmarish twist unfold and her stomach turned inside out,

"No!" Scott screamed. "Listen, Jack-"

"No. Is that what Erin said before you raped her?" The barrel of Jack's service pistol was aimed squarely at him, but it was not stationary. It was moving between the same three points on a vertical axis. Head. Heart. Balls. Round and round and round she goes. Where she stops? Only Jack knows. "So I guess 'no' means 'yes' to you?" he asked. "Should I just shoot you right now?"

"NO!"

Jack shrugged. "If you're asking for it."

He fired. There was a bang that sounded like an early firework going off.

As it turned out, she stopped on the head. Jack's bullet took Scott right above the bridge of his nose. Scott's whole upper body rolled in a wave of transferred force and a neat, red hole the size of a quarter appeared in his forehead.

The hole in the back of his head was not so neat. Blood flew from it in a massive spatter pattern. Jack was not surprised to see precious little brain matter coming out along with it.

In her head, Erin screamed. She screamed the kind of scream people only uncover once in their entire life. It was the scream of a person watching their solid, comfortable understanding of the world collapse. It was the last sound someone would make before they drowned in the ooze of a new, repugnant reality. In her head, she was still screaming as Scott's blood splashed across her face and chest.

In reality, her throat had constricted entirely. Her jaw hung open like the mouth of a discarded ventriloquist doll. Her eyes bulged with backed up terror straining to get out, but the only thing that could escape from the knotted tissue of her windpipe was a whistling shriek like a boiling tea kettle.

"It's okay, baby. It's okay."

Jack was there on the bed beside her. He cupped her face with one gentle hand that still reeked of gunpowder. "Listen to me, Erin. This wasn't your fault." He stroked her hair and pressed their foreheads together, whispering more comforting words that rang in her ears like graveyard dirt over a casket. "I'm here now. Jack's got you, baby."

He's insane, Erin thought. Then, on the heels of that, *I made him insane,* and shame coursed through her, temporarily overwhelming nausea and fear.

And then she felt the warm metal of the gun barrel against her thigh. She wanted to jump away from it, but Jack's hand stroking her hair had clamped down hard on the back of her neck. He held her in place and kept the gun against the inside of her leg.

"Still one more thing, baby," he said. "I believe

you. I wouldn't have shot that bastard if I didn't. But there's going to be an investigation into this." Jack's eyes flicked briefly towards Scott's body. "And Scott's obviously going to have problems making a signed confession."

The gun slid higher up her thigh as Jack continued in his reassuring tone.

"We're going to need to do a rape kit."

A Glock was not part of a rape kit. And she could have pointed out that Scott had still been wearing his pants when Jack found them. But those were reasons, and reason clearly had no place in what was happening here.

"Please, Jack," she whispered.

"I don't like it any more than you do, Erin," he said. "I know this is going to be uncomfortable. If you want to, you can hold my hand."

He held out the hand that wasn't holding the gun. Erin took it, praying that she would feel something of the Jack she loved there. Something of the kindness and gentleness she always felt in his fingertips like they were a living part of him.

But all she felt was the gun traveling still higher until it finally had no place else to go.

"And, Erin?"

She looked into his eyes and realized she was wrong before.

There was reason there.

"I know you're a fucking liar," he said.

He squeezed the trigger.

Aaron slammed into Jack at the last possible second. The bullet that should have ripped through Erin instead fired harmlessly through the mattress just beneath her thigh. It would still be a long time before Erin truly believed that she wasn't really dead.

Aaron wrestled Jack down off the bed and rolled him onto his stomach. He cracked his fist against the back of Jack's skull and smashed his friend's face against the floor.

He hit Jack again without waiting to see how much damage the first punch did. Jack was bigger, stronger, and better trained. Speed and surprise were the only advantages Aaron had, and he needed to use them before Jack got up. Aaron hit him again and again and then he took the gun from Jack's hand and pressed the barrel into the back of his head.

"Don't move, Jack! Don't fucking move!"

Jack stayed flat, but it was thirty long, unblinking seconds before Aaron felt secure enough to look to the bed.

Tess was there. She had Erin's face pressed into her chest, and she was rubbing soothing circle's against the other girl's back. "It's okay," Tess kept repeating, "It's okay." But Erin just squeaked with terror every time she said it, so Tess eventually stopped speaking and just held Erin close to her.

He saw Scott too. He'd fallen upside down with his legs still hooked up on the bed and his head resting against the floor at a crooked angle. His two blank, white eyes and the single, gaping, red one all stared right back at Aaron.

Aaron looked back down. Jack's back heaved up and down with the raging engine of his breath

"What's wrong with you?!" Aaron screamed.

"What's wrong with me!?" Jack raged. He twisted his head to the side. Aaron was so keyed up he nearly blew Jack's head off just for that. The hammer was actually rising before Aaron could stop his finger.

Jack wasn't getting up. He was only twisting his head so he could fix his eyes on Erin.

"WHAT'S WRONG WITH YOU!?"

- - -

The Single Rider laughed. The man ahead of him in line turned and fixed him with a questioning stare. The Single Rider shrugged his teenage girl's shoulders. "Just thinking of something funny. Sorry."

The other man turned back around without thinking too much of it. Bursts of unexplained amusement were commonplace at Turtleshell Mountain. It was like they pumped something into the air.

The Single Rider didn't laugh again, but his thin, pink lips peeled back in a smile that showed all of his neatly lined teeth.

Everybody had their ways of killing time while they waited in lines. Some people played games on their phones. Others made their children pose for pictures. Old-fashioned parents insisted on some kind of family activity.

The Single Rider tuned through the babble of every soul within the confines of Turtleshell Mountain until he found something really gut-wrenchingly ruinous. He listened for secrets, shames, and guilt, and sorted through the fog of thoughts like a child looking through souvenirs. He finally settled on the half-hearted rationalizations of a woman conflicted over cheating on her boyfriend. Her boyfriend whom, even better, the Single Rider could tell that she genuinely did love.

Perfect. The Single Rider hung onto that gem and felt around until he found the boyfriend's mind. It wasn't hard, because he just so happened to be thinking of her at the same time. Just lying there in bed, thinking about how much he loved her.

Come and see, the Single Rider whispered into the boyfriend's mind. *Third hotel door to the right and then straight on until morning.*

And see he did. And then, just to make it extra interesting, the Single Rider materialized a weapon in the gentleman's hand so he could express himself more thoroughly.

The Single Rider may have also egged him on a little bit. Perhaps mentally nudged him down some roads he might not have taken otherwise.

His toy had been taken before he could finish playing with the girlfriend, and that was disappointing, but not really a problem. He would not be able to tell anyone anything about the Single Rider. In point of fact, he would never be able to tell anyone much of anything. When the Single Rider stepped into someone's mind, it was like putting your foot into a full bucket. A lot would spill over the sides, and what overflowed could never be put back.

Which was also fine. What mattered was that

whatever line the Single Rider was waiting in had grown shorter still. He could feel it.

He could also feel that, whatever ride he was waiting for, it was most certainly going to be worth it.

17

Erin started crying as soon as security escorted them out into the hallway.

The normalcy of it all was too painful. Inside the hotel room, with the blood and the bodies and Jack's disoriented, lunatic's eyes, it was easy to pretend that so much insanity could not possibly be connected to the real world and the life they had there.

The hallway proved her wrong. It was the same mundane, burgundy carpet and creamy, yellow walls. The same anonymous hotel doors looked back at her, each one hiding lives that were still presumably whole and happy.

This was the real, regular world that she had always lived in. The real Jack had killed the real Scott. The real Jack was currently zip-cuffed to a chair beneath the terrified eyes of a Turtleshell Mountain security guard whose waxy pallor said that he clearly was not trained properly for this shit.

She, the real Erin, would soon see a police station from another perspective. One where evidence would be pulled off of her and not the other way around. She would be the treasure trove of information, and it would be others scouring over every detail of how she destroyed the man that she loved.

Then, the trials. Two trials. One for Jack, where

an entire life of honor and honestly would be outweighed by five minutes of anger and madness, and then one for her. Erin's trial would not be held in a courtroom. It would be held in Jack's parents' kitchen or maybe his brother's living room. Places where Erin had once been welcomed with love and affection and where she would now be torn apart as the bitch whore who'd broken Jack's heart and his mind. Erin would never get the chance to confront her accusers, but why would she need to?

She knew she was guilty.

She stepped out into the hallway. The ground beneath her feet held firm. It did not break apart underfoot. The walls in front of her didn't fade to smoke and drift away.

And they never will. They're too real.

Erin began to weep then. She discovered that if she cried hard enough, her tears made it impossible to see much of anything.

She found she preferred it that way.

- - -

Two security guards had answered Tess' frantic call. One stayed with Jack and waited for the police to arrive. The other one stepped out into the hallway with Tess, Aaron, and Erin but seemed to lose his sense of authority as soon as he shut the door behind him. He coughed nervously.

"Uh... is there a room you'd prefer to wait in?" He unconsciously raised his voice, trying to cover Erin's hitching sobs.

"Mine I guess," Aaron said.

"Okay," the guard said. He couldn't have been older than twenty. The way he fidgeted and mumbled, he was twenty going on four. "Your room. Right…. Which way?"

Aaron, twenty-six going on third grade himself, didn't answer. He couldn't remember.

"1919," Tess said quietly.

"1919," the guard repeated. Loud again. "Okay."

He led them in that direction. Following the numbers down. He kept a hand around Erin's arm, leading her along while she shivered and sobbed. It was designed to look like a comforting gesture, but Tess noticed the guard was also guiding them down the hallway at a quicker pace.

He doesn't want the other guests to hear, Tess thought. Which was stupid because if there were anyone in the rooms to hear Erin, then they would also have heard the gunshots, screaming, and cursing that had brought Aaron and Tess out of their rooms. It couldn't have been later than four o'clock. Nobody came to Turtleshell Mountain to sit in their room at four o'clock. You were either taking a break by the pool or you were out having the time of your life in one of the parks. No matter what you did, the only reason to be in your room was…

If you were having a miserable time.

It wasn't supposed to be. When the doctor had informed her that she was in remission, the phrase he'd used was "pleasantly surprising."

The word Tess thought of was Magic.

Shortly after her prognosis had gotten worse,

Tess had opened a book and then closed it just as quickly in a cold sweat. The book was the first part of a new series. It was getting rave reviews from everyone, and a legion of fans were already counting the days until the sequel came out.

Tess had closed it because it hit her that she would most likely be dead before the next book's release date. It felt like that was what cancer had made her life. Something beautiful and riveting that she was never going to see the end of.

And then, from out of nowhere, she was told that she could very possibly see the end of that story and many more.

To Tess, that was magic.

So, of course, she would want to break the news at Turtleshell Mountain. It was the place where Magic was everywhere. Their business was to spread joy and make wishes come true.

Instead, Scott was dead, Jack was going to spend the rest of his life in prison, and Erin was only sucking in breath so she could sob it back out.

And then there was Aaron. Even if their fight inside of the Mariner ride had been idiotic, it was the last exchange they'd had before they met in the hallway, drawn out by the sound of what they knew to be a gunshot. He was staring blankly ahead now and rubbing his knuckles. The same knuckles that he'd slammed into Jack's head again and again.

He wouldn't be able to ever look at her again without seeing Jack's bulging, broken eyes staring back at him. They would never share a bed that didn't have Scott's dead body lying in it with them.

They'd reached the door to Aaron's room. The guard opened it with the master key card on his belt and Tess remembered when she'd gone to this same door just a few hours ago.

"If you ever do want to say those things, I'll be sure to say thank you." The words hung around her head like ghosts in a haunted house.

Aaron never would say them now.

Tess could see the back of Erin's tank top. Timothy Turtle smiled broadly at her from between Erin's shoulder blades. He was wearing a cowboy hat and swinging a lasso that twisted and contorted to form the words "Let's Wrangle Up Some Good Times!"

They'd all slipped away from her completely. Everything was ruined, just like Erin's tank top was ruined by the blood stains.

She wished suddenly that she had no good news to share.

And she wished bitterly and sincerely that they'd never, ever come to Turtleshell Mountain.

18

The Single Rider reached the front of the line.
Oh. Oh, my.

He realized that he hadn't been waiting to get on a ride this whole time.

He'd been waiting to get in front of the control panel.

But no more waiting now. The Single Rider stepped up…. And started to turn things on.

19

Jim Carecki could not do The Howling Hop one more time.

He swore it to his wife. "I mean it, Liz. I absolutely cannot and will not walk into that torture chamber again. If all the kids wanted to do was listen to cheap robots lip sync the same terrible songs over and over, we could have taken them to Charlie Cheese's and saved three thousand dollars. And I double, triple swear, on my mother's grave, the next person who calls me 'Daddy-O' is getting put up for adoption."

Liz just smiled and said nothing. She knew that she didn't have to.

And, sure enough, when the boys started begging their "Daddy-O" to take them to *The Howling Hop* "just one more time, pretty, pretty please," Jim didn't just go along, he revealed to their two boys that he'd already grabbed their quiktrik tickets an hour ago.

They breezed into their seats after just a five-minute wait. And not just any seats in the tiny theatre designed to look like a fifties diner, FRONT ROW SEATS. As they waited for the show to begin, Liz's ears were tuned to the excited chatter of their twins but her eyes were fixed on her wonderful, perfect husband.

And it wasn't just the The Howling Hop. After five consecutive trips, every year since Ben and

107

Alex were three, she knew that Turtleshell Mountain had turned into a mountain of madness for her husband. But he never said a word about it. He never showed anything but total enthusiasm for every ride, show, and same three-song medley for the fourth time in one day.

She looked at him and realized, not for the fourth time nor the fortieth, that he was the most incredible, caring man that she ever could have married.

And then Liz lost sight of the clear lines of Jim's face as the lights in the theatre dimmed and small, eager hands wormed their way into hers. Then a voice came over the loudspeakers; a passable imitation of Dick Clark. *"Ladies and Gentlemen, now coming to the stage.... THE BIG BAD WOLVES!"*

The curtain opened on the same three animatronic wolves in motorcycle jackets, sunglasses, and bandanas.

Are they the same? Of course they are.

Of course they were. The guitarist, Frontman Wolfman, was raising one crudely articulated arm, just like he always did, to tap somewhere in the vicinity of the microphone.

"Helloooooo, Turtleshell Mountain!" The robot's voice was the same raspy, drawn-out imitation of Wolfman Jack. "How are you doing out there!?"

The answer from the fifty children and most of their parents was a loud, exuberant affirmative.

The robot pivoted jerkily on the lazy susan concealed in the floor and turned to the drummer.

"Mad Dog Mike, this feels like a special kinda crowd to me. Does it feel special to you?"

The wolf behind the drums rose up on a hydraulic lift and twitched from side to side. "It looks like one to me, Frontman. But I think you're asking the wrong person."

The kids knew a prompt when they heard one. They let out a cheer that rattled the ceramic collector's plates hanging on the walls.

But Liz saw that she wasn't the only parent in confused silence. This was not part of the script. This was not the normal introduction.

And still, the feeling that something else was different kept nagging at her.

"I see what you mean, Daddy-O," Frontman Wolfman said. "In fact, I think this crowd is too good to just watch the show. You guys know what I'm saying!? I think it might be time to turn this trio into a, what do you call it? Into a four-tet!"

Liz winced. If the kids were loud as spectators, they were deafening as possible participants.

A focus group, Liz suddenly realized. All at once, it all made perfect sense. *They're thinking of making some changes to the ride, and we're testing the new version. Jim might even hear some new songs to complain about.*

Meanwhile, the kids in the stands had lost their minds. Both of the twins were standing on their seats in a bid to make themselves more visible. "Me!" Alex was screaming. "Pick me!" After a moment's silent communication, Jim and Liz each grabbed a kid under the armpits and lifted them high overhead.

"ME, ME, ME, ME, ME!" Alex was howling. Ben had taken a different approach. "Sir! Sir! Please, pick me! I know how to play the recorder!"

Frontman Wolfman's eyebrows rose jerkily in surprise. "Whoa!" One arm rose stiffly and pointed right at Alex. "This little cub in the blue looks like he knows how to rock." In her hands, Liz felt Alex lose it in a paroxysm of ecstasy.

"What do you say, little wolf?! Wanna rock with the pack?"

He was nodding like a bobble head rocked by an uppercut. Liz set him down and Alex set a new land speed record sprinting for the stage.

Next to her, Ben was biting his lip which she knew meant he was trying his very hardest not to cry. Already, Jim was leaning close to murmur something in their son's ear. Liz couldn't hear it over the noise around them, but she knew it would be something to make Ben feel better.

On stage there was a small guitar and microphone she hadn't noticed before. Alex slung the strap over his shoulder and stepped up to the mic.

"You ready, little wolf?"

Alex grabbed the mic stand and stuck his fist out like one of the hair metal singers he watched with his dad on VH1 Classics. "Ready to rock!" he shouted.

"Well, all right," Frontman said. "You're going to help us sing a brand-new song. It's called *Eatin Good*. And a one, a two, a one, two-"

The band started to play. Liz and Jim clapped and cheered along with the rest of the audience,

110

but Liz wasn't sure if this new set-up was such a good one. If they handed out comment cards, she would say that having a live child onstage, especially one who was constantly on the move like Alex, only made the robots seem more jerky and artificial by comparison.

Also, this new song was just atrocious.

"I tell you, baby, I been eatin' mothballs and motor oil,
You hear my hunger, honey? It's coming to a boil.
So I don't mean to be rude,
And, baby, I don't mean to be crude,
But I hear that dinner bell a-ringin'
and tonight....
I'M EATIN' GOOD!"

Alex slid on his knees to the edge of the stage. In true eight-year-old tradition, he was so enthusiastically fixated on enjoying himself that he didn't realize he'd nearly gone right off the edge of the stage, but Liz noticed and her heart leapt into her throat and didn't climb back down until she was sure he wouldn't go tumbling to the ground head first.

But he was safe. Her beautiful boy, laughing, strumming on that guitar, and not even caring that the notes he made weren't even playing over the speakers. He was completely lost in his own world, playing on, even as his canine bandmates came to a stop. Mad Dog Mike froze with his drumsticks suspended over his snare. The bassist and

Frontman Wolfman slowed to a halt with their picks in mid-strum.

They're broken, Liz thought. *They really should have tested this more before trying it out on a real audience. And I'm still going to have to pry that guitar out of Alex's hands with a crowbar.*

And then the three animatronic wolves all suddenly pivoted and fixed their sunglasses-shrouded gazes on Alex.

Frontman Wolfman set down his guitar. Mad Dog Mike dropped his drumsticks and pistoned up off of his stool and onto legs Liz never even knew he had. The bassist, whose name Liz still couldn't remember, put down his instrument as well.

And Liz realized what had been bothering her since the curtain opened. It was suddenly so obvious it may as well have been lit up by one of the stage lights.

The wolves' mouths moved as they sang. Not at all in time with the lyrics, but who was going to nitpick that? They did move for effect though- fabric muzzles that opened and closed and even showed off painted-on tongues.

But now there was something else on display in their mouths.

Now there were teeth.

Liz was still trying to solidify the concept in her mind, the concept of *TEETH*, when the Big Bad Wolves pounced. The three of them swooped down on her son, and they weren't jerky or robotic in the slightest.

Mad Dog Mike grabbed Alex's arms. The bass player grabbed Alex's legs. They lifted him up and pulled his stringy, still-growing body taut.

Alex turned his head towards her. There was a single moment where Liz could see that her son was afraid. He understood that something very wrong was happening. Instinctively, he looked to his mother to fix it.

And then Frontman Wolfman ripped into Alex with his brand-new teeth and tore her son open like he was nothing but an oversized turkey leg.

Liz saw all of this with perfect clarity. It was onstage, right in the center of the spotlight... and they had front row seats.

Frontman Wolfman pulled his red-stained snout from Alex's torso. He howled and there was no doubt it came from the wolf's maw and not the speakers hidden in the diner booths.

Alex's body was trembling. Trembling and twitching. Blood bubbled from his gaping mouth. The drummer and bass player let Alex slip from their claws. In death, her son was nothing to them. The Big Bad Wolves were just getting warmed up. Snarling, they stage-dove right into the center of the theatre.

At least one thing was the same in a world where nothing else was. The Howling Hop was still a prerecorded act. *Eatin' Good* was still blasting over the speakers as Frontman Wolfman, Mad Dog Mike, and the bassist, whose name Liz still didn't know, tore into the packed crowd of families with fangs and claws bared.

Tonight.... I'M EATIN' GOOD!"

It was so loud, you could still hear it over the screams.

Jim and Liz ran with Ben tucked between them. They joined the stampede running for the door in a mad herd that was as old as time itself: prey fleeing with their young nestled between them.

And, running hard at their heels, the wolves.

Liz couldn't see too much of what was in front of her. But she could hear too much of what was behind her. Snarling and cries for mercy that suddenly turned into gurgled death screams.

Liz and Jim shouldered other couples aside as they ran faster for the door.

But then there was no room to run. The crowd in front of them had stopped moving and started compacting. From the front of the room came the sounds of pounding fist and screams.

"There's something in here!" she heard someone say. "Please, I'm with my children!" And, above everything else:

"Open the doors!"

"Please, open the doors!"

"SOMEBODY OPEN THE FUCKING DOORS!"

Behind them, there were no longer any cries for mercy. Only screams and the god-awful music of snarls and howls growing ever closer.

Liz blamed herself. She'd sensed that something wasn't right as soon as the curtain had opened. If they'd been any place but Turtleshell Mountain, she would have trusted her instincts and yanked them all out of there immediately. Instead, she'd trusted the safety of her family to someone else's dream. Now she had one son's blood

114

splattered over her blouse to show for it and, as Ben's sweaty fingers tightened against hers, she knew that she wasn't done paying.

Liz stopped running.

After a moment's silent communication, so did Jim.

They turned to face the monsters at their back.

The Big Bad Wolves were there. They were crouched in hunter's stances with blood on their motorcycle jackets and gore smeared across the cheap felt of their stitched-together snouts.

That was all there was to see. The rest was just human leftovers; ripped piece from piece, scattered across the seats, and splattered over the jukebox and the ceramic plates on the walls.

Liz pushed Ben behind them. Jim bent down and whispered something into their son's ear. This time, Liz could hear it all too well. "Close your eyes, kiddo." Then he kissed Ben's forehead and stood beside Liz. She dearly wanted to take his hand but she resisted. Their position was hopeless as it was; she wasn't going to make their odds any worse by trying to fight one-handed.

And fight they would. Unarmed. Untrained. Outnumbered. Uncaring. The trio of wolves rose to their full height. Their muzzles pulled back and put their red-stained fangs on full display.

It meant nothing to Jim and Liz. All that mattered was that nobody was going to touch their son without killing them first.

A human enemy would have at least taken notice of their courage. Perhaps he might even have been moved to show mercy and spare them.

At the very least, he would be touched by their love for each other.

The Big Bad Wolves were not human. They weren't even really alive.

And they didn't care what order they did their killing in.

Mad Dog Mike drove his claws into the underside of Liz's jaw and ripped her face off from the inside out.

The bass player tore Jim's stomach open and left him fumbling over his own intestines.

The child, cowering behind the crumpled corpse of his father, they left for Frontman Wolfman.

And still, the music played on:

> *"Ain't stickin' to no more diets,*
> *You heard me honey, we're about to start*
> *some riots!"*

- - -

Ron Cuesta had wanted to treat his wife Mia like a princess ever since the moment he had met her. But, for a long time, the best he had been able to do was keep a roof over their heads and lukewarm food on the table. No money for a baby. No money for vacations. Just lots of sixteen-hour days where Ron would come home, fearful that this would be the night where he'd slip into their bed and discover that Mia had finally just given up on him and left.

She never had. And every night she was still

there, Ron swore that one day he would give her everything she deserved.

Well, that day had finally come. The tech start-up Ron was partnered into hadn't just started-up, it had *exploded*. Ron would say they had more money than they knew what to do with, but that wasn't true. Ron knew exactly what he was going to do with it, and he knew that Turtleshell Mountain was the first place you went to when you wanted to treat someone like a princess.

The first place, but it wouldn't be the last. They were on The Whole Wide World ride and Ron was leaning over and whispering into her ear, telling Mia when they would visit each exotic locale as they passed it.

India, with the mahogany figures draped in sheets of red silk and shimmering marigold? This summer.

Italy, where tiny marionettes toasted their love atop a painstakingly detailed Leaning Tower? We'll be there for Christmas.

Egypt and the Sphinx whose mysterious gaze was just as enchanting at $1/200^{th}$ scale? Say the word and I'll ready the jet.

There were no dizzying drops or expensive effects but it was unquestionably the most magical experience of their entire trip. Ron looked down the river they were floating on and saw the path of their lives on either bank. A hundred magical adventures to every corner of the globe with the woman he loved at his side.

The ambush took place in the dense foliage of the Amazon jungles; but, the attackers were by no means restricted to Amazonian tribesmen. As the gondola containing Ron, Mia, and a dozen others with their own dreams and hopes floated down the riverway, projectiles from a dozen different cultures flew from the cover of miniature trees lining the banks.

An Inuit spear the length of a straw punctured Ron's jugular vein. His death felt like a rush of fleeing warmth that killed him before he even realized he was in pain.

A British musket ball no larger than a pencil point bored through Mia's left eye and lodged itself in her brain before she could even think to panic.

Miniature Swiss lances rained death on a family visiting from Missouri.

A couple from Australia flew all the way to California only to be struck and killed by a pair of boomerangs as wide as a single slice of bread.

In its own way, the assault was beautiful in its diversity.

The miniature citizens of the Whole Wide World had chosen the Amazon rainforest for their assault because it was the first diorama after a curve. And they'd struck silently for the same reason. By the time the next boatload of happily enchanted visitors was rounding the bend, the last one was a fair stretch ahead, and there was nothing to tip off the next group of victims that they were entering a killing corridor.

- - -

In Captain Regulus' Space Simulator, a

118

simulated crack in the video screen created a real depressurization inside of the cabin. Twenty-five people screamed against the building pain in their heads and then died with blood gushing from their noses and their burst eyeballs running down their faces.

- - -

If there was one group that was immune to the magic of Turtleshell Mountain, it was fifteen to sixteen year olds. It's the age where the punishment for breaking with peer-pressure enforced apathy is most severe.

Troy Carson was very much a teen-law-abiding citizen. Even his own father privately thought his son had been an eye-rolling dick bag for the entire family trip, and Troy was being no less dickish on the Himalayan Sled ride. He'd been on this dopey, baby, "roller coaster" like twenty times in his life. The ride wasn't scary, and the stupid Yeti with the glowing eyes before the last dip looked so fake.

There was nothing fake about the Yeti this time. Especially not the tremendous, blue-skinned paw that removed Troy's head from his shoulders.

- - -

On Main Street, families were sitting down to dinner at a dozen different restaurants. Tourists were taking pictures or debating between a light-up Turtleshell Hat and a pair of Falcon Falls swim

119

trunks declaring the wearer was a "High Diver."

And they all turned around at the thunder of approaching feet.

Parades were a common occurrence at Turtleshell Mountain. They happened daily at 11:00 a.m., 3:45 p.m., and 7:00 p.m.

This was not a parade.

This was a march.

They were all there. Two dozen Timothy Turtles. A flock of Fergus Falcons. A cete of Bella Badgers. A herd of Michael Moose. A toy chest of Cowboy Cals and Darling Delilahs. And there were others. The entirety of the history of Turtleshell Productions. Every much-loved character that had been delighting children for decades.

They were costumeers. The actors who professionally portrayed joy with only pantomime and the stitched grin sewn onto their oversized character heads. As they marched, the broad smiles on their faces were as fixed and unchanging as ever. The reflection from the streetlights put a happy twinkle in every plastic, unblinking eye.

The only thing that was different was the two-headed wood axe each one had clasped in their hands.

To be specific, they were carrying exact replicas of the woodsman's axe from the *Little Red Riding Hood* short. Any serious collector could have pointed it out if they weren't too busy trying to process the incongruity of the scene in front of them.

The same long, drawn-out thought process was

taking place in every head on Main Street. It was almost comical. If any one of them had been confronted with an army of axe-wielding men wearing masks on their hometown street, they would have run screaming in the opposite direction. But this was Turtleshell Mountain. And these were Turtleshell Mountain characters. The patron saints of four generations of children the world over. The idea that they were something to be afraid of was as difficult to process as the idea that oxygen was suddenly a carcinogen.

The hundreds of people caught out in the open on the streets of Turtleshell Mountain were still trying to reason out what to do when the chopping began.

The first victims, an obese father from Kentucky with his head split open and a college student from China with her arm hacked off, fell without so much as a scream from those around them.

Then a French tourist got his leg chopped off at the hip by a Felix Fox and a Hispanic mother of two took an axe blade to the chest from a Beaufort Bunny, and the people around them finally got it.

Then the screaming and running began.

Typically, the only time all of Turtleshell Mountain moved en masse like this was when the park first opened and people poured in from the entrance floodgate. Here, it flooded towards the exit in the same kind of mad tide. A tide of humanity that, this time, ran into a dam made up of a second front of axe-wielding costumeers marching in from the other end of Main Street.

121

Running turned into hiding then. The people scrambled for any concealment they could find and fervently prayed that they would be passed over.

It meant less than nothing. The costumeers found them in the bathrooms. They found them cowering in the gift shops. They cut them down while they huddled behind statues and dragged them out from underneath dining tables and butchered them atop their own half-eaten meals.

- - -

It was the same scene all over the park. The screams filled the Most Joyous Place on Earth as loudly and thoroughly as laughter ever did. The blood flowed in its gutters thicker than any Southern California downpour. Eventually, the mangled remains of the fallen cluttered over the drains, and the blood pooled in the streets. Every symbol of comfort, happiness, and light that ever walked the streets of Turtleshell Mountain was reborn beneath the moonlight as something new and savage.

And the Single Rider held sway over all.

20

1935

The eyes are the most important part.

When it comes to what's inside of a character- laughter, sorrow, love, even anger- it's the eyes that do the heavy lifting. The pose, the colors, the accessories, none of it matters if you can't get the eyes right.

They have to be large, but too big and people get uneasy. The eyes are the window to the soul. If the windows are too wide, the audience sees too much, and too much insight into any soul is a frightening thing.

"It's all in the eyes." That's Cartoons 101. The Gospel of everything from Mutt and Jeff to that smart-ass rabbit that the Turner Brothers kept pushing. Nobody gets anywhere with anything if they can't get the eyes right.

Charles Tuttle always saves the eyes for last. He draws everything else first, and then determines what kind of eyes he needs to pull it all together. He never rushes. He's never eager to reach the end the way someone building a hotrod might tire of installing doors and upholstery and rush to put in the engine. He takes his time to ensure that everything is right.

It is late. Well past two in the morning. Everyone else in the studio has gone home. This is what Charles Tuttle thinks of as the magic hour. The special time when he's not answering phone calls or signing off on merchandise or dealing with any of the other thousand responsibilities that distract him from the one thing he still cares about most of all.

Drawing.

He works for hours without even raising his head. Every line is made with the precision of machines that won't be invented for another seventy years. By the time he's done, the sun is almost coming up. Soon, the secretaries will begin filing in. Before they arrive, Charles reviews what he's done.

The character he drew is done lightly in pencil. Shades of noon-day shadows; barely even there. The graphite on the page is little more than a layer of dust.

The character has curved claws. It has twisted horns. It has fangs overlapping past its top and bottom jaw like the tangled concertina wire on the Western Front where Charles was stationed back in '14. Long, knotted fur, filthy with brambles, hangs from it in shaggy curtains.

Worst of all are its eyes. Charles has gotten them absolutely perfect. If he erased everything but the eyes and showed them to a thousand people, the consensus on what they represented would be unanimous.

Terror
Hunger.
Cruelty.
Wicked delight.

Charles takes all of this in.

Then, he sighs and starts to draw again.

The pencil lines are not ghostly this time. They're dark, solid, and firmly anchored in reality. The filthy fur is buffed into a uniform coat that hides all detail. He fills in the gaps between the uneven fangs and turns the creature's distended jaws into a long, friendly snout and then adds a set of whiskers for good measure.

The curved horns become wide, upright ears. Its cloven feet turn into penny loafers.

Charles saves the eyes for last. He softens the angles and adds dark half-moons to each snake slit pupil so they become round and inviting.

It takes maybe fifteen minutes. Little more than a blink of an eye in comparison to the rest of the night's labors. A layman would look and say that Charles had barely done anything.

But, those few marks are all it takes to turn something vicious and hateful into the best friend you never knew you were waiting for.

Charles sets his pencil down just as he hears the front door of the office open. Once again, he examines what he's done.

All there is to see now is a fox with his arms held wide for a big hug.

This is a good one, Charles thinks. A fox would seem to lean towards being a bad guy. It was in the same class as wolves and coyotes after all, generally considered Bad Guys in Cartoons 202. But, there's no question that this guy belongs with Timmy's gang. A little rascally maybe, but goodhearted all the same. Charles traces the outline of a suit over the character model and makes an annotation in the margins that the Fox should always be dressed to the nines- suit jacket, collared shirt, bowtie. That would go a long way towards enhancing his reputation.

Charles is scribbling some more notes as his secretary enters with his morning cup of coffee. She has worked here for five years and is not surprised to see Charles still hunched over his drawing desk.

"Is that one ready to go?" she asks.

"Almost," Charles says without looking up. He's finished the direction for the colorists: *Orange fur. Black nose.* But he's still stuck for a name.

Finally, it comes to him.

He writes "Felix" underneath the sketch in his customary, extravagant scrawl and then hands it off to his secretary.

"Go ahead, Jill. Let the vultures pick it over."

But Jill, of course, is the first one to see it. She's always the first one to see it. In those thirty seconds, she looks more critically at the fruits of his labor than anyone else will for the next six months.

Finally, she smiles.

"Another winner, Mr. Tuttle."

He smiles back. If she notices the strains at the edges of it, Jill attributes it to Mr. Tuttle's fanatical hours. "Nothing wrong with it?" he asks.

She shakes her head. "Looks like another cutie to me."

She leaves. Charles sits back in his chair and

126

doesn't start shaking until he hears the door close.

He fumbles for the bottom drawer. He pulls out a chipped glass and a cheap bottle of scotch. He fills the glass and empties it just as quickly. Then he drains the mug of coffee, drinking the liquid down along with the layer of skin burned off of his tongue.

Jill was taking the drawing to the animators and merchandisers. The process would soon begin. They would take Charles Tuttle's creation and begin prepping it for reproduction in cartoons and stuffed animals all over the country.

They would only use Charles Tuttle's drawing of the Fox as a template, of course. The finished product that would soon be playing before the eyes of millions of children would only be drawings of whiskers, smiles, and arms held wide for a big hug. The illustrators who followed him would not drape their banners of grins and embraces on a framework of fangs and claws.

But the Demon would be inside of them all the same.

<u>21</u>

No cops.

That had been Raylene's first order after she was able to confirm that no other guests were aware of the situation in the Kubla Khan Hotel.

No cops. Except, of course, for the fucking cops already right in the middle of this shitstorm.

She took an underground service tunnel from her office building to the hotel. There were strict rules for all Turtleshell employees, janitors and executives alive, governing the way they were supposed to portray themselves around the paying public. Frowning, grimacing, or any other kind of negative expressions were strictly forbidden. Elbowing fat kids in the face for being in her fucking way was also frowned upon, so Raylene played it safe and stuck to the underground pathways.

Jesus, this is going to be a nightmare. Shit. Shit. Fucking Shit.

Coming in had been a mistake. If she wanted to gloat, she could have just gone to her condo in San Clemente and toasted the sun with a bottle of $1,000 Magnum Grey Goose. Whoever mishandled this shitstorm was going to get crucified, and there was no place higher for her to climb by handling it right. It was all risk and no reward.

Bullshit. You've been getting the rewards ever

since you took that lunatic's noose and turned it into a rope ladder, Raylene reminded herself. *You're the Evil Queen Bitch of Turtleshell Mountain, and you've had the tallest room in the tallest tower all to yourself for years. Don't complain because you have to clean up a little birdshit.*

That was right. Birdshit was all this was. She reached the freight elevator labeled "Kubla Khan" and pressed the call button. While she waited for the elevator, she took a calming breath and welded a veneer of Turtleshell solicitude over her twisted core of anger and pride.

You're the Evil Queen Bitch.

You're the Evil Queen Bitch.

You are the Evil Queen Bitch and don't you dare forget it.

The elevator arrived. Raylene stepped inside with a smile on her face. She pressed the button for the ground floor and held it down until the bulky freight doors slid apart.

She was the Evil Queen Bitch.

And this was her castle.

- - -

Raylene was pleased to find the cops so diminished.

She'd had dealings with cops before and, in her experience, even the off-duty ones were incredibly arrogant pricks who just had to take control of every situation they were in.

Not these cops. One couldn't stop sobbing, and

the other two were sitting quietly with their hands folded in front of them.

She spoke with the security officer first. She got all of the pertinent information from him and then told him to call the local police. She also told him exactly who to ask for so he wouldn't fuck it up. Then, she crouched beside the woman who wasn't crying, the blonde, and gently squeezed her hand. "Miss? My name's Raylene Adams," she said. "I'm Director of Public and Guest Relations here at Turtleshell Mountain. I can't even begin to imagine how difficult this must be for all of you, but I'm here to do whatever I can to get you through this situation."

And to make sure none of you are still here and screaming in the hallways when the guests come back to their rooms for the night.

"Is there anything I can get you? A glass of water? Something to eat?"

The man shook his head. "We just want to get this resolved. Quietly, if we can."

Raylene nodded sympathetically, betraying none of the elation she felt. Quietly. Wonderful word.

"I understand," she said. "Turtleshell Mountain maintains a close relationship with local law enforcement. I've already directed one of my security personnel to reach out to the local precinct. I'm sure we'll have officers on hand shortly to take care of everything."

One officer, was what she had instructed the security person to say. *One officer to discreetly take the mad dog out through the service tunnels.*

No sirens, no police tape, no goddamn uniforms if they can help it. Tell them if they need anything from the crime scene, they can send someone back at midnight to get it. That was the kind of cooperation complimentary year-round passes for the entire precinct could ensure.

There was a subdued knock at the door.

"That must be them now," she said.

The Turtle woman, Aaron had already forgotten her name, got up and went to the door. He barely noticed. He was much more interested in his thumb.

There was a smear of red jelly there. It must have happened in the car. They'd taken breakfast on the road. Tess, fond of bad cop jokes, had brought donuts. Aaron and Jack had both taken jellies. By the end of it, both of them had dark red, strawberry jelly all over their hands.

Erin had grabbed Jack's hand; the one that wasn't holding the wheel. Aaron saw it in his head all over again with the stunning clarity of 1080p. *She'd taken his jelly thumb and sucked it clean. Jack had yanked his hand back and told her it was gross; but, he'd been smiling as he did it. Then, he took that newly clean hand and squeezed her bare knee with it.*

And Tess took your hand, he remembered. *For an electric, million-year-long moment, you thought she was going to do the same thing to you. Then Tess took your thumb and used it to smear a long, red streak across your own face.*

Disappointing, but it did get the jelly off. Which made this new red smear a mystery.

131

Then, he realized with a dim lurch that this spatter of red was probably some of Jack's blood. Mystery solved.

I think I'm going to be sick, he thought. He'd held it at bay this long, held it when he was breaking his best friend's nose, held it when security arrived to restrain Jack and Aaron had nothing left to do but look at the bend of Scott's legs sticking up over the side of the bed like relics of a long-dead civilization, but this was too much. This smudge of red the size of a penny was going to be the thing that finally pushed him over the edge.

As his stomach revolted, he struggled for something, anything else to fixate on.

Perhaps that was why he heard what he heard so clearly.

"-Seriously, do I actually have to tell you to just use your own cellphone?" That was Ms. Sincerely Concerned, talking to somebody through the half-opened door to the room.

"...I don't care," she said. "The two of you get him downstairs and then you go find a fucking phone that works."

Then the door was closed again, and the face that turned back towards them was the woman who wouldn't know if you spelled "fucking" with an "f" or a "ph."

"It would seem that we're having some kind of complication with our phone system. We don't like to advertise it, but we do have a containment area on the resort premises. I'm going to have our officers escort the...." Raylene struggled to find a polite euphemism for "bat-shit crazy murderer" and again wished she hadn't come in today.

"He's not 'The' anything!" Erin screamed. Tess held her to keep Erin from jumping off the bed, but there was nothing she could do to restrain the pain burning in her eyes. "It's Jack. His name is Jack." They were the first coherent words she'd said in an hour.

Raylene nodded reverently. "Jack," she agreed. She kept her voice carefully neutral and even. Aaron suspected her voice was always this even and neutral whenever she spoke in public. But something told him that he didn't want to hear what her voice sounded like when she knew she was in no danger of being quoted.

"As I was saying, we're going to take Jack someplace where he can't hurt himself or anyone else until the authorities can be contacted. While we're resolving this, I'd like to invite the three of you to wait in one of our corporate suites until you can provide your statements to the police. It's much more...." she looked around the room, almost exactly like the one where Scott's body was currently lying. "There are less associations to be made there."

Aaron nodded. "Okay." No associations sounded good. No associations actually sounded great right now.

Tess didn't seem to have the spirit to say anything, but she was getting up as well.

"I'm staying with Jack," Erin said.

The right side of Raylene's mouth twitched in a small, downward tick. None of them knew how much pure fury it took to create that small crack in her carefully constructed veneer.

"I'm afraid that would be against company policy," Raylene said with great diplomatic effort. She restrained herself from dragging the stupid cunt out by the hair with much greater diplomatic effort.

"Erin, that wouldn't be a good thing for either of you," Tess said.

"So I should just leave him alone? I'm not going to do that. He needs me."

Tess wavered, on the verge of saying something she knew would only hurt her. But in the end, she'd be hurt worse if Tess said nothing. "He's not going to want to see you, Erin."

"He needs me to distract him!" Erin shouted. "If he's alone, he's going to think about what he did and he's going to be afraid of what's going to happen next. And if I'm not there to hate, the only person he's going to have to be angry with is himself! He doesn't deserve that!" Maybe that was part of it; but, she was also squeezing her own arms tightly as she spoke. Aaron saw blood welling up where her nails broke through skin.

Tess bit her lip. She got it too. Erin wanted Jack to hurt her as much as she didn't want him to hurt himself.

"I'll do it," Aaron said. He stood up, finalizing his self-nomination before Tess could appoint herself to endure Jack in whatever shape he was in. Maybe crying and rocking back and forth in a ball. Maybe screaming and raging and hurling insults at whomever he saw. Either way, Aaron knew that if he didn't stand then Tess would.

He turned to Erin. "Does that sound, okay? You and Tess can sit and catch your breath, maybe even have that drink of water, and I'll sit with Jack and keep him company while we wait for-" he stopped short of saying 'police.' "-While we wait for someone to come get him."

Tess got up. But only so she could sit next to Erin and put an arm around her. "I think that would be all right, don't you?"

Not trusting herself to speak, Erin nodded.

Raylene, the one they really should be asking for permission, tried to assert her authority. "I'm afraid that the holding section is in the employees only area of the park. Allowing you back there would be a liability issue."

"Could that liability issue be resolved if Aaron was willing to sign a waiver?" Tess asked. "You know, if we quickly drew something up outlining all the details of the situation? I could call a lawyer if you're not sure."

The implied threat was not lost on Raylene. The bitch's blonde hair was fake, either a bad dye job or a bad wig, but there was obviously nothing wrong with the brain underneath it.

"My guards have already brought your friend to the holding area," Raylene said, conceding without consenting. "I'll have to walk you down myself. And while you're there, you will obey the directives of my officers at all times. Is that understood?"

The Turtleshell woman was clearly ready for a fight but Aaron wasn't. He would agree to all of that just fine.

Or, at least, that's what he would have done.

But that was before Jack started screaming.

22

True love (or friendship) is like a tower with a heavily fortified bunker in the basement.

You can do whatever you want with that tower. You can build it a hundred stories tall and put a ten-story spire on top of that. You can cover it with glass panels of every color until it glistens in the sun like a pillar of jewels. Hell, you can even build it out of actual jewels if you want to.

Then, you can demolish that tower. Take every single precious inch you spent years building tall and beautiful and rip that motherfucker right down to the ground.

But there's still that bunker in the basement. And if you've built it right, a person napping in that bunker wouldn't even wake up as all of those tons of cheap, dollar-store flash came crashing down overhead.

Even with Scott's body cold at the other end of the hall, it was that principle that drove Erin, Aaron, and Tess out into the hallway. Raylene actually made it out faster than any of them. The cops were just worried about their psycho friend. Raylene was looking out for her career.

"Where is he?" Erin cried.

None of them knew. They couldn't see him. And it wasn't coming from the direction of Scott's room.

But Jack was screaming. Softly. So softly that

if the TV was on they might not have even heard him.

But that only made things worse. Because it wasn't really that Jack wasn't screaming loudly. It was just that he was very far away. So far that for them to even hear him at all must have meant that he was screaming at the top of his lungs.

And he was screaming because he was terrified. That much was obvious.

They listened. The screams were getting louder.

And louder.

And then there was a short "Ding," and howling as loud as a winter storm wind.

"The elevator!" Raylene screamed. And then, in her head, *Those brain-dead fucks took him down in the guest elevator?* She was going to wrap up this shitstorm and then she swore that she was going to hand those guards their own heads.

The elevator doors opened. Jack came flying out, still screaming at the top of his lungs.

He came out drenched in blood. It soaked his face, chest, and legs. He left bloody footprints in the carpet behind him as he exploded out of the elevator.

Jack was still running. There was a wall in front of him and he ran straight into it without even slowing down. His hands were still tied behinds his back and he struck the wall face first. He didn't even seem to realize it. He kept pumping his legs and rubbing bloody smears against the wall with his face like he was trying to run through it.

Tess got to him first. She grabbed Jack by the

138

shoulders and tried to haul him away from the wall. She may as well have been trying to tug an oxen back by its tail. Jack shrugged her off and kept driving face first into the wall. He was still screaming. Aaron heard a crunching sound like a fistful of dried leaves. *That's Jack's broken nose grinding against the sheet rock.*

"Jack!" Erin threw herself between him and the wall. He smacked into her and she took the jarring impact of his weight without complaint. She cupped his face, trying to calm him down the way she would when the Patriots blew a playoff game or some ADA fucked up a surefire case.

"Jack," she repeated softly. "Jack, stop." She worked her hands up and down the sides of his face. "Jack, look at me," she soothed. "Look at me."

He finally stopped slamming himself into the wall. He sunk to his knees and Erin went down with him. He'd stopped screaming, but now he was shaking uncontrollably and his eyes still seemed to be focused on something a million miles away.

This isn't the same, Aaron thought. *This isn't the anger that made him shoot Scott.* No, this was a fear so overwhelming that it was radiating from Jack in palpable waves.

"They want a Golden Hinoki," he said. Jack's throat was so raw from screaming, the words came out like pieces of jagged glass. "They want the Golden Hinoki! We have to find one right away!"

"What's he saying?" Aaron asked.

Erin ignored him. She knew what he was talking about, but it made so little sense that it wasn't worth trying to explain. Not while she could feel his body thrumming with terror beneath her hands.

"Where are my security guards?"

Raylene had hung back. She was not about to literally get her hands dirty, and she was such a stranger to them that Aaron and the others had forgotten she was there.

But Raylene had all of their attention now as she brought up a glaringly obvious question that none of them had considered.

"There were two guards that went down with him. Where are they?"

Aaron and Tess took a large step away from Jack as the most obvious answer occurred to both of them.

Erin stayed where she was, but it meant ignoring every self-preservation instinct she had. And the blood underneath her palms suddenly burned like it was scalding.

So much blood.

More blood than Jack could lose and still be alive.

They suddenly realized something else as well.

The elevator was still dinging.

They turned. They saw that something was keeping the elevator door from closing.

Tess screamed.

Aaron was finally sick.

Erin buried her head in Jack's bloody shoulder. It was the only refuge she could find from what she was seeing.

Jack kept babbling, lost in whatever darkness

he'd been pushed into. "Golden Hinoki... Has to be gold. Has to be."

Raylene realized that she could still hand those guards their heads. But she would have to find their bodies first.

One guard's severed head was in the path of the closing doors. This was the one keeping the elevator from closing. The doors would start to slide shut, then the decapitated head would trigger the collision sensor and the doors would slide open. The chiming sound coming from the elevator was actually a warning.

Look. Look here. Something's not right.

It was actually two somethings. The second severed head was facing them. The strained, dead eyes stared at them through the split in the door.

They were frozen with the same unending terror they saw in Jack's eyes.

23

They tried to reach the front desk from nine different phones. Once from Aaron, Tess, Erin, and even Scott's rooms. Then they tried again from each of their cellphones. Then they tried once more from Raylene's cell phone. Each time, they got nothing but static.

Then they tried to call 911, and there was nothing on the other end but grating white noise that filled their ears like powdered glass.

Now they sat silently in Aaron's room, each one of them running through the same options silently in their heads.

Go downstairs. That was the simple, most obvious answer. *Go downstairs. Get the hell out of here.* Except that nothing inside of that idea was simple. It was like a baseball. Smooth and clean on the outside and an impenetrable mass of knots on the inside.

It all depended on who had killed the guards. Had Jack done it, with his hands literally tied behind his back? If it was somebody else, were they still in the lobby? If they dawdled too long, was it only a matter of time before there were killers knocking at their door? If they split up, then who was safer? The people who went downstairs or the ones that stayed upstairs?

The only one who possibly had any information was Jack. But all he did was stare into space and occasionally mumble something about the Golden Hinoki.

So round and round they went, just like on the mad tea cups.

Aaron looked at the clock on the night stand. Ten minutes that felt like ten hours had passed.

"We could take the service elevator," Raylene said. "That's what those morons... those guards should have done anyway." She kept her arms folded and her hands clamped tightly to her elbows as she spoke. She wouldn't shake that way.

"Where would it take us?" Tess asked.

"Anywhere. The whole park's connected by underground tunnels. It's how the support staff gets around without ruining the, you know, magic."

"Why didn't you mention that before?" Aaron asked.

"Because you need a keycard to take the elevator down, and I don't have one. It's with the...." she gestured out into the hallway. Towards what was in the elevator. "With their bodies I mean."

"So down in the lobby," Aaron finished.

"Then we should just go out that way then if we're already going there," Erin said. "There might even be more people down there." She tried to smile but the rusty hinges of her jaw could only produce a twisted grimace. "We're probably just psyching ourselves out anyway. I mean, we're at Turtleshell Mountain!"

"Are we?" Tess was by the window. They were on the nineteenth floor. Outside, she could see lights and rides in motion and even the occasional silhouette running across Main Street. But her nerves were screaming at her that she couldn't trust any of it. "I'm not so sure," she said.

"Oh, we are," Jack spoke so suddenly and so forcefully that they all jumped. "We're here and they're here. They're allll here." Then he lapsed back into his fugue state, leaving his words to linger among them.

"We go to the lobby," Aaron decided. Maybe only to fill the void left by the jet of poisonous gas that was every word Jack said.

"No," Erin said immediately. A second ago, she hadn't any idea what she wanted to do, but now she knew for sure. She definitely did not want to go to the lobby.

"We go together," Aaron continued. "And all we do is poke our heads out of the elevator. If things look normal-"

"If there are two headless bodies on the reception desk, I think we can count out normal." That was Tess. She was smiling, but it was the thin, morbid twist of lip that he remembered all too clearly from chemotherapy.

"Then I'll settle for quiet," he said. "All I know is staying here and getting room service isn't going to get us anywhere. We can't keep looking at the walls and waiting for a magic escape door to appear. And we're going to have to find out what's going on before we can decide to do anything else."

Silence again. But this time it was the silence of consent. Tess was the first one to get up. She was followed by Raylene. Then Erin, who had to

144

stoop and grunt as she hauled up the empty meat that was Jack. "Come on, Jack," she said, hoping for even a small spark of consciousness to help take some of his bulk off of her.

What she got instead was Raylene pushing them apart. Without Erin to hold him up, Jack crumpled instantaneously. He missed the chair and dropped down onto the floor without making any attempt to hold himself up.

"He's not coming with us," Raylene said.

Erin stood her ground. With her haggard eyes, skin like curdled milk, and hair greasy with fear sweat, she cut a very poor figure against the statuesque, polished career woman.

She stood anyway.

"Yes, he is," Erin said. She set her jaw. "I'm not leaving him alone for...WHATEVER to find him."

Raylene just laughed. "Oh. Okay, I see what this is." She sketched a sign of the cross in front of Erin's face. "I absolve you of your sins. Say ten Hail Marys, don't ride any more dicks you shouldn't be on, go in peace, and feel free to leave the psychopath behind when you do."

"Fuck you, bitch."

"Save it. I don't like you enough to spar with you. The only thing I care about is I've got no reason to think your psycho boyfriend didn't kill my guards himself and then pull this PTSD shit so we won't see it coming when he tries to do the same thing to all of us."

"His hands are tied behind his back!"

"And that's where they're staying. And his ass is going to stay right in this room."

145

"I'm not leaving him," Erin swore.

Raylene shrugged. "So stay here and have couples therapy together. Nobody's making you come."

"Nobody's leaving without her either," Tess said.

She stood hip to hip with Erin. Tess had honestly not been sure what the right thing to do with Jack was. She still didn't, but she could see that Erin would not go anywhere without him, and Tess didn't even need to think about it to know that there was no way she'd abandon Erin.

And Aaron, of course, was not going anywhere without Tess.

"Have you all lost your fucking minds?" Raylene asked as Aaron joined the other two morons in forming a protective half-circle around the gibbering lunatic. "He stays here. End of story."

"That's not the end of the story," Aaron said. "The end of the story is when we do get out of here and we have to explain what happened. Do you really want to be on record as the acting employee who left a known murderer unsupervised on Turtleshell property?"

What Raylene wanted was to be on a beach somewhere, taking her pick of men half her age. Instead, she was stuck choosing between the short-term safety of her life and the long-term safety of her spot on the board.

Of course, that was not really a choice at all.

- - -

146

Even with everything that had happened so far, the walk to the elevator was the worst thing any of them had ever experienced. Each step was made with the precision of a soldier crossing a field of invisible tripwires. The silence was analyzed for even the slightest hint of any sound.

The worst part was Jack. Erin was guiding him but he muttered unintelligibly the whole time and occasionally banged his foot against the wall. Every time he did, the rest of them jumped for fear that the noise was something other than Jack.

The sensation was far worse than having something concrete to be afraid of. It made it so everything around them was terrifying.

And that was before they reached the elevator.

Some internal protocol had been activated. The doors were no longer dinging and opening and shutting. They were buzzing harshly while the twin doors squeezed even more harshly against the guard's severed head.

Aaron, Erin, Raylene, and Tess formed up in a line and stared silently at the head. The same stupid, obvious thought ran laps in all of their heads.

Somebody's going to have to move it.

But how? Aaron was not a street cop. He wasn't even trained to handle a gun or authorized to hand out a parking ticket. Still, the three of them were members of a police force. This man's head was not just a piece of unwrapped butcher's meat. It was the face of someone who held a place in the hearts of others. A place that was going to be empty.

They all understood it. If Aaron ever met this man's wife or children, he wanted to be able to say he did *something*.

Raylene stepped forward and picked up the trashcan next to the elevator. She angled the narrow metal can between the doors and swept the security guard's head out into the hallway. Without the obstruction, the doors slid closed without so much as a whisper. Raylene quickly hit the call button to open them again.

She entered the elevator, still holding the trashcan. She used it to bat the other severed head out into the hallway. It rolled towards Erin, and she clung protectively to Jack as it tumbled past her.

Raylene pressed the button for the lobby and then held the door open for the others.

At first, they just stared at her. And that was all right, Raylene stared right back. Someone had to set a course if they were going to get out of here alive.

"All aboard," she said.

<u>24</u>

Tess had discovered a new favorite ride. A week ago, she wouldn't have been able to answer that question. She would have had to break the park down into the different theme sections. Then she would have to break it down into ride categories: thrill rides, relaxing rides, kiddie rides, simulated screen rides. Finally, she *might* be able to provide you with a top four in each category.

Not anymore. Now, beyond a shadow of a doubt, Tess' favorite ride in all of Turtleshell Mountain was Elevator to the Lobby.

It didn't matter that there was blood all over it. What mattered was that the soothing hum of the elevator surrounded her like a blanket, and the gentle descent of the car was almost lulling her to sleep. Even the blood wasn't so bad if you didn't look at it. Tess found that the best remedy was to look at the blood-free floor indicator mounted over the door and watch the floors tick down.

Twelve... to eleven... to seven... to four....

"We don't have a Golden Hinoki,"

Tess screamed.

The others jumped. All except Jack who stared blankly ahead as if he hadn't heard a thing.

"We don't have a Golden Hinoki," he repeated. "She won't be happy with us if we don't bring her a Golden Hinoki."

"What is it he keeps going on about?" Raylene

149

snapped.

"Shouldn't you know?" Erin asked. "He's talking about *Lavender Twist and the Golden Hinoki*. That's his favorite Turtleshell Pictures movie."

Raylene snorted. "If that's his favorite movie, then he really is psycho. The only reason we even gave that flop a parking lot was because we built it before the box office numbers came in."

"Quiet," Tess hissed. Not because she wanted Raylene to shut up, but because the floor indicator had just shifted to a "2."

The lobby was coming up next.

"Everyone just stay calm," Aaron cautioned, even as he looked like he was doing a terrible job of following his own advice. "If anything looks wrong, we don't even have to leave the elevator. We close the doors, go back upstairs, and figure something else out."

Nobody actually answered. They all just waited for the ding, the ding that they were all quickly starting to associate with unrelenting doom, to announce that they had reached the lobby.

And then, of course, it came with all the solemn inevitability of a funeral bell.

The doors opened.

Lavender Twist was waiting for them.

25

When the world fell apart, Minister Eddie and his eighteen children were on the Coney Island Coaster.

Ed was expecting a repeat of The Comet Drop and every other combination of eye-drying speed and lunch-reversing drops he'd been subjected to all day. Actually, he was expecting worse than a repeat because, after nimbly evading it all day, he was finally stuck in the front seat of a ride. Historically, the front seat was the worst. It was where he got the most terrified and the seat where his stomach was most likely to hit the emergency escape hatch.

Still, he was determined to tough it out. There was a trick Mrs. Carmody in the rectory had taught him on Friday. Mrs. Carmody was a theme park veteran after serving more tours than she could count with four kids and twelve grandkids, and Ed knew better than to dismiss any advice she had for him.

You count the rails, Mrs. Carmody had told him in her hoarse old smoker's voice. *I don't know what you can do with those new steel ones, but with the old wooden roller coasters what you do is you don't focus on what's coming in front of you. All you do is look to your left or your right and count the wooden beams of the track. You keep your mind right there and you won't even realize that there is a drop until you're halfway down it.*

On one thing, they were in agreement for sure. Ed had no idea what to do about the steel coasters either. He had even less of an idea what to do about the rides where there was nothing to count but open sky or really tiny people ambling along a hundred feet underneath them. But on the retro, clanking Coney Island Coaster, the wooden beams were solid, tangible, and close enough to feel real. Ed could actually forget about his circumstances so long as he stayed focused on the procession of beams moving past his eyes.

Things got even easier once they got closer to the-

No, that's not a thing we're thinking about

-Ed's attention was pulled even further away from the ride once the statues started lining the sides of the track. Each one was a member of the cast from *The Coney Island Caper*. Here was Wladimir the strongman in his tiger-skin unitard and a massive barbell hoisted over his head. Next to him was Elsa, the contortionist. The blonde was balanced upside down on one arm with her legs tied together in a bow. Ed found that the statues worked even better than the wood beams because he didn't have to work as hard to be focused on them. The paint had faded after several year's exposure to the weather, but the craftsmanship behind each one was stunning. Their faces were so detailed.

They almost looked alive.

The -

Don't think about it

-the coaster got, the more sincerely Ed focused on the statues. Here was Mauricio the Lion Tamer. Behind him was Edna, the World's Fattest Bearded Lady. *It's just like an art show,* Ed thought. *An art show on an escalator. Nothing else to think about.*

His seatmate, Paulie Maldonado, chose that exact moment to grab his arm. "Here comes the drop!" he yelled excitedly.

Great, Ed thought. But he returned the nine year old's squeeze and tried to twist the edges of his grimace to make it look like a smile.

The world around him was suddenly much larger. He could see that the coaster was indeed cresting the hill and was only seconds away from plunging to the ground like a fallen angel. Ed resigned himself to the fact that the art show was over and the horror show was about to begin.

Mercifully, there was still one more statue for him to focus on. Eddie trained his eyes on the graven image. It was set to the side, away from the coaster's arc of descent, and Ed was happy to look out instead of down.

Of course, they'd saved the main character for last. Right as gravity was about to seize the train of cars and drag it down to earth, Bally Cast himself was there. A cigarette, a holdover from the days where smoking was not just allowed but expected, dangled from his lip. His sledgehammer was held high overhead, poised to ding the bell of the tallest high striker in the state, save the boardwalk, and win him the Tattooed Lady's inked heart all in a single swing, as it was in the beginning, is now, and ever shall be. His smirk looked lifelike. Full of the clever charm that had made him a fan favorite for decades.

Any tricks to get me out of this one, Bally? I'm open to whatever suggestion you've got.

The statue moved.

The plaster Bally Cast leapt from the platform and onto the tracks. He brought the hammer down with him, swinging with all his force as if his home and sweetheart really did depend on him hitting the bell of the high striker with all the force he could muster.

But there was no bell above him and no see-saw lever below. There was only the roller coaster track and Bally smashed a hole through the boards that was so big you could drive a Cadillac through it.

Or a roller coaster train.

"NO!" Eddie leaned back instinctively, as if somehow his weight would be enough to reverse the coaster's momentum as it hurtled towards the hole in the track.

It wasn't. Ed and Paulie screamed as their lead car plummeted through the crevice in the track and into the empty air. Coming from behind him, Ed heard the other children's screams. It was like a wave. One that began with yells of excitement and turned into howls of horror as row after row of kids, HIS KIDS, realized that something was wrong. The descent was too steep. All of a sudden, the angle they saw the world from took a radical downward dive.

The coaster fell.

Minister Ed had a new thing to focus on. The

sparsely grassed ground eighty feet below them. Eighty feet and rushing towards them at incredible speed.

So fast and yet so slow. Ed had the time to understand what was happening. He knew they were falling and he knew there was nothing they could do about it, and the whole thing struck him as so incredibly cruel. What was the point of God giving them so much time to understand what was happening to them when there was nothing they could do about it?

Nothing you can do to stop it maybe, Ed had the time to realize. *But there's always something you can do.*

Minister Ed placed a hand over Paulie's eyes and held the trembling boy close to him. "It's going to be all right!" he tried to shout, but he didn't know if any of the kids heard him over their own screams. He felt Paul shuddering against his side and dearly wished he could have held the others as well.

Lord God, this is your friend, Ed. In about a minute, you and I are going to have a conversation about how You treat Your friends. In the meantime, please take care of the innocent young souls that are about to enter your Kingdom and treat them like the precious treasures that they are.

Ed crossed himself and then closed his eyes and waited for the darkness to turn into light. But first he waited for the crash. The wind whistled past his ears. The rush of air filled his nostrils and made it hard to breath. There was something heavy expanding in his chest, waiting for-

The crash came.

The sound of grinding steel decimated everything else around him. Ed's whole body rocked forward and his face smashed into something hard. Pain exploded in his skull...

But the sensation of having a body never left him. His head felt like it had been cracked in half, but there was no disputing that he still had a head. No, this couldn't be the afterlife. There was far too much pain.

Ed opened his eyes.

The world was swinging before him like a pendulum.

But it was also swinging far, far below him.

His nose was throbbing, obviously broken, but the blood gushing from it meant his body was still intact enough to retain blood.

He patted his shoulders and his chest. He felt his heart hammering against his ribs. His *solid* ribs.

He was still alive.

And they weren't falling. The coaster was swinging gently side to side. The only thing keeping Ed and the others from tumbling loose was the lap bar. It wasn't foolproof, Ed sensed that he could wiggle loose from it if he tried, but the coaster was obviously hung up on something. They were safe for now.

"Nobody move," Ed shouted to the kids. "Everyone just stay very still and try not to shake the cars too much!"

Ed twisted around in his seat to try and get an idea of what had snagged the back of the coaster. It could be only something tenuous, but, surely, God had pulled them back from the abyss. He had reached down and lifted them above ruination on the backs of eagles. He would not have gone to such lengths only to clip those wings now.

Ignoring the whiplash pain in his neck, he cranked his neck all the way back. He needed to see that the other kids were safe. He needed to know what was holding them up and how secure their position was.

There was not one hook holding them up. There were ten. Wladimir's fingers, snared into the last car of the coaster. The strongman was holding up the whole train with effortless ease.

"Ahoy there!" he shouted when he saw Ed looking at him. He waved at them and held the coaster effortlessly with one hand, the patron saint of all Strongmen brought to life.

"A miracle," Ed whispered. "A miracle!" he shouted for all the children to hear. He laughed uproariously, caring not one whit for his broken noise or strained neck. "A MIRACLE!" *Oh thank you, Jesus. Praise to your name for all days and ages.*

"We're saved!" he shouted. The kids didn't believe it. They still clung to their lap bars. Their faces were trembling and tear-stained. "Look!" he shouted even louder. "Up there! Behind you!" he screamed it until his children started to pay attention. They swiveled back and saw the strong man holding up the roller coaster train. Keeping them safe.

They got it then too. Some laughed. Others cheered. Not a single one cared to question

157

"How?" All they knew was-

"We're saved!" Ed yelled again. "Praise God, we're saved!" Overcome with exhilaration, Ed shook Paul's shoulder, wanting to certify their salvation by feeling the glorious life racing through the boy's body.

Instead, he felt the empty shuffle of raw meat.

"Paul? Paul, are you hurt?"

Paul was not there. There was only his weight and clothes, slumped forward in the seat where Paulie had been. "Paul! Look at me!" Minister Ed shook him and Paul's head rolled far too easily and dangled listlessly off the boy's shoulder. It hung so far, it was completely upside down

His neck was broken.

Minister Ed shrunk back as far as the cramped car would allow. Paul's eyes were open and glassy, staring at him from that dangling, wrong-side-up head.

I was trying to be merciful. That was the protest that kept running through Minister Ed's mind. *It was an act of mercy!* Ed had still been covering Paul's eyes as the coaster was plummeting to earth. It was an act of mercy! But then the coaster had jerked to a stop so suddenly. Ed's entire body had rocked forward and then back and his grip on Paul's head had tightened involuntarily. He hadn't even noticed it. And the crunch of metal had been so loud. It would have been easy for a smaller crack to go unnoticed.

Easy, so horribly easy, to not realize that he'd snuffed out a life he treasured far more than his own.

158

Far above, in another world, Wladimir called out again. "Not the ride any of you were expecting, was it!? I hope nobody was doing anything cute when their safety bars were being checked!"

Ed pushed his guilt aside. Pushed it like a physical thing the size of a house. Tomorrow, he would accept the blame for the death of Paul Michael Maldonado. Today, there were seventeen lives still in his care, and he swore that he wasn't going to lose a single one more.

"Can you pull us up!?" Ed shouted. He didn't waste time pondering the mystery of the living statue. The strongman, with his waxed mustache and tiger skin singlet, was their only hope. If he wasn't strong enough to haul the coaster back up to the tracks, then Ed would have to coax the kids to jump onto the relative safety of the ride's framework.

Wladimir chuckled. The weight of the coaster didn't seem to be bothering him at all. "Just pull you up? Do I look like a New Deal-er to you?"

What? "What did you say!? I can't hear you!"

"Little too much steel ringing in your ears?" That was Elsa. The contortionist spoke with a Brooklyn rasp that belonged back in the thirties. She was walking backwards on her hands up the incline of the track with her legs curled over her head like a scorpion's tail. She reached Wladimir's side and flipped gracefully onto her feet. She looked down at the dangling rope of lives and laughed. "You heard him fine. You just didn't like what you heard." The other statues joined them at the edge. The lion tamer, the tattooed lady, and the

159

others. They all looked down with great interest but no one made a move to aid them.

"For God's sake!" Ed screamed. "Please, help us!"

"That's not how it works, Father." With a nimble bound, Bally Cast leapt over to the other side of the hole in the tracks and landed alongside the other characters. The hammer that started all of this madness was still balanced on his shoulder. "Freebees may be the law of the soup line, but this is the Carnival Walk. We offer prizes, and they're not prizes if we just hand them out."

"I'll do whatever you say! But the children! Jesus Christ, pull the children up!"

"Slow down!" Wladimir boomed. "I like your enthusiasm, but we haven't even decided on a game, much less on the prize." He shifted his grip and the coaster shifted with it. The kids screamed and cried. Ed could pick out each voice individually.

"STOP IT!"

"I think the prize might be the kiddies," Bally drawled.

Wladimir frowned. "The *deti* were supposed to be part of the game. He doesn't have anything else to play with."

"Let them be both," Elsa said with chilling rationality.

Wladmir was unconvinced but Bally seemed interested. "What are you thinking?" he asked.

"I'm thinking I could use some exercise." The contortionist was already limbering up. She twisted one arm behind her back until it touched the underside of the opposite breast and bent at the waist until her nose touched the wood. "Here's the game. I go down there and then me and the preacher have a little race. He starts climbing up and I start tossing kids down."

"NO!"

"If he makes it to the top before I do, him and whatever kids still seated get to walk."

Bally seemed skeptical. "It seems too easy."

"Bally, look at him! He's young but he's walking around at least twenty pounds past fighting weight."

"That's what I mean. Too easy for you."

"There's like twenty kids there! And they're not going to go quietly. I'll have to pry their fingers off one at a time."

But there's only seventeen, Ed thought. *There's only seventeen.*

"For what it's worth, I like it," Wladimir said."

"What do you think?" Elsa pressed when she saw Bally was still not totally won over. "Fair?"

Ed twisted and lunged so far from his seat that ne nearly fell out right there. "FOR THE LOVE OF GOD, YOU CAN'T DO THIS!"

They weren't talking to him. Bally spat in his hand and held it out. Elsa spat in hers. They shook.

Then she was crawling down the side of the coaster with the ease of a poisonous spider.

Elsa came down the right side of the train. Brian, Monica, Lorenzo, Gina, Maria, Jackson, and Louis all shrank away from her as she passed by them. None of them screamed. They were too frightened to make a sound. Instead, the terror

161

radiated from their pale skin and bulging eyes.

I'm going to save you, Ed tried to send out to them. *I'm going to save all of you.* Then, sending it upward harder than he'd ever sent any message, *Please God, grant me the speed of Angel's wings. Give me the strength of Samson. Please, Lord Jesus. More than ever in my entire life, I need you right now.*

Elsa was right beside him. This close, he saw that she didn't look alive at all. She was made of nothing but chipped, weather-faded plaster, and her eyes looked like walled off tunnels with nothing behind them.

"I'll give you a sixty Mississippi head start," she offered. Then she reached for the bundled heap that was Paul's body.

"Don't you touch him!" Ed bellowed. He surged forward to yank her hand away. Instead, his arm was twisted behind his back and the contortionist wrapped her thighs around his neck. The plastic was warm and dirty, the way a bus seat felt if the person there before you was someone heavy and not particularly clean.

She squeezed until Ed's strained vertebrae nearly cracked.

"Ah-ah-ah," Elsa said. "One more rule. If you touch me or try to grab any of the prizes before you reach the finish line, then you're a cheat. If you're a cheat, then the game's over. If the game's over, then Wlad lets the coaster go and, ashes, ashes, you all fall down." She squeezed tighter, stopping just short of breaking Ed's neck. The corners of his vision were starting to turn black.

162

"And, just so everything's out in the open, I'm touching *him* because he's going to be the first one up and over. That means I'm giving you a head start AND the first game piece off the board is somebody who's already dead. I'm so generous you should be kissing my fucking feet."

She let him go.

Ed gasped for air. The more breath he sucked in, the further the black faded from his vision. Gradually, his sight turned from standard radio to widescreen again. He could hear nothing except his own backed up blood roaring in his ears.

"-fty-eight Mississippi... Fifty-seven Mississippi."

Ed threw himself forward without even thinking.

He started his climb.

His kids looked at him from every car as he weaved his way between them on his way up the coaster. Some whimpered. Most were crying. A few were in shock, staring at something a million miles away that no one else could see. A few others were shaking, sucking their thumbs, and muttering "Mama," over and over again. "Mama. Mama. Mama."

Minister Ed tried to lock eyes with each one of them as he passed. He tried to silently assure them that they were going to be all right. He prayed that that would be enough. The climbing was so arduous that he couldn't spare the breath to speak a word. Two of Ed's ribs had been cracked in the crash, leaving him short of breath, no matter how deeply he tried to suck in air. The arm Elsa had

163

twisted throbbed every time he reached for another handhold.

Worst of all, there was not enough adrenaline, determination, or love in the entire universe to grant Ed the athletic ability to make this climb with any kind of grace or speed.

He could use the lap bar as a foothold, but from there he had to do a chin up off the nose of the next car and kick at the air until his feet caught on a seatback. From there, he could clamor into the next car and then start the whole process all over again. He was sweating profusely, and he'd only made it through three cars out of nine before he heard Bally pounding his hammer against a steel railing like a starting bell. "Aaaaannnddddd there she goes!" he howled jubilantly.

From another universe, he heard a brief whisper that might have been Paulie's body hitting the ground eighty feet below.

Ignore it, he told himself. *Go faster. That's only thing you can do.*

And then he heard the first scream and realized how impossible that would be.

So Ed traded tactics. As he climbed, as his body went from aching, to numb, to feeling like every muscle was made out of powdered glass, Ed took everything in. He marked every scream. Every "NO!" Every "Minister Ed!" He put a face to every cry and used it to push himself harder. He was halfway to the top.

"No doubles!" Wlad yelled.

"Twins count as one!" Elsa shouted back.

Ed's footing slipped. One leg slipped between a

pair of cars and his sweat-slicked hands lost their grip as his weight shifted towards his back.

He fell.

NOOO!

His trapped leg saved him. He stripped a foot of meat from his shin before his foot caught in the gap underneath the casing of the car, dislocating his ankle and saving his life.

Don't look back. That was what Ed had told himself. *Don't look back and keep going forward.* That was what had kept him moving. Until now, when Ed was dangling upside down and he could see how many empty carts there were behind him.

The contortionist had Jeffrey Dean by the armpits. Ten years old but embarrassed by how short he still was. This was the first year he was tall enough to even go on the roller coaster.

He reached out for Minister Ed as Elsa let him fall.

Then, the blood from his gouged legs flowed down over his eyes and Minister Ed saw no more.

Blind, Ed lunged upwards anyway. Anchored by only one leg, he did an inverted sit up that would have been the envy of any gym apostle. He felt the plastic of the next car underneath his fingers and held onto it for all he was worth. He righted himself, smeared the blood away from his eyes, and threw himself towards the next car.

"Don't worry!" He screamed at the children in front of him. "Don't worry!"

Then, for the first time, he heard a cry of hope from the children he had left. They cheered for him. They believed in him.

It was the last thing Minister Ed heard before The Zone claimed him. There were four cars left, and Ed cleared them like they were nothing more than stepping stones. He no longer had a body, he was lightning bounding from one conductor to another.

He climbed to the top of the last car and there was a final gap between the roller coaster and the edge of the track.

Ed ignored it and leapt. His hand gripped a loose length of the roller coaster's chain track and held tight, even as jagged spars of broken wood gouged into his belly.

It doesn't matter. You don't know if the finish line is the end of the coaster or the start of the track so don't you dare stop.

Ed bit his own lip. He kicked and clawed and hauled his resisting bulk up until he finally beached his exhausted, broken, bleeding body onto the tracks.

He landed and all of the pain came rushing back. His legs, his arms, his stomach. His neck, back, and head. It was impossible to tell what hurt the most. *Pain. Pain. Pain.* It screamed through him so strongly in so many different voices that there was no way to tell who was loudest.

But it didn't matter because a single voice spoke louder than all of those voices combined.

Made it. I made it. Thank you, Jesus. Thank you.

Ed heard clapping. Bally was suddenly leaning over him, applauding furiously. "Incredible!" he raved. "Absolutely incredible! Forget Coney

Island, we should run you at Belmont!" He looked back over his shoulder. "WLAD! What did he win!?"

Still holding the coaster, Wladimir peered down at the train of cars. He took a moment to count.

"Nothing."

Nothing? No. No, no, no. That was impossible. He tried to say so but his throat had closed completely. It felt like a cork of sandpaper was rammed down his mouth. But he could crawl. He dragged his dislocated foot behind him and peered down to the roller coaster where he had to have been fast enough to save at least one child.

Ed kept looking even after he knew there was nothing to look at. Maybe one of them was hiding down in the footwell of a car. Or perhaps Tina was still there. The girl was barely tall enough to get on the ride. She might not be tall enough for her head to rise above the seat back.

There had to be something he wasn't seeing. This couldn't be all of it. He had not dug and dug and discovered strength and love and determination that he never knew existed only to be confronted with an empty roller coaster and Elsa creeping back onto the level alongside of him. She stood on the track while Bally, Wlad, the Lion Tamer, and the Tattooed Lady all applauded her efforts. Elsa bowed so low that her nose touched the wooden track.

"He made it a race at the end," she said. "I had to push to get the last two off."

"But get them you did!" Wladimir boomed. He

let the roller coaster drop. "And now, for your prize." The hands that had held up the steel train of cars with such ease grasped Ed by the belt and collar. "You pick, Elsa! Where should I throw him?" He hoisted Ed over his head. "To the flying rhinos? Dr. Fantabulous' Laborator-glee? If I try I think I can even throw him right over the peak of Falcon Falls!"

"Wait."

It was not Elsa that spoke. Upside down, Ed saw Bally take a drag from his cigarette that never went out. "He beat Elsa to the top," Bally said. "That was the game. And the prize was that he got to walk away with whoever was left. Even if that's just himself."

Ed shook his head. The motion hurt his neck, but not as badly as he deserved to be hurt. "I don't want it," he murmured. "You win."

Wladimir wasn't ready to set him down yet, either. "You see?" he said. "He wants it."

"I don't care if he wants Eleanor Roosevelt's left tit on a shelf. That's not the way the game is played," Bally said. "If he wants to take a long walk off a short track, that's his business. As far as we're concerned, he's a winner."

"Please," Ed prayed. But not to God. "Please," he repeated.

Wlad still seemed sorely tempted to oblige him.

Elsa walked up behind him. She jumped up and wrapped both legs around his waist. She hung there and ran her fingers across the barrel of his chest. It was meant to be enticing but the rasp of

168

plaster on plaster was devoid of love or life. "You don't want to be bad, do you, Wladimir? Bad boys don't get prizes," she said.

Bally gagged. "Get a room."

"We could you know," Elsa whispered in Wlad's ear. "This is a big resort, and there are about to be a lot of vacancies."

Wlad took all of two seconds to think it over. Then, he didn't just drop Ed, he set him down gently and even wiped some more of the blood off of his face. "Enjoy your winnings, friend!" he bellowed in the same booming voice that Ed remembered from his own childhood. "I have to give this lady a prize of her own!" He held Elsa tight to him, and the contortionist laughed and wriggled like an eel against him.

And then they were gone. The others didn't speak to him, but Bally patted Ed's shoulder as he, the Tattooed Lady, and the Lion Tamer followed their fellows down the track and into the park.

Ed stayed where he was.

He took a short walk to where the track was shattered. He stopped at the edge of the gaping chasm and looked down.

He could see them. Far below, he could see the distant specks that were once his children. Their arms and legs were broken at such twisted angles, they almost looked like stars.

One step, and Ed could take his place among them.

He stood there and looked down as a gust of wind screamed in behind him.

To Minister Ed, it seemed like that cold,

unfeeling gust was God's way of giving him a
push.

<u>26</u>

Lavender Twist and the Golden Hinoki was a 1992 Turtleshell Pictures animated film. It concerned a tribe of three-inch tall, vaguely wood nymph-ish creatures that lived amongst the flowers and shrubs of a small town plant nursery. Lavender Twist was the youngest of the vaguely wood nymph-ish people, and she was always getting into trouble alongside her best friends Leyland Cypress and Harley, the plant nursery cat.

That's all well and precocious until "trouble" turns into "fucking catastrophe." Lavender leaves the front gate unlocked one night, and the nursery's most prized shrub, the Golden Hinoki, is stolen by the corporate growers on the other side of town. Deprived of their claim to fame, it looks like the kindly old couple who runs the nursery will have to close up shop, and the vaguely wood nymph-ish people are going to be out on their asses.

Naturally, Lavender won't allow that to happen. Together with Leyland and Harley Cat, she sets off on a cross-town adventure where she learns about responsibility, family, and how to handle having a crush on your best friend. For their part, the corporate growers learn that larceny and animal cruelty statutes still apply even if you really want to be the most popular plant nursery in town.

Raylene was correct to say it wasn't the most

171

popular feature in the Turtleshell catalogue, but you didn't have to be deranged to pick it as your favorite either. It was well-liked enough that there was a Golden Hinoki garden tucked into a corner of the park, and there was always a Lavender Twist or a Leyland Cypress costumeer in the big character parades.

The thing in the lobby was not a person in a costume. The vines wrapped around its supple limbs glistened with sap. Tess smelled real lavender coming from its bob of white blossom hair. The features on its bulbous head were not sewn on. The thing's giant eyes blinked at the sight of them, and its smile widened to showcase a mouthful of neat, square, wooden teeth.

"Hi!" Lavender Twist said to them.

Aaron and the others didn't answer. They just stared.

Jack didn't just stare. He screamed. He shouldered Raylene aside and kicked at the panel of buttons. "I told you! I told you!" he screamed. His foot slammed into it again and again until one of the buttons for a higher floor lit up.

"Told you! Told you!"

The doors were closing. Lavender made no movement to stop them. A different hand, one with evergreen shoots for fingers, took care of that. It slid into the doorway, causing the elevator doors to automatically slide back open, and took Tess by the arm.

"Oh, no. We're not falling for that one again," Leyland Cypress said.

Tess froze like her arm was in the jaws of a bull

mastiff ready to bite down. She needn't have worried. Leyland pulled her out of the elevator with the gentle insistence of a courtier.

Lavender hopped into the space the two of them left behind. She grabbed Jack's arm in both of her hands. "You're not getting away this time, cutie."

"No!" Jack tried to twist away, but Lavender held him firm and tugged him into the lobby.

"The rest of you are welcome too," Leyland said. "It's a big lobby."

They followed. There was no other choice. Erin would not leave Jack. Aaron would never leave Tess. And Raylene didn't want to be left alone in a world that was totally going off the rails.

The lobby was big. Leyland led them to a seating area with two cushy arm chairs facing a large couch. Lavender had sat Jack down in one, and now she was bouncing excitedly on his lap. Jack winced every time she came back down.

"Sit them down, Leyland! Make them sit!"

Leyland didn't make them do anything. He gently guided Tess to the couch but let her sit of her own accord.

"Go on," he said to Aaron, Erin, and Raylene. He looked down on them with a gentle, patient smile. Lavender was the size of a middle school girl, but Leyland was tall. The top of his conical, evergreen head brushed at the ceiling. Despite this, he spoke with the same high-pitched voice as Lavender. "We don't bite."

Something does, Aaron reminded himself as his eyes scanned the empty lobby. *They're working the*

173

cute- Lavender looks ready to host a children's party- but those guards didn't cut their own heads off.

He sat in the chair and immediately regretted it. Tess was on the couch with Erin and Raylene. She was too far from him.

There was no seat for Leyland, but that didn't seem to bother him. He stood next to Lavender with his pine branch arms folded across his tree bark chest.

"We need tea," Lavender decided. "Tea and coffee for our new friends. And cake! Leyland, is there any left?"

"No more cake," Leyland reported. He went to the complimentary coffee station beside the empty reception desk and shook the heavy, steel beverage dispensers. "But hot water and coffee by the gallon." He gathered four cups. The clinking ceramics were the only sound in the silence. "What're we having?" he asked them.

Nobody answered but Leyland didn't seem to mind. "Let's say coffee then," he said.

While the conifer giant did his barista's work, Aaron cleared his throat. "Do you know what happened here?" he asked.

"What happened here? The party started!" Lavender squealed.

"And it's still going on," Leyland added without looking up from his brewings.

Filling in each other's blanks. Aaron remembered the movie now. He'd missed it in theatres but caught it on video one rainy Friday when they couldn't go out for recess. It was

174

impossible not to recognize them now. Not with the *actual* Lavender and Leyland in front of him, acting exactly like they did in the movie. Lavender, bubbly and vivacious. Leyland, more reserved and steady. They were the characters come to life in every detail.

Except they're not six inches tall. Leyland Cypress is over seven feet. And they don't seem like two plucky little kids in over their head. They look like they're completely in control of whatever's going on. And that includes us.

"Would anyone like sugar?" Leyland asked.

"NO POWDER!" Jack screamed. He shook his head frantically from side to side. "No powder! No powder!"

"It sounds like they take it black, Leyland," Lavender said.

Tess looked around the empty lobby. Aaron knew her body language well enough to see that she'd come to the same conclusion he had. They were in some trouble here. More than some, really. But, the smart thing to do was preserve the neutral equilibrium until they understood their position better.

"This is the party? It seems a little dead," Tess said. She winced inwardly. "Dead" felt far too close to the truth.

"Wellll, it's not happening hereee," Lavender sang. She waved her arm, out past the doors. Into the park. "That's where all the excitement is."

"And who's there?" Tess prodded.

"Everyone," Leyland put in. He came back to the seating area with two coffee mugs balanced in

175

each hand. He kept speaking as he handed the cups out. "Felix Fox. Bally Cast. Nobody's seen Timmy Turtle yet, but we all think he's just waiting for the right time to make a big entrance."

"Hell of a guest list," Aaron said. Like the others, he took the cup but let it rest in his lap. He felt too anxious to drink anything.

And there's something else, isn't there, Aaron? Something you're not remembering.

"Well, we've all been waiting a long time for this," Leyland said.

"This?" Tess asked.

"This!" Lavender yelled. Jack flinched beneath her. "Freedom!" Lavender rolled off him into a somersault and then jumped up with her arms raised over her head. "Frrreeedddommmmm!" she sang.

"Shouldn't you be out enjoying the party then?" Raylene asked in an unfamiliar, plaintive voice that she didn't even recognize as her own. Purely on reflex, she took a sip from her cup of coffee. The brew was crap, not like the stuff they served in the board meetings, but it was soothing just to raise a cup to her lips while she was talking.

"Can't show up at a party empty-handed," Lavender said. "That's what Mrs. Cipriano says."

Aaron blanked. "Who's Mrs.-"

"The old woman who runs the nursery, of course!" Tess supplied. She didn't know if they were being graded on their answers, but it seemed very important to pass.

And there's something else that's important. What is it you've forgotten, Tess?

176

Lavender nodded emphatically. "Exactly. We need to bring something if we want to be good guests. And me and Leyland know exactly what we're going to bring."

Leyland harrumphed. Lavender blushed, turning her green skin temporarily brown.

"What I mean is, we know what we *want* to bring. We're having some trouble finding it."

Jack moaned suddenly in his seat. Erin took a sip of her coffee to keep herself from moaning with him. She was glad she did. The hot liquid hit her belly and spread warming tendrils throughout her whole body.

Lavender and Leyland ignored him. "We thought we might be able to find it in one of the hotels," Lavender said. "Nobody's really looked here."

"Well, the Kubla Khan is certainly an excellent place to look for a unique gift," Raylene's smile came back as she found herself on footing she could understand again. She took another sip of coffee. That simple act felt amazingly refreshing. The hot liquid didn't go down- it went up, into her head, and hit like a colonic for her mind. "We have several one-of-a-kind pieces of Turtleshell Memorabilia on display in the lobby and in the restaurant. I can-"

Lavender blew a raspberry at them. It went on like the scream of a dying cat.

"He doesn't want anything like *that!*"

"Are you sure? I can't believe that Timmy Turtle wouldn't like to have one of Charles Tuttle's drawing pads. Or perhaps-"

Lavender and Leyland exchanged a look. It wasn't quite fearful, but it wasn't affectionate either.

"It's not for Timmy Turtle," Lavender said.

"It's for the one who started this," Leyland clarified. "The party. There's something he's looking for. He says that if we find it, then the party never has to stop."

Raylene tried again. "Well, there's nothing in Turtleshell Mountain I don't know about." Raylene's professional solicitude had held firmly against a thirty-year tide of incompetent superiors, moronic celebrity spokespeople, and entitled Make-A-Wish brats without so much as a single crack. It held just as firmly now. The coffee, as always, helped keep her steady. "If you tell me more about what you're looking for, whatever it is, then I'm certain I can help you find it."

Leyland shook his head. "We can't describe it. It's just something he put in our heads."

Tess was listening as Leyland spoke. She listened in the way you listened when a single word might reveal everything. But she was also trying to get Aaron's attention.

Look at me, she silently willed. *Look at me.*

"It has to be something," Raylene persisted.

"We can't describe it," Lavender repeated. "It's a head picture."

Aaron. Pay fucking attention to me.

"So it's a portrait," Raylene said. "I know where all of those are. Who were you looking for? A character or a creator?"

Aaron's hands were resting on his knees. Still

178

not looking at Tess, he raised a single finger and tapped it against his knee.

That was enough for Tess.

Lavender giggled again. It was seriously starting to grate on Raylene's nerves to the point where her annoyance was outweighing her fear and confusion. She did not like to be laughed at. Yet, she felt like there was nothing she could do about it. Her arms felt... *heavy*. More than that, her *mind* felt heavy. The idea of doing *anything* just seemed so far away.

"You're not getting it," Lavender said. "We're not looking for a picture of a head."

"But you said-"

"It's how he described it in our minds." Leyland said. His voice came from behind the couch. From behind their backs. *He moved,* Aaron realized. *Jesus. When did he move? We were so busy listening to them talk and watching Lavender hop around that we never realized he'd-*

"We're looking for heads," Leyland said.

His hands came down on top of Erin and Raylene's heads. Too fast to be avoided. Not so fast that Aaron didn't notice that Leyland's hands had changed.

His fingers were no longer evergreen shoots. They were now brown and slim and seemingly boneless. His fingers twisted in every direction, settling around Raylene and Erin's skulls in a complete circle and molding to them perfectly.

They were roots.

Leyland lifted them up. Lifted each woman effortlessly until their feet kicked only empty air.

The tips of Leyland's root fingers twisted and writhed and then burrowed into his captives' skin. Erin screamed. Raylene screamed in concerto right into her ear.

Her body screamed along with her, all of her weight straining the muscles of her neck. Worst of all was the pain in her head. There were *things* pinching through the skin of her forehead. She felt dirt grinding into her flesh and, worst of all, she felt things pushing deeper.

Trying to push through bone.

No longer giggling, Lavender pounced on Tess. This was the second part of the ambush. Leyland seized two while they were distracted by Lavender. Now Lavender would take one while they were distracted by Leyland.

Except Aaron and Tess were already moving.

Installing police surveillance didn't always mean bantering back and forth in an empty hotel room. Sometimes it meant wiring the perimeter of a cartel safehouse when it was actively occupied by known murderers. When conversation was a liability, a good surveillance team knew how to communicate with nothing but looks and small hand gestures.

Whatever else they may have been, Aaron and Tess were an extremely good surveillance team. Aaron knew exactly what Tess was trying to call his attention to with the shift of her eyes. And Tess knew exactly what Aaron's raised finger meant.

I know. But not yet.

They'd been waiting ever since that moment for the right time to move. Now, Erin's scream was as good a signal as any.

Aaron and Tess had plotted in silence and plotted well. If Jack was in his right mind, he would have found very little fault in their tactics.

The only thing they hadn't counted on was just how fast Lavender really was. The flower creature landed in the body of the chair instead of in Aaron's lap but she somersaulted away just as quickly and snared Aaron's ankle as he was scrambling towards the check-in desk. He fell and slammed his chin painfully against the wood floor. His vision swam.

"Careful! Don't hurt his head until we look inside it!" Leyland yelled

Lavender wasn't laughing now. She was snarling. "I know that!" She dragged Aaron back fully into her grasp and flipped him over. She lunged for his face.

Aaron's hands went for her wrists, keeping Lavender's twisting fingers away as they twisted and stretched for his eyes. Hers were roots now as well. Long, brown worms eager for the good soil of his flesh. He tried to buck her off but Lavender wrapped her legs around his waist and held tight.

"Do it!" Aaron roared.

"I'm trying," Lavender snapped back. "Let go of my hands and I'll get it over with!"

Aaron didn't bother to correct her. He wasn't talking to Lavender.

He was talking to Tess.

Tess, who earlier had been trying to call Aaron's attention to the large cylinder of complimentary hot coffee that Leyland had so helpfully informed them was completely full. Lavender may have had some trouble putting the code together, but Tess understood it just fine. She reared up behind Lavender with the five-gallon coffee dispenser and spilled the boiling contents over Lavender's head and back.

Lavender howled. Aaron was prepared to move and he seized the chance while she was distracted by the pain. He scrambled free and then he was up and running.

"Lavender!" Leyland screamed. He tightened his grip on Erin and Raylene and they both shrieked still louder. Blood was staining both of their hair as it welled up like oil from the holes he was boring in their skulls. It ran down their face in streams.

The boy, coward he was, had run from the lobby into the dining room. Leyland thought it would have been smarter to run out through the front doors but-

It doesn't matter. The park is ours. And there's nowhere he could go that I won't find him. Not after he helped make Lavender scream like that.

He willed his fingers to do their work faster. Getting through the skull was the hard part. After that, the brain was good, soft soil. Easy to get what he wanted.

Tess ran at Leyland. The coffee pot was empty but it was still heavy enough to work as a bludgeon. Tess didn't know how much good a club would do against something as solid looking as a walking tree, but she took a swing at his unprotected head. If nothing else, if Leyland

182

wanted to defend himself, he would have to put either Raylene or Erin down or else Tess was going to smash his wooden teeth to splinters.

Or Leyland would lift Erin up in front of his face and, instead of striking him, Tess slammed the metal can into her best friend's ribs.

Erin's mouth flapped open and closed like a TV with the sound off. Screaming, at its core, is just exhaling. Tess' blow had punched out whatever air Erin had left in her lungs.

"I'm sorry!" Tess blurted. It was a ridiculous thing to say, but it was all Tess could think of.

Lavender came up behind her. The scalds had peeled the green flesh off her back and shoulders in large swatches that revealed pale cellulose underneath. The coffee had stained the white buds of her hair a muddy brown. "Not yet you're not," she hissed.

She twisted Tess' arm behind her back and yanked it upwards. Tess howled and let the coffee dispenser drop.

"You won't be really sorry until I bury you. Alive." The small tendrils of her root fingers were already burrowing into Tess' wrist.

And they were going deeper.

"I can hear in the ground, you know," she whispered into Tess' ear. "When I put you down there, you can tell me all about how sorry you are.... and do you know what I might do if you're good and scream as loudly as you can?"

Tess twisted and tried to escape the tendrils worming under her skin. And, despite herself, she waited to hear what Lavender was going to

183

threaten to do.

Instead, she heard Leyland scream.

"LAVENDER!" he howled.

The Kubla Khan was a luxurious hotel with a lot of amenities. One such amenity was the large, attached restaurant which the website described as a "mature setting." Tess had joked that, translated, what that really meant was "there's not a single damn character for five hundred feet in any direction."

That had not turned out to be as true as advertised.

But the website had also boasted about a carving station. In that regard, they were right on the money.

Aaron had run out of the lobby.

He came back with a nine-inch carving knife.

Leyland saw him coming. He screamed, "Lavender, look out!"

It was too late. Aaron plunged the knife all the way down through the back of Lavender's skull at a slanted angle. It made a sound akin to stabbing through a head of lettuce. The tip of the blade broke through Lavender's skin to the left of her nose and just below her eye. Wintergreen blood ran from the wound in a thin trickle.

Lavender swayed gently on her feet. She was staring at something a thousand miles away.

"Oh," she whispered. The knife tip shifted slightly with the movement of her lips. "I can see so many colors, Leyland."

Her grip on Tess loosened.

Lavender fell like a redwood.

"LAVENDER!" Leyland screamed.

He did for revenge what he wouldn't do for defense. He dropped Erin and Raylene.

Leyland shoved the couch aside like it was made of Styrofoam. Maybe this scrawny meat bag was the gift they were looking for and maybe he wasn't. Leyland didn't care. He was going to rip him apart until he was nothing but mulch.

He bore down on Aaron with both of his hands knotted into wooden hammers. He loosed a roar that belonged to an elephant; not a tiny elf living in a nursery.

Aaron tightened his grip on the knife, even though it suddenly seemed about as substantial as the tiny sword in a cocktail glass.

But Aaron had a trick in mind. Something he'd seen work in movies a thousand times and, with all the fiction becoming reality around them, he hoped it would prove true one more time.

Hold the knife out. Hold it out like a spear and let him run right into it.

Aaron took a step forward. He meant to brace himself, the better to take Leyland's weight as the berserker wood nymph impaled himself on the knife, but he made a critical error.

He forgot about the coffee on the floor.

Aaron's step forward brought him square into the puddle. His foot flew out from under him and he pitched forward with all of his weight coming down squarely on his face. The pain exploded in his brain with such force that, for a moment, Aaron forgot where he was.

Leyland hadn't forgotten. Leyland knew

185

exactly where he was, and he knew exactly what he was going to do to the fiend who'd murdered his true love. He was going to smash the meatbag's spine first to keep from squirming. Then, Leyland was going to rip his limbs off one after the other. Leyland almost wanted to shout "Timber!" as his clenched fists swung down towards Aaron's back.

Jack slammed into Leyland. His hands were still bound behind his back, but he dove shoulder first right into Leyland's knees and sent the tree creature sprawling forward. Leyland staggered past Aaron and smashed into a glass display case holding a number of vintage Tina Turtle collectibles. The case exploded in a spray of shattered glass. The collectibles fell. The plastics broke. The ceramics cracked.

Leyland rose up no worse for the wear and even more furious than before. His teeth were ground together so hard, they were starting to splinter.

Jack was still on the floor. He couldn't stand with his hands tied. All he could do was shimmy away, legs kicking furiously behind him as his face skidded across the floor.

Leyland stomped after him, quickly closing the distance.

"Okay. If that's the way you want it," Leyland panted. "You were supposed to be first anyway." He brought his foot down on Jack's ankle, pinning him in place and eliciting a fresh howl of pain.

Aaron groped his way to his knees. The world was still swimming, and he couldn't see where the knife had gone. He tried to force his hazy sight to

186

refocus. *A weapon. Find a weapon. NOW.*

Erin found one first. Inside the display of Tina Turtle memorabilia had been a ceramic toothbrush holder. It had broken so the cute turtle girl with the bow and polka dots was gone and in her place was a perfect circle of jagged, ceramic points.

Erin lunged forward, bloody curtain of hair flying behind her. "Get away from him!" she screamed. She jammed that ring of pointed peaks perfectly over Leyland's eye.

The ceramic bit into wood. Leyland trashed and swung blindly. Erin jumped back and narrowly avoided losing her head to his sweeping arms.

Leyland roared. He reared back, bellowing and groping blindly with his giant paws. "I'll kill you!" he screeched. "Mulch you! Compost you!" One tree root hand went to the ring of points puncturing his face. The tendrils looped around the ceramic.

Tess had found the knife. She came in from Leyland's blind slide and swept the blade across his throat.

Everything went still. Tess froze at the end of her follow through. Erin remained crouched on the floor where she'd ducked from Leyland's assault. One of Leyland's hand stayed wrapped around the ceramic in his eye. The other was poised over his head in a twisted claw.

Every eye was fixed on the gaping, dry canyon that Tess had slashed into Leyland's wooden throat.

Leyland twisted towards Tess. She shrank back and raised the knife but Leyland swatted it effortlessly from her hand. He pushed Tess to the floor. His humongous mitt of a hand descended towards her throat.

"Youuuu," he wheezed.

And then the canyon flooded.

He didn't bleed green like Lavender did. Thick, amber sap oozed from the wound and grew fat and blotted beneath his chin like a beard.

Leyland gurgled. The wound to his face was forgotten as both hands pawed at his oozing throat.

Leyland didn't die quickly. He croaked and gasped as sap seeped between his fingers and the mad, rolling orb of his remaining eye fixed on each one of them.

Leyland sank to his knees. A bubble formed in the sap-blood beneath his chin and then burst. Leyland's life seemed to go with it. The wood nymph fell to all fours and then sunk down to his belly and lay still.

Tess let out a breath. Three lifetimes of tension exhaled with it. It was quiet.

But the quiet wouldn't last. She knew that they were not even close to being out of trouble. That made the moment's quiet even more important.

Leyland rose again. He stretched his arm out towards Erin. She screamed. Tess scrambled for the knife. *Stab him. Destroy the brain and you destroy the toon.*

Leyland collapsed again, and this time he did not move. Tess realized he had not been reaching towards Erin.

He was reaching towards Lavender. Leyland lay there now, truly dead, with his tree root fingers just short of hers.

Leyland was still for a long time before any of

them felt comfortable moving.

Tess went to Aaron. She found him crouched and clutching his head in the lukewarm coffee. He looked up as she got closer.

"Are they dead?" he asked.

Tess nodded. She knelt down so they were eye to eye. "They're dead."

"I'm sorry," Aaron said. "I forgot all about the coffee. I wasn't even thinking about it."

"It's all right."

"It's not all right! I screwed up and he could have killed all of us!"

He could have killed you.

"I can't-" he stuttered. "We have to- We won't-" He looked her in the eye and she saw everything.

There are no re-dos, Tess. If I fuck up, you won't get to tell me "It's all right." You'll be dead. We'll all be dead. I have to be smarter than that. There can't be any excuses. Excuses won't-

She hugged him, silencing his mouth and his mind. Aaron hugged her back, not caring that it made the scalds on his arms and chest hurt like hell.

"Are you okay now?" she asked him.

He shook his head against the refuge of her shoulder. "Not a chance. You?"

"No," she said.

Aaron held her close to him. Beneath the stench of sweat, terror, and coffee, there was still the smell of Tess. Aaron wanted to throw himself into the fog of that smell and let it obscure everything else. The way Tess clung to him said that she felt the same way.

"A party." That's what she said. Parties have more than two guests.

Aaron separated himself slightly from Tess and helped her up. Their fingers still trailed over each other's skin. Even as they stood and took stock of their situation.

The burns were already tightening the skin of his arms and chest. Tess was clutching the wrist Lavender had twisted and her face was pale and diminished in the folds of her wig. Erin was crouched on the floor beside Jack, cradling his head. Blood stained her face in stripes like a candy cane. Jack himself had mentally checked out again. He laid motionless in her arms like a slab of beef. Still by the couch, Raylene had a ring of neat punctures around her forehead and her own barbershop pole of blood.

Oh yeah, we're off to a great start.

Raylene rolled off the couch. She walked over to Lavender, swaying from side to side like a sailor at sea. She tugged at the imp's face. Lavender's features stretched with the pull of Raylene's fingers, but otherwise, stayed attached to her bones.

Raylene pulled harder. Lavender's head lifted on her neck. Raylene let it drop and it smacked back down with a sound like a cabbage falling off a countertop.

"It won't come off," Raylene said. "One of you help me. Let's see who they really are."

"We know who they are," Erin said. "Lavender Twist and Leyland Cypress."

"Bullshit!" Raylene screamed. Louder than

when the roots had been digging into her skull.
"Mice don't turn into carriage horses. Camels can't
talk. And none of this Turtleshell shit comes to
life." She yanked on Lavender's face and shook her
entire skull. "It just doesn't! These are terrorists or
cultists or just freaks in masks.... or.... or...
SOMETHING REAL."

"The holes in your head are real," Tess
reminded her. "What'll happen to us if something
else finds us? That will be real too."

Raylene whirled on her, mouth open with a
rebuttal loaded and ready.

"I'm not saying you're wrong," Tess said
quietly. Even though anyone with eyes could see
that she was. "I'm saying that it doesn't really
matter. The only thing we need to care about is
getting out of here. We can discuss what's real and
what isn't then."

"Can everybody walk?" Aaron asked.

"I don't know if Jack can," Erin said.

"Cry me a river," Raylene muttered. She had a
silk scarf, eight hundred dollars at Neiman Marcus.
She was tying it around her head like a bandage.

"We might all be dead if it wasn't for him,"
Erin snarled. "And now you know he didn't kill
anybody. Leave him alone."

"I know he didn't kill my guards," Raylene
sneered. "But, if I'm remembering right, it seemed
like you were all in agreement over who turned
your fivesome into a four top. Is that correct?"

Erin didn't respond, but Raylene wasn't ready
to let her go that easily. She cupped an ear towards
Erin. "Well? You were there, weren't you? Tell me

191

what happened. Or does your mouth not open as easily as your legs?"

"Shut up."

"I'm just saying, if I owe your boyfriend an apology, let me know. Your boyfriend who was accused of murder, I mean. Not your other boyfriend who got shot in the head."

"SHUT YOUR FUCKING MOUTH!" Erin seethed up into Raylene's face. If Raylene cared to look close enough, she might have even been able to see the other woman's blood boiling as it seeped from the holes in her head.

If she cared. "Just so we understand each other," was all Raylene said.

Feeling worlds better, Raylene looked past Erin to Aaron and Tess. "We need to find one of my guard's... other half. For the key card."

Aaron shook his head. "We don't need to look," he said.

\- - -

Aaron hadn't had time to dwell on it when he ran into the dining room. He could hear Erin, Raylene, and Tess screaming, and he was too busy looking for a weapon to even think about anything else.

But he had noticed them.

It was impossible not to notice them.

There was very little blood, just like in the lobby. Aaron would never know for sure what had happened down here. Jack probably had the best idea, but he obviously wasn't going to be explaining anything anytime soon.

Nevertheless, a picture was starting to form in Aaron's mind.

He saw several empty glasses scattered across the floor. His mind associated that with Leyland's insistence that they all have some coffee. He associated *that* with the way Raylene had been slurring her words and how Erin's eyelids had been fluttering shut while she sat on the couch. And *that* explained why Jack had been screaming about "no powder" and prompted the thing that Aaron had been trying to remember. He had to think all the way back to a classroom in the early '90s, but he remembered it now. He remembered that day when it was too wet to go outside and a little boy and his classmates had to stay in and watch Lavender Twist and Leyland Cypress sneak out of the nursery by putting their parents to sleep with… sleeping powder in their tea.

He could almost picture it. Lavender and Leyland, beloved characters, bursting into the lobby, all smiles and cheers. Maybe going to one of the families first. Or maybe the reception clerks. Moving over each drink, subtle as could be, until everyone was suddenly laughing and light-headed.

Until everyone was too slow and drowsy to do anything once Lavender and Leyland began their "search."

That probably wasn't perfect, but it would explain the guards. No time to offer them a drink, better to kill them fast, even if it was messier than the others. It was probably only dumb luck that had let Jack shut the elevator doors and send it back up.

Whatever the full details were, the end result was obvious.

Two sets of mothers and fathers, six children younger than ten, two desk clerks, and a young couple that might have been on their honeymoon were all laid out on the serving table like entrees.

There was a perfect circle of tiny, red holes ringed around each of their heads. Each victim was as pasty white as vanilla ice cream. He suspected that there wasn't a full cup of blood left between the fifteen of them.

And Aaron knew why not. He'd taken biology in high school.

He knew what roots did.

Raylene looked at the stack of bodies and turned nearly as pale. She shivered and touched the scarf wrapped around her head. The wounds beneath it were still sensitive enough to tingle.

This is where they would have put us, she realized. *Right up on the table. With the others. No blood. No life. Just… this.*

"What were their names?"

Raylene jumped. She'd forgotten she wasn't alone.

Aaron was not looking at the table. He was looking directly underneath it where the two security guards were leaning shoulder to shoulder. Their white shirts were soaking red but, sitting up, very little blood had gotten on the floor.

"Do you know?" Aaron persisted.

Raylene thought for a moment. She honestly

tried. But, in the end, she could only shake her head.

"I don't interact with security that often."

Aaron would have dearly liked to think of them as something other than "guards," but it would have to do. He pointed to the plastic cards dangling from their belts.

"There?"

Raylene nodded.

They both stared at the small squares of white plastic. Neither one seemed able to move.

It should have been simple. After the frantic, life-or-death struggle in the lobby against things that shouldn't exist, kneeling down and unclipping a card from a belt should have been the simplest thing in the world.

It wasn't. The smell of stale blood was a buffer he couldn't get past. He couldn't stop thinking about heads that were no longer there or how limp bodies might move if they were disturbed. The thoughts were a barricade of thorns between him and any action, and he found that he simply could not get any closer to the corpses.

"Well," Raylene spoke brusquely. "How about this? We'll call them 'Hector' and 'Jose.'"

So saying, she went forward in three brisk steps, crouched down like a proper lady does when she's wearing a skirt, and reached for the closest belt.

Raylene took the card and only wanted to scream once, when her knuckles brushed the fabric of his pants and it sounded like something small and vile scurrying through dead leaves. She wanted to scream then; but she reminded herself that she was the Evil Queen Bitch, and the Evil Queen Bitch took care of business. Especially when nobody else had the stomach for what had to be done.

- - -

Tess, Erin, and Jack had stayed behind in the lobby. Aaron hadn't seen any reason in exposing them to any more gruesomeness. He only brought Raylene along because he needed confirmation that he was getting the right keycard and not at all because he wanted to show the bitch something to wipe the insufferable sneer off of her face.

At least, that was what he told himself.

He didn't have time for much more thinking. The second they re-entered the lobby, Tess immediately got up and wrapped him in another hug.

"No more separating, ok? Horror Movie 101," she said. She was joking, but the quiet from the other room had been far too much and that thought had been screaming, far less comically, in her mind the entire minute that Aaron was gone. *You left him. You left him alone.*

Aaron nodded and squeezed her reassuringly, letting her feel the reality of him. "You've got a deal."

"Did you find it?" Erin asked.

Raylene held the key up as proof. "Get your baggage and let's go." She looked squarely at Jack

196

as she said it.

"One second," Aaron said.

Tess still had the carving knife. Aaron took the knife from her and went over to Jack.

Jack had risen with Erin. His leg had been hurt, but it seemed to hold him up ok. Aaron looked him up and down, and "vertical" was about the only positive thing he could say about his friend. Jack's large frame, usually so wide-stanced and solid, looked hunched and dilapidated. He stared somewhere to the right of Aaron's knees and kept shaking his head like he was trying to ward off a horsefly.

We all met through Tess. First year out of training. The whole precinct was out for drinks. I hadn't even wanted to go, but Tess convinced me it would be fun and I was already finding it impossible to say no to her. I was waiting at the bar for drinks. So was Jack, but neither of us was giving the other the time of day until Tess got tired of waiting for me and wormed between us.

She called us twins which was ridiculous because he had six inches and sixty pounds on me. Jack even said as much.

"I know!" *Tess chortled.* "Danny DeVito and Arnold Schwarzenegger twins!" *Which still wasn't really accurate, but Tess cracked herself up and me and Jack couldn't help but laugh along.*

And then it turned out we were both Red Sox fans living in California. And all three of us liked country music and got annoyed by how many people just dismissed the whole genre just because they didn't like the same five songs that were always on the radio.

And he liked Tess. So much so that I was worried I might have to hate him even though he seemed like such a good guy. But then Erin recognized Tess from somewhere and came over to say hello. Jack got one look at her and that took care of that.

Then Scott came in like a hurricane. Drunk and dancing too wildly and knocking into Jack and spilling my drink and Tess' drink all over the place.

If he had been less apologetic or if Jack was in less of a good mood, everything might have happened differently. Instead, Scott bought us all a round. Even Jack and Erin, because "They weren't too old to double fist," and that was it. Maybe from the beginning there was something rotten festering inside of it, but from that day the five of us stayed together like family.

Aaron looked into Jack's bulging eyes, dimmed like someone had vacated a house but left a single light on to give the false impression that someone was home. He tried to see if there was any trace of his friend there.

There wasn't. Not now.

But he'd seen it in Jack's mad, armless rush into Leyland's path when it was clear that Aaron was about to be ripped in half.

"You saved my life," Aaron said to that empty face.

Jack didn't seem to hear him.

"You probably saved all of us," he persisted.

Jack still said nothing. His bottom lip started ticking, like he was trying to speak, but no words came out.

Aaron turned away. "Do you know which way will get us out of the park the quickest?" he asked Raylene.

"Friendship!" Jack shouted suddenly.

Aaron turned back around. Jack had Raylene and Tess' attention as well. He'd never lost Erin's.

"Friendship's a tough seed. It'll grow tall even in the worst soil! All you have to do is take care of it!"

He fell silent again. Like he wasn't even there.

"That's from Lavender Twist," Erin said quietly.

There was silence for another moment. Aaron went behind Jack's back.

He used the carving knife to cut Jack's plastic cuffs.

He looked squarely at Raylene as he did it, ready for an uproar from the Turtleshell woman, but she stayed carefully neutral while the rasp of the knife echoed in the lobby.

Unbound, Jack's hands fell limply at his side. He gave no indication he was even aware his hands were loose.

That was ok.

Aaron trusted he would be there if they needed him.

<u>27</u>

The Single Rider was feeling light-headed.

He shook the bag slung over his shoulder and guessed that he only had three or four left. He didn't see any more to be found on the ground in front of him either.

But that was okay. It just meant that there would be some a little farther down the street.

The Single Rider ambled on, delighting in the smallest signs of what he'd writ into existence. A souvenir *Diggle Dino* mug abandoned here. A child's sneaker discarded there with the foot still inside of it.

He passed one of the carnival stands in the *Brooklyn Boardwalk* section. A pyramid of Plexiglas bottles with Turtleshell characters painted on them still waited behind the counter, as neat and orderly as if nothing had happened.

The Single Rider stopped. What the hell, he was feeling lucky.

He opened his bag and took out a severed head. It was a woman's. The Single Rider seized it by the long mane of blonde hair. He twirled the head until it whirled in a whistling blur and then let it fly. Poorly aimed, the head sailed past the bottles and cracked against the painted backdrop, leaving a long streak of blood across Tommy Turtle's encouraging smile.

The Single Rider pulled out a second head and,

overwhelmed by a surge of good humor, he missed again on purpose. So what if he did? He could hear the screams echoing from every corner of Turtleshell Mountain. He could close his eyes and be there to witness a hundred last breaths. He felt the exhilaration of the kill pulsing through him from each of his avatars.

He threw the third head and struck the pyramid of bottles low and slightly left of dead center, exactly the right spot to bring the whole pyramid crashing down. He laughed as it collapsed.

The last one laughing in the Most Joyous Place on Earth.

He climbed over the counter to claim his prize, and he was a forty-year-old black man in jeans and a polo shirt.

He came down inside of the booth, and he was a twenty-two year old with terrible acne and a Turtleshell Mountain Employee's vest.

He walked over to the wall of prizes and considered carefully. He didn't want a Tina Turtle or a Princess Annika. He'd never really been a fan of *Gene-A: Girl Grown in a Lab*.

His eyes fell on a stuffed figure, hidden away in the far corner of the display.

"That one." The voice that came from his chapped, pimple-ridden lips was that of a small girl. *"Oh, I love it!"* he gushed in the same young girl's voice.

Criss Cringe. Halloween King of Shadowsberg.

The Single Rider picked the doll up and placed it on the counter. He climbed back over to the walkway and then claimed his prize with the tiny, unblemished hands of an eight-year-old girl with braids. He stuffed the doll into his bag and continued along his merry way down Main Street. He'd chosen polished, black, strappy shoes, and the hard heels clicked jauntily against the brick path.

He reached the entrance to Horror Heights. The entryway, a pair of plane hangar doors, loomed huge over him in all of their deliberately dilapidated glory. Most days, the screams from this ride could be heard all over the park. Tonight, Horror Heights was silent, and it was the rest of the park that was screaming.

The Single Rider pushed on one of the rolling doors with the permanently chipped paint. They were designed to squeak for dramatic effect, but the Single Rider really leaned on it to draw out the sound as much as possible.

Beyond the doors was a long stretch of runway leading to a grimy, dual prop plane. A maze of winding ropes and posts marked the path between the doors and the plane. Technically, the Single Rider could have walked underneath the ropes but he chose to instead walk properly through the winding path of the line.

About halfway to the front, the old mind in the little girl's body started skipping and giggling. When he reached the front of the line, he held onto the girl's form, but he grew it to 48 inches in order to satisfy the height requirement for the ride.

The gangway into the plane was down, and the Single Rider hopped on board. Inside, there were more heads if he wanted them. Along with arms, legs, and his choice of internal organs. Clearly, the gremlins who were supposed to send the plane into a terrifying tail spin had decided it would just be more economical to slaughter the passengers before they even got off the ground.

The gremlins themselves were nowhere to be seen. There were far more places for them to lurk now than on the wing.

The door to the cockpit hung ajar. The silhouette of a figure in a jaunty cap leaned into view from behind the pilot's chair and sketched a salute. The Single Rider returned the motion and went to find his seat. Behind him, he heard the whine of the gangway rising and the cabin sealing itself.

The Single Rider pushed an overweight father from his seat. The man fell to the floor and one eye rattled loose from his gouged face. The Single Rider used his bulk as a step ladder and hopped into the seat. He drummed his little girl's feet excitedly against the dead man's buttocks as the plane began to vibrate.

"Ladies and Gentlemen, this is your Captain speaking," a voice intoned over the intercom. It gurgled like it was speaking through a throat filled with blood. "We've finished our pre-flight check and, at this time, we'd ask you to please ensure that your seat backs and tray tables are in the upright and locked position as we will be taking off shortly."

The Single Rider dutifully checked his seat and strapped in as the vibrations below him picked up.

Horror Heights was a motion simulation ride. The windows were all video screens and the plummeting effect was achieved by forced perspective. The body of the plane jerked back and forth on pistons to add to the effect, but it never truly left the ground.

But tonight there was more magic than reason to be found in Turtleshell Mountain. The plane taxied on its for-show runway, and its nonexistent engines worked harder. The plane picked up speed and lifted up into the air shortly before it would have smashed into a gift shop.

Stay low, the Single Rider ordered without speaking. The Single Rider wanted to see more, but he did not want to see so much that he lost the details.

Do a lap. The plane tipped at his command. It swung out to the perimeter of the park and then took the Single Rider on a lazy, wide, arcing course of the entire park that let him see how his influence was spreading in a more complete way than any one character's perspective could provide.

The Single Rider looked... and liked what he saw.

He saw shadowy blood under blazing lights.

He saw costumeer death squads roaming the grounds with bloody axes in hand.

He saw bodies floating in the wishing well and Alicia and her Mermaid pals playing in the red water.

He saw that Turtleshell Mountain was his.

There were still guests alive to be sure. He knew that because the one guest he was looking for had not been found yet.

But he (or she) was out there somewhere.

Somewhere inside the park, just waiting to be found. Turtleshell Mountain was built like a cone. And a cone was just a fancy word for a ring. Maybe some people had holed up in the hotels and the downtown shops in the center of the ring, but the Single Rider controlled the edges. The whole park was in the palm of his hand, and as he closed that hand into a fist, he would find every man, woman, and child and drag them from their hidey holes like rats from a bag of powdered sugar.

More were being found even now.

But, still, not the one that he needed.

Keep searching, he told the thousand fingers of his new hands.

And they listened.

<u>28</u>

Anyone who ever worked in an upscale hotel or restaurant would feel a disheartening familiarity with the underground tunnels of Turtleshell Mountain. The service pathways, where the costumeers, groundskeepers, and retail workers traveled so as not to tinge the guest's magical time with even a single dose of reality, were painted a drab white smeared by decades of dirt. The tile floor was dingy, the ceilings were too low, and the corridors reeked of stale sweat. The difference between above and below would have been jarring if they weren't all already so thoroughly jarred. As it was, all of their capacity for pondering the strange and contrary was thoroughly occupied.

Maybe they were wearing costumes, Aaron thought. *Not the cheap ones they have here, but real Hollywood style makeup stuff. It could be terrorism with an extra psychological edge. Like those wanna-be Jihad nitwits we bugged in that Denny's. They couldn't shut up about how important it was to go after the things that people thought were safe. Maybe someone had the bright idea to not just destroy one of the most American places of all time, but also ruin all of the characters associated with it.*

Or maybe Scott thought it would be hilarious to slip us all some acid, but he never bothered to check the expiration date.

Or maybe Aurelius' Toga Tornado flew off the rails and I'm hallucinating this while I bleed out in a pile of wreckage.

They were all more plausible solutions. The only problem was the same reason why Aaron wouldn't say any of them out loud.

Because he knew what he really saw. So did Tess, Erin, and even that miserable Turtle Bitch.

What he saw was perfectly and undoubtedly Lavender Twist and Leyland Cypress in every mannerism and detail.

They had just been brought to life with a taste for death.

And they're only two. Two from a roster of dozens.

Aaron suppressed that particular piece of gruesome logic along with as much of the last hour as he possibly could. Maybe later he would think about it more. Think about parallel realities and high-tech robots gone berserk and maybe a really fucked-up kid who threw a quarter in a wishing well. Right now, he was just going to follow Raylene on what she said was the path to the ticket booth. Until they made it to fresh air on the other side, Aaron was thinking about nothing but the ugly, comforting reality of the tunnel around them.

Raylene kept the procession marching at a brisk pace. She made left and right turns without hesitation and never once let on that she had no idea where she was going.

Raylene was not a gnome. She did not spend hours every day navigating this underground knot of pathways. There were signs to be sure, but they were all short-range locators. "Western World" this way. "Future Field" that way. If you were looking for a specific destination, like the exit, then you were out of luck. She tried to visualize the park in her head, *If Future Field is that way, then the Main Entrance should be past it.* So they went that way but then the next elevator they saw went up to the Candy Castle and that meant they were heading deeper into the park. Didn't it?

Raylene was starting to sweat. It made the wounds in her forehead sting. It made her lips feel dry even though they were wet. She wanted to double back and maybe take a left at the intersection where they had just turned right. She wanted to let someone else take the lead. Maybe the fake blonde who thought she was so fucking smart.

She almost did once. Her mouth was actually open with the beginnings of the first word before the Evil Queen Bitch swept forward and slammed her mouth shut.

Put that crown back on your fucking head and keep it there, the Once and Forever Majesty of Malice commanded.

Raylene plowed ahead.

When the reality of the tunnels became monotonous and other thoughts started to creep back in for a little color, Aaron strove for something else to focus on.

Of course, he thought of Tess.

She was walking a little behind him, and Aaron slowed so they were walking side by side. With Raylene marching relentlessly ahead and Erin coaxing Jack along with little tugs and gentle murmurs in the rear, it was as close to alone as they could get.

"Doing fucking awful?" He asked.

Tess snapped out of her own personal reverie. "What?"

"I mean, if I say 'How are you?' it feels like I'm pressuring you to say that you're doing ok. I want you to feel like you can say that you're doing fucking awful."

"Don't worry, I don't mind telling you. I'm doing fucking awful."

Aaron smiled. "That's my girl." Then he winced inside. Burnt, exhausted, and terrified and calling Tess that when it wasn't true still hurt most of all.

They walked a few more steps before Aaron realized there was something else he had to say.

"I'm glad you're ok."

"I thought we just agreed I wasn't?"

He couldn't look her in the eye. "I mean I'm glad you're healthy. I didn't say anything... before, and I should have. I mean, for a year all I wanted was for you to be-"

"I'll tell you what," Tess cut him off. "Let's wait to make sure we don't get killed before you say anything else, ok?" She winked. "Every time we start this conversation, it doesn't seem to work out that well."

Tess walked a little faster.

Aaron grabbed her wrist. He swung her around so they were face to face.

"We'll make it work."

In all the times he had imagined kissing Tess, he had never pictured it like this. Not with her soaked in blood and sweat. Not with a dank corridor beneath an amusement park as the backdrop.

But as he looked into her eyes and saw the same desire there, as her wrist tingled with eagerness in his hand, he had no doubt that it would be a kiss more magical than anything Charles Tuttle could dream up on his best day.

Walking behind them, Erin saw what was happening and reined Jack in like an agreeable pony. Not that it really mattered. Aaron and Tess had no idea she and Jack were even there. Aaron and Tess didn't notice anything except for each other. Watching them was like seeing a single ray of sunshine bursting through the blackness of the end of the world. Like Aaron, she felt the magic of the moment between him and Tess, and she waited to see the kiss that she too had been eagerly anticipating since these two idiots had met.

Beside her Jack was humming. She didn't recognize the tune at first, not with his cracked voice and wildly fluctuating pitch. But, eventually, it clicked.

He was humming "I Can Feel the Love Tonight" from *The Jungle King*.

Erin took his hand and, instead of just lying in her grasp like a quarter pound of lukewarm ground beef, Jack actually squeezed back. It might have just been the moment, but she thought she could feel some of the real Jack thrumming through their intertwined fingers.

They watched Aaron and Tess lean towards each other. Finally, after all the horror stories, a love story brought to life.

And then the tapping sound began.

<u>29</u>

Leo the Mole did not work for Turtle Shell Mountain.

As a matter of fact, Leo didn't work for anyone. Leo the Mole was a homeless man who lived somewhere in the network of highway overpasses and parking lots around Turtleshell Mountain. He got his nickname because his small, wrinkled brown face made him look like the Turtleshell character of the same name. Also because of the way he dug through the trashcans in search of bottles and cans in the same two-handed scurrying manner that Leo the Mole searched for bugs.

Turtleshell Mountain had a strict policy against vagrants and panhandlers, even on the fringes of the property, but Leo was the exception because of his tenacity and his surprising amount of charm. He came back no matter how many times he was chased away and, when he did interact with guests, he tipped his frayed hat, bade them a pleasant rest of the day, and never so much as asked for a single cent from anyone. Many guests left thinking that he was supposed to be a character from *Beggar's Masquerade*.

Over the years, the staff had reluctantly come to adopt him like a stray cat that just wouldn't go away. He knew the guards by name and shift, tonight was probably Franco Agostonachio, and towards the end of the night Leo could usually count on a to-go box filled with day-old churros waiting for him by the gate. Leo was really counting on one of those care packages tonight because so far he was getting dick all with bottles and cans. It wasn't just recyclables either, none of the trash cans lining the main exit were more than a quarter full. It was as if nobody had left the park at all.

"Leeoooo."

The voice could have charmed the birds out of the trees. Leo pulled his head out of the trash can and, appropriately enough, it was Princess Francesca standing there outside the exit. The same Francesca who actually did sing doe-eyed birds down from their perches and made rabbits blush with a single smile.

Leo had not had an easy childhood. His father had gone down in Korea, and his mother had gone down in a bottle of gin and on any guy who would hold still long enough. But no matter how much of their money went into a bottleneck, on Saturdays there was always fifty cents so Leo could take his sister to the movies. Leo always let Sophie pick and she'd chosen *Princess of the Western Wilds* so many times that, even fifty years later, forty years after his sister had been buried in a pine box, Leo still knew the words to all of the songs.

And he knew that this girl in front of him was a mirror image of Princess Francesca. The blue and yellow gown was the same, of course, but that was easy. What was remarkable was that her eyes were the exact same perfect shade of animator's green, her brown hair was the same chocolate-colored silk, and her lips were the same perfectly formed red bow.

"Leeeooo," she sang again. She walked closer towards him. Usually, the princesses didn't want much to do with him and Leo understood their caution. He was a homeless man and they were young, pretty women. Those were not groups that typically played well together.

"Leeeoooo."

Princess Francesca did not look cautious. She looked inviting. She looked like she wanted Leo to step into the park with her *(Don't worry, Mr. Mole. We have a ticket waiting for you)* and take a tour of the Princess' Castle.

She also looked like she'd tore at her bust line to show off a little more of the Princess Francesca than they usually did in the cartoons.

"You can do better than cast-offs and scraps today, Mr. Mole." Francesca said. That obviously wasn't the costumeer's real name, but Leo found there was no other way to think of her. "Tonight is a very special night. Tonight, everything is open to everyone and it's oh, oh, so magical."

It didn't look magical. Leo could see past Princess Francesca into the park and it looked like there wasn't a soul alive inside. He heard no laughter either. The lights were on and the rides were spinning, but Turtleshell Mountain looked like a haunted house with some candles lit in the windows.

Leo stayed right where he was and thumbed his dirty coat. "Even if admission's free, I'm sure there's a dress code I'm not up to."

Francesca shook her head. The shining tresses of her hair stayed exactly where they needed to be to maintain a perfect frame around her face. "We'll dress you up like a prince, Leo the Mole. You'll wear the finest clothes you've ever known." She stepped closer. "Please, William." She whispered his full name. Not Leo, Will, or Billy, and it made him shiver and sweat inside. "Please," she repeated. "The Grand Ball is coming and I desperately need a courtier." She reached out to him. Perfectly manicured fingernails attached to fingers and a hand of perfect butterscotch cream. "Say you'll come with me, William. Please say you'll escort me."

Leo was a drunk. And he had some anger issues that kept him from holding onto a job. But he was by no means an idiot, and he knew that there was not enough Turtleshell Magic or LSD in the world to make a girl this beautiful invite Leo the Mole to escort her anywhere. This whole situation was crooked, and you survived on the streets as long as Leo had by pointing yourself straight in the opposite direction anytime something in front of you looked crooked.

Leo was adding an addendum to that rule right now. He was moving in the opposite direction, but he didn't want to turn his back on the Princess Francesca either. He walked backwards and tried to angle the trash can between them as he did. "I'm sorry, princess, but I'm afraid I have somewhere else to be. But I wouldn't worry if I was you. I'm sure any man would love to have you on his arm."

He kept moving back, and he kept his eyes

fixed firmly on Princess Francesca as he did. He didn't permit himself to get distracted by the chasm of her cleavage or her bear trap eyes either. He kept his focus on her feet and her hands. So far, her hands were still clamped demurely in front of her and Francesca's feet stayed planted on the far side of the trash can. That was good, but Leo was ready to run the second she so much as took another step towards him.

Hands pressed into his back. Leo yelped. Warm breath tickled his ear.

"Don't leave, Leo."

Still another set of hands creeped under his shirt. Manicured nails ran up his sides and over his nipples.

"We need you, Leo."

Princess Scheraze and Princess Melisande held him in place. Coal black and fiery red hair tickled the sides of his face. Inviting, full lips brushed his ears. He looked wildly from side to side and sparkling brown and blue eyes met his own. He was in the dream foursome of every sixteen-year-old's inner six-year-old, but the dream was a lie. He could feel it, the dream was just the curtain that hid something far worse. And Leo could hear that something licking its chops.

Francesca was right in front of him again. She dragged his hand towards her strawberry syrup lips; the most beautiful woman to touch Leo the Mole in decades, but all he felt was a terror so primal that it stripped away everything adult inside of him and left nothing behind but a frightened child.

216

"Don't," he pleaded. "Please, just let me go." Leo tried to resist her, but the strength of her grip could not be denied. Francesca stuck his finger in her mouth. Leo moaned. Whether in lust or fear, he didn't know. Her mouth was warm, wet, and vacuum sealed around his finger. Part of him would have let her tongue massage his knuckle forever. Except, beneath that delicious sensation, there was a gritty feeling like sand rubbing against his skin. Leo forced himself to hold onto that sensation. The grit was what was really happening.

Francesca let his finger go with a pop. Leo the Mole looked at his hand and saw what had really happened beneath that mollifying moisture.

His index finger was gone. In its place was nothing but a mushy stump with a hint of bone poking through. There was no pain, but he saw Francesca lick a small dab of something peach-colored from the corner of her mouth.

That was my finger, he realized. Leo would have collapsed if Scheraze and Melisande weren't holding him up. Phantom agony for his missing finger curdled in his head. Had he really thought he was afraid before? He'd had no idea what afraid really was, but he did now. Leo screamed. He yanked and twisted and tried to worm his arms out of his coat sleeves, but there was no escaping the clutches of the Princesses of Turtleshell Mountain.

"FRANK!" he screamed. "JESUS, FRANK, ARE YOU THERE!? IS ANYBODY IN THERE!?"

Scheraze and Melisande pulled him down. Right there on the walkway where he'd seen ten years of laughing children race by with balloons and souvenir t-shirts.

"HELP ME! SOMEBODY HELP ME PLEASE!"

Frank didn't hear him.

Nobody heard him.

Scheraze held his wrists down. Melisande pinned his kicking feet. Francesca ripped away at his clothes until he was lying there, completely bare ass, on the main causeway out of Turtleshell Mountain. Leo looked into the Princesses' faces. Their eyes were overflowing with joy and innocent glee.

Their mouths were gone.

In place of lips and teeth, each Princess had a toothless, elongated funnel of stretched skin with an endless black hole in the middle. Leo gaped at those holes. Here, on the outside, was the insectoid sucker that had digested his finger.

"NO! NOOO!"

No one heard him. Then the streetlight over his head was blocked out. Princess Francesca loomed over him. The black pit of her snout sucked noisily at the air. It made a sound like water struggling through a clogged drain.

She latched onto his face, making a seal so tight that it posed a new philosophical question:
If a man's screaming, but no one can possibly hear it, is he really screaming?

Scheraze latched onto his shoulder. Melisande sucked on his thigh. The fat deposits in Leo's belly went first, collapsing like the whipped cream on top of a milkshake. The meat in his arms and legs went next, disappearing until his skin lay draped over bone like oversized clothes. Then that went too.

Alone, any one of them could have slurped Leo up in minutes. Together, the three of them turned him into baby food and inhaled him in less than thirty seconds.

When all that was left of Leo were his shoes and some stains on his discarded jacket, the Princesses looked up. They stared down the causeway. Twin rows of sodium lights underneath Turtleshell character hoods illuminated a barren strip of asphalt with rows of dark, empty, parked cars on either side of it.

Beyond that, there was a steady stream of traffic moving back and forth between restaurants, shops, and houses that lay outside of the park.

The three beautiful princesses could not use their horrible, true mouths to form words, but they could communicate just the same through snorts and huffs.

Food.

Meat.

More.

MORE.

They crawled towards the movement and life without bothering to rise from all fours. They dragged their gowns across the dirty asphalt and left long streaks of filth across the beautiful fabric.

The voice in their heads made them stop.

Come back.

Search the park.

Then, like when the magic kiss that first woke

them all up, the picture appeared again in their minds. The picture of an open head with a star shining out of it. The features on this face were generic, it was impossible to tell even anything as simple as race or gender, but the star was unique. The star was a pulsing prism of light unlike anything else that had ever existed. The star was one in a million. They would know when they touched it. They would know if they-

Find the star for me.

Find the star first. And then-

Another picture.

The gates of Turtleshell Peak in Florida, Tokyo Turtleshell, and Euro Turtleshell. All of them alive with their brothers and sisters.

All of them full of screaming.

Eyes alive with carefree joy, black mouths tasting the air for sweat and terror, the Princesses returned to the park.

<u>30</u>

In Jack's head, this was all a movie. Or maybe a video game. Jack had never played it, but he remembered there was a game that came out when he was in high school where all the Turtleshell Pictures characters teamed up with the characters from the *Visions of the End* games. That was all any of this was to him.

The sense that none of this was real had begun with the voice in his head. The one that had spoken to him while he was watching the football game in his room.

Come and see, it said. *Go to Scott's room. There's another game being played there that you DEFINETLY don't want to miss.*

Jack listened to the voice because he knew that he wasn't crazy. If he was hearing actual, no bullshit voices in his head, then he'd obviously just dozed off. If all of this was a dream anyway, then there was no sense in not playing along.

Then, when he went to Scott's room and saw Erin… well, obviously, he wasn't dreaming. But it definitely wasn't reality either. It couldn't be. Not with Erin. Not with Erin and Scott. And not with his service pistol suddenly in his hand when he knew it was locked away securely at the station.

And he still had the voice in his head.

Shoot him. Shoot that woman stealer in the fucking head. You know he's got plenty of empty space in that skull of his so take advantage of the low property values and fill it up with some lead.

That seemed like a good idea to Jack. And, if none of this was real anyway, he didn't see why he shouldn't do what he wanted to do.

Then had come the business with Erin and the "exam," and that was a bit much. Even for a nightmare. *Wake up,* he'd chanted to himself. *Wake up now!* But it didn't matter. The nightmare just kept dragging on.

Then he'd been brought down in the elevator, and Lavender Twist and Leyland Cypress were there. They grabbed the guards. They tried to grab *him*. Jack kicked the door closed and got away but that was all too much insanity to even be a nightmare. That was too insane to be *anything*. In desperation, Jack had retreated into a haze of fog somewhere below his conscious mind.

Occasionally, something deeper than his mind, something in his heart, would stir. When that happened, Jack would take a peek topside. But when he looked and saw that he still hadn't woken back up into a world where the football game was over and Erin was sleeping peacefully beside him, he went back under. He could still see and hear everything that was happening around him, it was just that none of it triggered anything in his mind.

Tap.

Tap.

Tap.

That was why Jack was the only who didn't flinch once the tapping came echoing out from somewhere in the underground tunnels. He saw the dread pass between the others as they traded looks to confirm that they'd really heard something. It was just that, obviously, none of it was real so there was no reason to change the slack, slightly interested look on his own face. Not even when Erin squeaked and then clamped a hand over her mouth, frightened of what might have heard her.

Erin, Aaron, and Raylene drew tightly together. There was no place to hide in the barren hallway. They were completely exposed.

Meanwhile, the tapping only got louder. It was fast paced too. The sound of something moving quickly.

"It might just be more people trying to get out," Tess whispered.

"So what if they are?" Raylene hissed back. "You want to try and stay unnoticed with that fucking noise following you around?"

"We can all get out together," Tess argued.

"I need to be able to think if I'm going to figure out what tunnel gets us out of here, and I won't be able to do it with that sound driving me crazy."

"What do you mean, 'figure it out?'" Erin hissed. "You don't know where we're going!?"

"Don't," Raylene warned. "I don't have a cock, so there's no reason for you to open your mouth around me."

"We should see who it is," Tess interrupted. "Maybe they know where they're going,"

"And if it's more fucking things? What are you going to say then?" Raylene countered. "'Whoops, don't mind us?'"

All the while, the tapping got louder.

Louder.

Tap.

Tap.

Tap.

It was getting close enough that they knew which way it was coming from. Right around the corner at the far end of the hall. Aaron looked in that direction. They all did. If they didn't make a decision, a decision was going to be made for them.

It might have been a couple and their kids helping their elderly grandfather along with the aid of a walker.

It might have been one of the stars from *Biography of a Bug*, skittering along on legs tipped like daggers and looking for more than an autograph.

Tap.

Tap.

Tap.

"Fuck this," Raylene said. "You can all do what you want."

They were near one of the elevators leading up to… somewhere. Raylene pushed the call button.

Tess was stunned. "You're just going to leave them?"

"I don't know what 'they' are," Raylene said. "You want to find out, be my guest."

We are your guests, Tess thought. But the elevator arrived and Raylene got inside.

After a moment's hesitation, Erin said, "Come on, Jack," and pulled him in.

The tapping moved faster. Someone moving

grandpa along faster to try and catch up. Or Allen Arachnid moving faster to catch his prey.

Tap tap.

Tap tap.

Tap tap.

Tess wanted to wait. Aaron knew that she did. Truthfully, so did he. He'd seen what Lavender and Leyland had done to the people in the lobby. Erin hadn't. Apparently, neither had Raylene. Tess hadn't seen it, but she still didn't want to abandon them anyway.

But the others are going. And if we're separated we're not finding them again.

And below that rationale, yes, the fear of whatever was coming down the hall. *Get out. Get the hell out. Jesus Christ, are you waiting for an invitation?*

He took Tess' hand. "We can't risk it," he said. He hated himself the second he said it, wondered what he was really risking if he thought like that, and saw the same questions in Tess' eyes as she let him lead her into the elevator.

Raylene was hammering the button for the ground floor but the doors refused to come together. "Clossse," she hissed. "Close you fucking thing." Then she remembered this was the service elevator. You didn't just press the button, you had to hold it.

She leaned on the "G" button with all of her weight until the blood pooled at the tip of her finger and turned purple. The doors started to close.

Aaron stuck his arm into the doorway. The

doors sensed the obstacle and slid open again.

Raylene whirled in him. "What the FUCK are you doing?" she snarled as viciously as she could without raising her voice.

"One second," Aaron whispered.

"If you don't move that hand right now, then you're going to need to go prosthetics shopping with Captain Claw."

"One second," Aaron repeated. "We can still close the door before it gets here. If we have to. Let's just see who it is."

Raylene was ready to threaten something much more precious than his hands, but she didn't have the time.

The tapper came around the corner.

They saw.

It was an old man.

An old man with a walker, struggling to get by as fast as he could.

Jesus, Aaron thought. *No wonder it took him so long to get here*. The old guy was maybe four feet high and three feet wide with stubby legs like tomato cans. He leaned heavily on the walker, and Aaron saw his chest heaving with every step.

That's why he didn't call out to us. He needed every breath just to keep moving. At the other end of the hall, the old man squinted at them from behind thick, square glasses.

"Is someone down there?!" he called out in a low, raspy voice.

Jesus, he can't even see us. Aaron's heart went out to him, and he felt a surge of satisfaction that they had not cut and run. They would have been no

226

better than the monsters running around in the park.

So why was Tess clutching his arm so tightly?

Aaron looked at her and saw no relief on her face nor compassion. Only bleached skin and bulging eyes.

"Close it," Raylene said. "Move your fucking arm."

Why? Aaron looked again and all he saw was a squat old man tilting his head on his hunched, crooked shoulders and trying just to see more than two feet in front of him.

But…

There was something familiar about that move, wasn't there? And the quizzical expression on his face. And the brown sweater he was wearing. Aaron had seen that before, he just couldn't place where.

The old man's eyes suddenly shot open. They were muddy brown and excitement rose from those murky depths like the bones of things long dead.

"Wait a minute. Have you got bitches down there?"

Hearing the old man's froggy voice again closed the circuit. Aaron knew it from dozens of movies, TV shows, and commercials stretching back from before he was born. Most recently, he recognized it from Turtleshell Picture's *The Old Man in the Moon*.

"You do!" the Old Man yelled. He got his walker going and he no longer seemed frail at all. "Bitches!"

Tap tap tap.

Tap tap tap.

"Bitches! Bitches! Bitches!" He was shouting it the way a child might scream for candy. He was drooling just as much.

Raylene pushed on the elevator button. Her finger throbbed in protest and she just pushed harder. The heavy freight doors started to rumble closed, but the old man was coming in fast. The flush in his wrinkled, hanging skin meant that was true in more ways than one.

And the doors were slow. Jesus, so slow. The Old Man was even closer. Close enough to see his hot breath fogging his glasses.

But he wasn't going to make it. Aaron could tell. The Old Man was close, but not close enough.

We'll be okay. It's going to be close, but we're going to be okay.

Aaron's hands were balled into fists, but that was just a precaution.

The elevator door panels were coming together, slowly but surely eclipsing their view of the old man even as he was almost on top of them. Finally the doors did indeed close. They heard the Old Man's wail of disappointment from the other side.

Raylene turned on Aaron. "Satisfied? Or do you want to wait a little longer? Try that Good Samaritan shit again and you better hope whoever finds what's left of you is feeling charitable."

The doors opened again.

They'd all forgotten that the elevator door had buttons on the outside as well.

The Old Man's walker clacked through the rift

228

first. It was followed quickly by his arms, his block-shaped head, and his lecherous smile.

They all screamed. This was not Lavender and Leyland and their deceptive calm. There was no time for dread or the formulation of a plan. There was only blind revulsion and panic as he wormed more of his body into the rift between the doors before they even finished opening. The Old Man in the Moon was exactly eye level with the hem of Raylene's skirt. He smiled up at her as Raylene tried to press herself as tightly against the elevator wall as she could.

"Evening, madam," he said in the same memorable voice that had won Emmys and Golden Globes. "Fancy a chimney sweep?"

Tess kicked the Old Man in the face. There was none of her self-defense training or kick-boxing class in it. It was the kind of knee-jerk kick one would aim at a rodent creeping up in the kitchen.

It was enough. The Old Man flew back like he was made of bird bones and shredded wheat. The walker went flying, and he fell flat on his face. It would have been pathetic if he hadn't immediately reared back around and roared at them, revealing flat, yellow teeth as broad as industrial grinders.

He crawled back towards them. His glasses had been knocked off by the kick and without the lenses his eyes were tiny, soulless, black pinpricks.

Erin tried to close the doors again. The Old Man got his jagged, yellow fingernails into the gap first. His lips peeled into a wide, lecher's grin.

"Help," he said to Erin, using the winning charm that had stolen audience's hearts for a decade. "I've fallen and I can't get up."

This time Erin kicked him. She aimed her foot right for the swollen tumor of his nose.

The Old Man took the kick and he took Erin's foot with it. He grabbed her ankle, digging bloody chips in her skin, and held on tight. "Close, but I think you meant to put your foot in my mouth. Here, my darling, let me help."

He sucked at the blood flowing over his clenched fingers and then moved up to lick at the source from Erin's ankle.

Erin didn't scream. She threw up. Vomit rained down on the Old Man's sparse hair, and he didn't even care. He was too busy trying to undo Erin's shoelaces.

Erin tried to yank her foot away and almost lost balance. She would have fallen-

If I do he'll climb on me. No, oh God, no.

But Tess was there to support her. She tried to pull Erin free but, backed into the corner, she couldn't get enough distance to yank her away from the Old Man.

Aaron kicked him in the ribs. The Old Man flopped up and down with the force, but he had his hands tight around Erin's ankle and he wasn't letting go.

Raylene tried to get the doors to close again; but, The Old Man was still sprawled right across the path of the doors and they only slid back open again. Aaron realized how dangerous this was getting.

We can't close the doors without getting rid of him, and we can't get him to let go of Erin.

Erin screamed again. The Old Man just laughed at it. "Don't listen to them, darling. I love the way you sing! DO IT AGAIN!" He bit her. Erin screamed even louder.

And the more noise we make, the more likely something else is going to find us here.

Raylene understood all of this as well. She understood the situation, and she also understood that she was finally dealing with some part of this nightmare that she'd dealt with before:

A horny old man.

And the best thing to do when you were dealing with a grabby-handed old bastard?

You threw him a bone.

While the others were fighting and screaming and pulling, Raylene was looking at Erin and waiting for just the right moment. She got it when Erin tried to twist herself from the Old Man in the Moon's grasp and actually wound up wrenching herself loose from Tess. She was completely unsupported and wobbling for balance, perfectly in position in front of the open doors.

Raylene made her move. She stepped forward with her hands cocked back and her eyes firmly fixed on the small of Erin's back as she wobbled for balance.

But it was Raylene that got hit. Something big and fast crashed into her from behind and knocked her sprawling to the side. Raylene hit the wall and spun back around, raising her hands to defend herself, trying to see what the hell had hit her.

All she caught was the fleeting end of a leg, and then Jack was locomotoring past her. Jack, roaring with both hands outstretched and his eyes wildly alive and fixed ahead on only one thing. He snatched the Old Man up by the collar and the belt and hauled him into the hallway. Still in the decrepit old thing's grasp, Erin went with him. She fell painfully on her tailbone and then she slid into the hallway as the Old Man kept his claws wrapped around her foot.

"Erin!"

Tess grabbed her hand. Aaron grabbed Tess around the waist. Together, they pulled at Erin while Jack hoisted the Old Man straight up and away in the opposite direction.

"Hey, who said you could butt in!?" the old man raged. "The lady's mine!"

Jack ignored him and cranked the Old Man sideways. Erin's torso corkscrewed with him, stretching her body to the limits of its flexibility. The pain was everywhere now, all the way from the Old Man's death grip on her ankle, along the burning path of her vertebrates, and up to Tess and Aaron's lock on her wrist.

"Don't let go!" Erin pleaded with her friends. The pain was better. She would take any pain over the hot breath on her ankle. "Please, Tess, please don't let me go!"

Tess didn't hear her. Tess was too deep in her own head, hiding from her own exhaustion.

I'm fine, she repeated grimly in the darkness of her mind. *I'm not weak. I've got you, Erin. I'm holding on.* And the weaker her grip became, the louder she repeated it.

I'm not losing you. I'M NOT LOSING YOU.

232

She still wasn't loud enough. Not so loud in her head that she couldn't block Erin from her ears.

"TESS!"

Tess reared back, galvanized by her friend's scream to put all the muscle she had into one final, titanic pull, but she already knew that her hardest wasn't going to be hard enough. The raw truth was finally too loud not to hear:

She had no strength left.

But what she had was blood and sweat. Erin's blood and sweat, lubricating her ankle. Jack had never stopped trying to wrench the Old Man away and enough slippery blood and sweat had gotten in under his grip that the Old Man's wrinkled fingers slipped loose. Erin came free.

"Darling!" the Old Man moaned, heartbroken, as she slipped away from him.

Without any resistance from his side, Tess, Aaron, and Erin flew into the corner of the elevator and collapsed in a tangled heap.

Jack kept running with the Old Man in the opposite direction. He put all of his giant frame behind it and slammed the Old Man against the far wall with enough force to make his teeth chatter together and send his over-sized eyes rolling.

It would have been comical if the Old Man's face hadn't reverted so swiftly back into fury.

"Butt out, butthead!"

He attacked Jack's arms and hands with his jagged nails. In seconds, he ripped the flesh of Jack's arms into bloody ribbons. He peeled back entire strips of skin, exposing raw muscle underneath.

Still, Jack gritted his teeth and held the Old Man exactly where he was: with his stubby legs kicking helplessly in the air three feet off the ground.

"READY THE COUNTDOWN!" Jack roared

Raylene didn't know what he was saying, but she knew what he meant and she didn't hesitate. She pressed the button to close the doors.

5...4...

Erin, Tess, and Aaron were still in a dazed knot on the floor. It was Erin who saw what was happening first.

3...2...

"NOO!" Erin dove for the doors but it was too late. They closed a bare instant before her clenched fist struck it, and her last sight was Jack looking over his shoulder at her before the doors scissored close.

The hum of the motor told her they were already moving.

Blast off.

"JACK! JAACCKKK!" She was screaming his name because there wasn't time to tell him how sorry she was. There was no time to explain that she hadn't strayed because of anything he'd done wrong.

She didn't have time to tell him that she would always love him.

Jack slammed the old man against the wall again, rattling the rotten brain in his skull. He could hear Erin screaming through the closed door but he wasn't able to respond in kind. The ability to say something as simple as, *"Yes, I hear you,"* was

234

lost in the cracks of Jack's fractured mind.

That didn't mean he didn't know what she was trying to say.

"Keep looking up!" he shouted at the elevator doors. "Keep looking up and you can't go wrong!"

Which, of course, was the Old Man in the Moon's mission statement as he launched his homemade rocket.

When he was sure they were up and away, Jack swiveled his head back to the Old Man. The Old Man was twisting in his grasp but Jack could barely feel it. The veins in his wrists were gushing blood and his hands had lost all feeling.

He shifted his grip and forced one forearm into the Old Man's throat. Leaning forward added more weight to his hold on the creature, but it also put him more closely into the Old Man's range. Nails ripped more detours in his circulatory system. The Old Man lunged forward with his thumb and gouged out one of Jack's eyes.

None of it mattered. Jack pushed more of his weight onto the Old Man's neck. The flesh beneath his arm didn't feel like flesh. It was too rubbery, like latex over plastic rods. But the reaction was the same when the Old Man's throat finally collapsed. The withered creature twitched, gurgled, and went still. A thin trickle of something orange ran from his lip. Hydraulic fluid maybe.

Jack let the body drop, and the world suddenly spun around him. He leaned against the wall for support without really seeing it. The wall was on the right side of his vision and, thanks to the Old Man, the right side of the world had become crusty-feeling darkness.

Dizzy. Too many trips on the Spinning Umbrellas will do that to you.

He pushed that aside. He was lucid for just a moment. *No, that's not what's happening.*

Even with the wall, Jack's legs couldn't hold him up. He sunk down lower and lower until he was sitting in a puddle of his own blood. His limbs felt warm and fuzzy. It was hard to catch his breath, especially with blood dribbling into his mouth from his ruined eye.

He still could have perhaps eventually crawled over to the elevator. Maybe make it upstairs and get help. From his friends. But he didn't bother trying. He knew that he wouldn't have enough time before he bled out.

And he knew that the Old Man hadn't made the trip to the moon by himself.

Jack swiveled to look out of his good left eye and, sure enough, the others were waiting for him at end of the hall. Jack scoped them out, turning at the waist to make better use of the eye that wasn't a gory ruin.

Shirley, the granddaughter was there, of course. The spunky eleven-year old was wearing the moon armor she discovered in the lunar temple and riding atop her mount- the yellow, white, and adorably befuddled Giant Moon Ostrich.

The Moon Bird didn't look very adorable or befuddled now. It glared at Jack with the flat, unblinking eyes of a bird of prey.

Shirley didn't seem so spunky either. She seemed more like a Valkyrie atop her hell-steed.

236

The shadow of her helmet hid most of her face, but not the burning hatred in her eyes as she looked from her grandfather's body to Jack.

"Family First," she said. That was the prevailing theme of *The Old Man in the Moon*, but Shirley spoke it like an executioner's edict.

Jack understood that just fine. Family First, wasn't that why he'd killed the Old Man in the first place?

Blood loss made Jack woozy. He tilted his head back and closed his good eye.

He could still hear the click clack of the Moon Bird's talons across the linoleum. He started singing to block it out:

"You're a friend to me,
I'm a friend to you,"

His voice was utterly atrocious. Croaking and not even remotely in key, but it did the trick. Jack was no longer in the service hallway. In his mind, it was the ending scene of *Lavender Twist and the Golden Hinoki* and Jack wasn't just watching it, he was inside the movie. He sat at the round table that was actually a sunflower bloom. Sunlight speckled down through the treetops that towered as far above him as skyscrapers and the hollowed-out acorn shell cup in front of him was filled with the most delicious hibiscus tea in the entire nursery.

Erin was there too. So were Aaron and Tess. Lavender and Leyland were there as well. Not the obscene creatures they'd met in the lobby; but the real Lavender Twist and Leyland Cypress. The animated friends who had been there for a young Jack who had not yet had the growth spurt or athletic success that would earn him popularity and acceptance as a teenager. This Jack would sit in his grandma's living room every day after school and watch Lavender and Leyland and a friendship that was as precious as emeralds to an undersized boy with an oversized back brace. It made Jack happier than anything to imagine this scene where he could share his old friends with his new ones.

And they were all so good here. Everything wrong had been fixed by a hefty dose of Turtleshell magic. Erin was on his arm. Jack could feel the warmth of her side and see the glisten of his favorite apple-red lip gloss on her lips.

Aaron and Tess were sharing a begonia bud chair on the near curve of the table. Jack had her sitting on Aaron's lap and Aaron's hand comfortably at the small of her back.

Even Scott was there. He was sitting on the opposite side of the table, but there wasn't a bullet in his head, and there was a double helping of his favorite food, buffalo wings, on his plate. He seemed happy enough.

Jack raised his glass in a toast. He was sensing the fade to black, and it was time to say the final lines:

"For love of loved ones."

The others, his friends real and imagined, raised their glasses.

"For love of loved ones!"

They clinked their cups together, and their smiles only widened as the end credits started to roll.

And Jack Nelson felt absolutely nothing when

238

the Moon Bird's rocky beak punctured his skull.

31

Erin spent the entire elevator ride slack and lifeless. She only stayed upright because she had the elevator doors to slump against. When those doors opened, Erin made no attempt to hold herself up. She pitched forward and lay there, forehead pressed against the cool, stone floor of what turned out to be a gift shop storeroom, and just didn't get back up. All things considered, she would rather breathe in the dust from the concrete floor rather than get back up and look at the world that she knew was waiting for her.

Raylene stepped over her. She walked farther into the storeroom and swiveled her head from left to right. "I don't think anyone else is here," she whispered.

Aaron didn't step over Erin. He looked down at her, sprawled out like a toy nobody had bothered to pick up, and tried to think of something to say.

He loved you too.

I'm sorry.

I wish there was something I could do.

He lives in you.

Spring always follows winter, even the coldest ones.

No matter how your heart grieves, always-

Oh, God.

He was quoting Turtleshell movies.

Tess' fingers briefly intertwined with his. "Why

don't you try to help Sacajawea figure out where we are?" she asked.

Standing by the computer on the manager's desk, Raylene glared at her but said nothing.

Aaron moved as carefully as he could around Erin. His foot came down within inches of her head, but the knotted curtain of her hair didn't even stir.

Aware of their precarious position, Tess first hit the emergency stop switch on the elevator and then knelt down beside Erin. Erin knew she was there. She could hear Tess breathing but refused to acknowledge it. *Just leave me here. Let me be dead. I don't care. I DON'T FUCKING CARE.*

Tess could hear Erin's breathing too. It came in and out behind the funeral shroud of hair like engine exhaust, filthy with grief and guilt. Tess leaned closer to her.

If she touches me, I'm going to scream. I don't care what hears it.

Tess didn't touch her. Like Aaron, Tess didn't have the words to reach Erin.

But she knew who did.

"We have to pick it up."

We have to pick it up. That's what Jack would always say towards the end of a game when the Patriots or the Red Sox or the Buckeyes were down towards the end of a close game. If his team was still in it but down by a touchdown or a run with only an inning or two minutes to go, Jack would crack open a beer but he wouldn't touch it until the game was over one way or another. He would just tighten his face into short, foreboding

241

lines, hold that beer so tightly that the aluminum would dent in his hand, and he would say, "They have to pick it up."

It became their inside joke. If the bartender was slow with their drinks, Tess would say, "He has to pick it up." If Netflix wasn't loading on group movie night, Scott would throw popcorn at the TV and say, "They have to pick it up!"

When they were making love, if Jack was being too excruciatingly considerate, Erin would squeeze him, not with her hands, and groan, "You have to pick it up."

And, oh, how he would.

But that was for things that were close. Bartenders just a few feet away, Netflix buffering at 96%, Erin's knees twitching as she felt so damn good that it was maddening to not feel better.

Erin's voice came, thin and barely there, from behind her hair. "Does any of this really feel close to you?" she asked.

"I was supposed to be dead eight months ago," Tess said. "I'm still here because I never stopped thinking that it was close." She went to join Aaron and Raylene. She didn't look back to see if Erin was going to get up.

And Erin didn't. The concrete floor was so soothingly cool. And quiet. It felt so much better than the heat of thought and fear and guilt.

It's the cold of the grave, a second voice put in. *Is that what you want? Is that what Jack would want for you?*

Slowly, Erin picked herself up.

She joined Tess and the others. They were

gathered around the computer screen, too tightly for Erin to get close and see what they were looking at. "Can you get online?" she asked. "Is there any way we can call for help?"

"We can't do anything," Raylene said. She wasn't looking away from the screen, though. None of them were.

"It's not working?"

"Nothing's working," Aaron said. "E-mail. Skype. The mouse doesn't even move."

Erin didn't understand. "...So what are you all looking at?"

Tess moved so she could see.

At first, Erin thought it was just a screensaver. It was the toy chest from *Live Action Figures* with the entire cast of living toys jumping out from the box in a wide fan of characters.

Except there was a new figure standing in the middle of the frame, right where you would expect Cowboy Cal to be. He was handsome, and his smile suggested more than a little roguish charm that was just waiting for an audience to be unleashed upon.

Maybe it's a sequel. Live Action Figures 3. He's some new character. If that was the case, then they still needed to do some serious work on the animation. There was something... unfinished about the new addition's face. Yes, the eyes, nose, and mouth were all there and arranged to show that he was having the absolute time of his life, but that was the problem- *life*. It looked like the animator had made the broad strokes, but hadn't bothered with any of the tiny tweaks and details that made it

243

feel like there was a living soul inside a character. It felt like his smile and bright eyes were nothing but a framed photo hung over a gaping hole in a wall.

"What's wrong with the new character?"

"What new character?" Aaron asked.

"Right there," Erin pointed. "Isn't that what you're all looking at?"

"That's not..." Aaron began- began, but couldn't finish.

"No, that's not what we're looking at," Raylene said.

"Then what? What is it?"

"The toy chest," Tess moaned. She sounded ill. *If Tess had sounded like that while she was trying to pick me up, I don't think I would have ever gotten off the floor.*

Then Erin looked at the toy chest and understood why.

And wished to God that she didn't.

The toy chest was an optical illusion. It looked like plain, sanded wood but, if you looked closer, you realized that the waves of wood grain were all made up of screaming faces. Genderless, twisted mouths and gaping, blank eyes all in terrible, unending agony.

The worst part was that this poster wasn't meant to scare anyone. This poster was meant as a celebration. If the brilliant color palette and the joyful expressions on the characters' faces did not make that fact clear enough, then the banner across the bottom of the screen made it abundantly clear.

All the banner said, all it needed to say, was,

"Time to Play."

Aaron reached behind the monitor. He felt for the power cord and yanked it out.

The screen stayed on. If anything, the screaming faces got wider.

Tess grabbed a souvenir shirt and threw it over the monitor, blocking it from view.

"Great, that makes everything all better," Raylene drawled. Secretly, though, the walls around her didn't feel so close without those faces staring at her.

Tess ignored the jab. "We're above ground now," she said. "Do you know where we are yet? Or should we ask somebody who works here?" She had perhaps not ignored the jab completely.

Raylene decided to leave them at even. She inspected the merchandise on the shelves for a reference point. She saw bees. Lots of the same bee, technically. A sporty fellow wearing boxing gloves, yellow-and-black striped trunks, and a "Hit me if you can," smirk.

It was all she needed to see. "Rumble Bee's Ringside Ruckus. It's closer to the exit than the hotels but still not close enough. We'd be out in the open for another five blocks."

"I'm not going back into the tunnels," Erin said. Not that any of them would, but the others were only afraid of what characters might be waiting for them down there. Erin was most afraid of what she knew would be waiting for them. Jack's body.

But if we step foot outside up here, we might run into the real Rumble Bee, Aaron thought. It

245

was just like being in the hotel room all over again. Except now they knew what a wrong choice meant.

"Maybe we can just stay here," Erin said. "We shut the elevator off and this room has no windows. What if we blocked off the door and just… waited? Somebody has to know what's happened here. People will come."

"I haven't heard any sirens," Aaron said. "No helicopters. Nothing. I don't even… I don't even hear anybody screaming." At the last moment, he almost didn't say it. The words hung like a fist cocked and ready to fly. In the end, perhaps against his better judgment, he threw it.

"I don't think anyone got out of this place alive."

"I got a report this afternoon," Raylene said. "Attendance for the day was twenty thousand people."

"No," Erin said. "No. That can't be. Twenty thousand people don't die without SOMEBODY knowing about it." He saw fear jittering at the corner of her mouth and her eyes. He saw the terror lurking behind the belligerence on Raylene's face. He wished he could have taken back the blow he'd just thrown at them.

Instead, he hit them again.

"You remember what happened when we tried to call 911. Even if there are other people hiding somewhere, I don't think their phones will work either."

And everyone here is on vacation. There's not even anyone to get suspicious when they don't

246

come home. He was able to keep at least that much to himself.

Tess spoke into the silence that followed. "The longer we stay here, the more likely we are to end up just like them. We have to get out."

"How!?" Raylene exploded, finally tired of all this can-do bullshit. "You want to stroll down Patty Cake Lane and hop on a trolley? We can't fly. We can't-"

Raylene stopped talking, but her mouth stayed open and her eyes stretched wide. It looked like she was having a stroke.

"Oh, shit. OH, SHIT. Yes, we can!"

"Can what?" Tess asked.

"It's right here! The stairs are fifty feet across the street. I'll blow Timmy Turtle if it's fifty-one!"

Raylene paced back and forth, vibrating with pent-up energy. She could see it clear as day. The steps lined up neatly on a white board inside her mind. She had it. *She had it*.

"What is it!?" Erin demanded. "If you know a way out, you have to tell us!"

The slut's needy, entitled whining dragged Raylene back to awareness. *I don't have to tell you anything*, was what she wanted to say. But, of course, she did. They would be coming with her, if only so she'd have someone to certify that Raylene Adams had done everything in her power to maintain the Hospitality Standards of Turtleshell Mountain. She took a breath first, going over it in her head first like she always did before a high-stakes presentation, making sure she had everything perfectly prepared.

Maybe she did, and maybe she didn't. She'd never know because the tinkling of a bell made itself heard first. Raylene recognized it. They all did. It was the kind of antiquated, old-time bell mounted over the door in every gift shop in Turtleshell Mountain. It meant another customer had come inside the shop.

To the survivors of Turtleshell Mountain, it meant that something else hunting for their heads was lurking on the other side of that door.

Raylene froze. They all did. Nobody drew a breath. They waited.

Waited.

They heard nothing else. Nothing moved in the gift shop.

The wind, Aaron thought. *Thank God, just the wind*.

He turned towards Raylene, the scare had only underlined how desperately they needed to get out. "Hurry, what is it you're thinking?"

Then they heard footsteps moving across the floor of the gift shop.

<u>32</u>

Minister Ed had climbed down from the top of the Coney Island Coaster. He walked past Horror Heights (and what a sick fucking joke that was) and all the way to the Flying Rhinos that Gabrielle had wanted to see so badly (and wasn't that an even sicker fucking joke) without encountering another soul or even anything walking around without a soul.

But that didn't mean he didn't have anyone to talk to.

Minister Ed had God.

When I die, You better send me to Hell because if You don't the first thing I'm going to do is march up to Your mighty throne and knock it over with Your ass still in it.

That was the latest in the litany of threats he'd leveled against the Almighty. Edward Harrison's last true prayer had been uttered when he was standing at the top of the roller coaster. *Tear it down, God,* he'd prayed. *Bring the whole works down the way Samson brought down the Philistine's temple. And tear me down with it.*

God had not answered and for Ed that was the final straw. Now, he had nothing to say to God the Father, God the Son, and God the Holy Ghost except for curses and slurs.

But that did not mean that Ed did not believe in God.

Trusted, loved, and served? Absolutely not. But his belief in God was based on a lifetime of observation, deep consideration, and, finally, understanding. Part of that understanding was the academic truth that sometimes God allowed tragic things to happen.

"God has His reasons," Minister Ed had once said in a sermon. "That's not the easiest Gospel to take to heart. It's not anything you'd say to sway converts or something you'd want to shout from the mountaintops. But when we're faced with a 9/11 or a Sandy Hook, sometimes the only answer that isn't a platitude is, 'God has His reasons.'

"But do not despair, Brothers and Sisters! Hard as that truth may be, we also need to remember that for every one person who cries, there are another hundred who laugh! We must never forget that every new day is also full to brimming with joy, wonder, and incredible, indescribable beauty. Amen I say to you, God has his reasons for all of that joy as well, and we cannot trust Him to create one without trusting that He allows us to suffer the other for a purpose as well."

It had sounded fine when he said it in the chapel. That clean, well-lit space lined with the families all intact and whole. But now that Ed's understanding was personal and not academic, he realized that he didn't give one shit what God's reasons were. When something finally killed him, Timmy Turtle or Pedro Parrot or Ed didn't care what, he and God would have a conversation to be sure. But it would be a conversation with very little talking.

That was why, at the last moment, Ed had not thrown himself from the top of the Coney Island Coaster. Ed had still lived the same life he had led before everything had turned to ash. He had honored God. He had served his neighbor. He had lived an all-around commendable life and, when he died, he had no doubts about his prospects for entering paradise.

Paulie Maldonado's blank eyes staring at him. Rolled up in his head so all Minister Ed could see was the whites. The boy's mouth half open and his tongue poking limply from between his-.

THAT WAS AN ACCIDENT!

But suicide? Suicide was a sin. Maybe not so much in cases of mental illness but, for all his despair, Ed was not insane. He could not take his life and then plead that he was not rational enough to know what he'd done. The horrible truth was that Ed was still completely in control of his faculties.

So he needed to stay alive until something killed him. He trusted that wouldn't take too long. He heard human screams and inhuman laughter all throughout the park. Surely, something would find him that didn't share the Coney Island Code of Conduct. And when it did, Ed would still have his pass to Heaven and he would use it to raise as much Hell as he could.

But he couldn't just be looking to die. No, no, no. That would be cheating. Ed needed to have a purpose and, as black luck would have it, he had the perfect excuse to stay alive.

He needed to bury his kids.

And, Ed laughed, here was more luck. Underneath the Rhinos was a tipped over landscaper's cart. He jogged over to it. The landscaper himself was presumably fertilizer in one of his flower beds by now, but whatever creature had taken him had no use for the cart. Ed sorted through the handles until he found a good, sturdy spade. Perfect for burying children or, if something found him first, for the pretense of self-defense.

He slung the spade across his shoulder and walked brazenly back the way he came. As if it were a Sunday morning in his own church yard. He would not be rushed in his walk or in his work. He would dig deep, square graves until something came along to stop him.

And the ones you don't get to bury because you're just throwing your life away? What will you say if you meet them again on your way to try and punch out God? How will you justify leaving their bodies behind like chewed gum that nobody could bother to scrape up?

If this is a part of myself talking, then we'll just have to live with it. And not for that long anyway.

And what if this is the true, quiet voice of God speaking through you?

Then You already had Your chance to get involved, and all You did was sit on Your ass. Now You can kindly keep Your mouth shut.

There were no more voices after that. Ed kept his focus on the looming height of the coaster, rising up against the night sky like a pillar of fire. He was almost there when the shadow exploded

252

out from behind one of the game booths. The black shape sprinted at him, too fast for Ed to make out anything but its tremendous bulk and pumping limbs. In seconds, it was right in his face.

This was wrong. Ed's death was not supposed to come from the shadows. His killer was supposed to step from the light. Ed was supposed to have the time to understand what was happening and welcome it with grim stoicism.

His death was not supposed to be like this. Not huge and startling and terrifying. Not sweeping over him so quickly that he felt nothing but common, animal fear as the darkness claimed him and he knew no more.

He was not supposed to want to take it back.

<u>33</u>

It was a paradox. If Aaron moved, he would be dead. Yet, he yearned to move because he was so perfectly still that he was starting to be afraid that he was already dead.

He wasn't breathing. He wasn't blinking. It felt like his heart had stopped dead in his chest. This was close. This was way too close to being like one of those dead people stacked on the tables in the restaurant.

Too close to how Jack must be lying in the hallway beneath them.

Aaron wanted to lift his arm or turn his head. Something, anything that would prove that he was still living and breathing.

But even that might be too much. The thing in the gift shop might be Barry Bat. Blind, yes, but with ears so sharp they might easily pick up the pop of cartilage in his neck. Maybe even sharp enough that they could hear air shift with the movement of his arm.

And he'd already *spoke*. Just a whisper, yes. But what if it heard?

If it did, it would already be pounding on the storeroom door. Just stay absolutely quiet. If you make a sound now, then you really will be dead. And not just you, Tess too. Do NOT fuck up.

There was another noise from the other side of the door. Boxes falling over.

254

Closer this time.

What about the door!? Aaron's face remained impassive (what if changing expressions made sounds?), but the thought was deafening his mind. None of them had bothered to check if the door was locked. Aaron could see it plainly from here. The lock was a twist knob in the handle. The tiny bar was horizontal. Did that mean locked or unlocked? He tried to remember his own apartment door but couldn't visualize it with any clarity. Even if he could, were the locks uniform? Maybe the door was already locked and if he tried to fiddle with it, he would be risking detection just so he could clear the way for whatever was lurking on the other side.

And who said locking it was even better? These things had intelligence. If it encountered a locked door, it might reason that it was locked because someone was hiding behind it.

But if the door's unlocked, it will just come in anyway.

He was considering every option so intensely that he didn't even realize he could feel his heart beat again. It was pumping so hard that it would have been physically painful if he were paying attention to it.

Then Tess took a step. Aaron's heart surged so hard that it almost cracked a rib. He stopped just short of screaming out her name, and only because of the way Tess looked at him. *Don't you make a sound,* her eyes warned.

So come back here and I won't have to, he silently sent back.

Incredibly, Tess winked. *Trust me.*

And he did trust her. He trusted that she was going to do something that would help them.

He didn't trust that her own well-being factored into her thought process at all.

But he stayed where he was.

So did Erin, even though concern for her friend was etched clearly on her face.

So did Raylene, but only because it would be noisier to beat the suicidal cunt unconscious.

Tess tread quietly to the door. The others didn't hear her make a sound, even from a few feet away.

We'll hear the door handle, though. No way not to. Tess, I hope you know what you're doing.

Tess, of course, understood the problem. She knew that there was no way to quietly do anything with the lock.

So rather than try, she grabbed the handle and flung the door wide open.

The others had no time to react. They were too shocked to even scramble out of sight as the closed door became an open window right into the gift shop.

They looked...

And there was nothing to see. The gift shop was empty.

Aaron breathed a sigh of relief. Whatever had been searching there had decided there was nothing to see.

Then Felix Fox snapped up from behind a display stand and looked right at them. There was a large smile on his face, a smile that was never going to go away. This was not another animatronic brought to life. This was a costumeer. A baggy body of gaudy orange fur, oversized, white-gloved hands, and a bulbous, hydrocephalic head with unblinking plastic eyes and a rictus grin that looked like it was clenched against a mouthful of mad screams.

The axe it was holding also looked like a smile. Long and broad with sharpened points for dimples.

Felix Fox raised his smiling axe and charged them. It was not an animal's lithe uncoiling of muscle and sinew. It was the clumsy charge of a mental patient with very little grace and a very large appetite for murder.

The scene unfolded in total silence. There was not a whisper from the costumeer as he charged and Aaron, Erin, and Raylene were too stunned by the sudden sight of him to even voice a scream. The whole grisly tableau was unfolding like an early Turtleshell silent cartoon.

Then the shelving unit came crashing down and brought sound back into the world in a cacophony of clattering metal and plastic

Felix Fox never saw it coming. He hurtled through the doorway into the stock room at the exact wrong time and was hit first by a hard rain of plastic merchandise. Then the full weight of the industrial shelving unit hit him and slapped him down to the ground. The axe went flying, and the framework of steel pinned Felix from the shoulders down.

Tess scrambled on top of the shelving, adding her own weight to the load holding Felix down, but it didn't appear necessary. The fox costumeer was splayed and motionless like a crushed insect. Tess stayed where she was anyway. Perched atop the wreckage and the crushed costumeer, she smirked at Aaron with her eyebrows raised.

I told you to trust me.

Aaron was too stunned to respond with just his eyes. "What if he wasn't alone?" he asked.

Tess just shrugged. "I picked a pretty big shelf."

In spite of everything, that familiar, one-shoulder shrug in the face of catastrophe, sent a small bolt of warmth through him. He could only imagine the heat he would have felt if they'd been anywhere else.

"Let's get out of here," Erin said. Her foot was already up to climb over the lattice work of the shelving.

"One second," Tess said. "Not yet."

"Why not?" Raylene asked. "Do we want to wait again and see if there's a friendly old man coming behind him?"

"How about I'd like to get some actual information about what's going on," Tess said. She nodded down at the still form of Felix Fox underneath her. "If there's any chance to ask some real questions, this is it. And if we're going to be making a run for it above ground, I think we should know what's waiting for us."

Aaron looked skeptically at the Felix Fox. He still wasn't moving. The costumeer's costume head was still on and its endless grin gave no indication as to the health of the... *thing* inside.

"Is he even alive?"

Felix Fox lifted one hand. The others jumped. Erin let out a short scream. She was convinced that the axe was going to fly across the room back into his waiting hand.

But it didn't. And the Fox just stayed where he was. Alive but trapped.

Theirs.

"We can't stay long," Erin said. "Felix Fox and Bella Badger are good friends in the cartoons. She'll.... she might be coming."

"So let's be direct with our inquiries," Raylene said. "I'm good at that."

She paced in front of him like the Fox was a rat stuck in a trap. Like he was a rat and Raylene was the cat.

That suited Raylene just fine. For the first time since all of this began, she was in her element. She needed information. The cornerstone of her career, and thus the foundation of her life, was acquiring and distributing information. She'd been too busy running and hiding to think about it but, now that Blondie had brought it up, Raylene remembered how much she hated being kept in the dark about anything.

She also hated being chased.

Attacked.

Almost killed.

Forced to scurry through the tunnels like a fucking gnome.

Dragged from place to place by these cops like she was a piece of baggage.

The Evil Queen Bitch was not happy. The Evil Queen Bitch wanted to be in control of something.

And Mr. Felix Fox had the bad fortune to be something the Evil Queen Bitch was in control of.

"What are you?" Raylene asked.

No answer from Felix. Only his smile and their strained faces reflected in his plastic disc eyes.

"I said, what are you? Don't waste your bad attitude on the easy questions."

Nothing.

"Fine, you want to play hard ball?" Raylene stooped down. When she stood back up, she was holding a Rumble Bee branded tee-ball bat. She thunked the bat against the floor, letting them all hear the metal ring out against the hard floor. "I can play hard ball."

She rapped the bat against the Felix Fox head. It made a hollow tapping sound that seemed much less sturdy than the sound the floor made.

"What are you? How did all of this start and who started it?"

"The party favor," Tess put in, remembering what Leyland and Lavender said. "A picture of a head. What does that mean to you?"

"Four questions," Raylene said, ignoring the fact that this was supposed to be a one-on-one meeting and not a conference call. "You answer all of them, or I smash your Felix Fox head like a fucking piñata and we see what comes out."

Still no answer. *Fine. You think I'm fucking around?* Raylene raised the bat without hesitation.

"Wait," Aaron said.

"Jesus Christ, what now!?"

Aaron knelt beside the trapped Fox and grabbed for its oversized costume head. The fur

260

bristled unpleasantly under his fingers like a thousand skittering spider legs.

He turned the head slowly, with the exaggerated care. Gently, carefully, he pulled the Felix Fox head off completely.

Erin almost screamed but stopped herself at the last second. If she screamed then something might hear her. She bit her lip instead, bit it until trails of blood ran down her chin.

"Oh, my God," Tess moaned. She grabbed Aaron's hand on impulse and squeezed as hard as she could. Aaron focused on the feel of her hand in his. That was a better feeling than most things, it was certainly better than the thing in front of them.

Underneath the character's head, there was nothing to see.

There was no person inside of the Felix Fox suit.

Aaron, Erin, and Tess all stared at the empty space where a head should have been but, unsettling as their view was, Raylene's was worse. Raylene was standing right in front of it. She could look right into the hollow interior of the suit and see a solid nothingness that was like what Raylene imagined death to be. No afterlife. No shining light.

Only darkness.

"Let's go," Aaron said. "We're not going to learn anything from him."

"Where are we going to go?" Tess asked.

"Not the tunnels," Erin said. Her face was bleached white at the thought of it.

"The Monorail," Raylene said. "That was what

I was going to say... before." Her eyes went involuntarily to the empty suit that had tried to butcher them. It no longer seemed alive with its head removed. If *alive* was ever the right word for it.

"The final station is right across the street," she went on. "And there's always a monorail waiting at the end of the line. It's Turtleshell standard operating procedure."

Aaron and Tess exchanged a look. This time, it was one that Erin had no problem deciphering:

Our car is parked right next to the station in the Lavender Lot.

"Can you drive it?" Aaron asked.

Raylene snorted. "We let the Make-A-Wish kids drive it and some of them have flippers. It's a go button and a stop button."

Fifty feet, that was what Raylene had said. They'd be exposed on the ground for less distance than the sprint from third base to home plate. *The moving monorail is going to be like a beacon for every freak in the park, though.*

But a fast beacon. And a tough one to break into. And it would let them out right next to their car.

It'll get us out. It'll get Tess out.

"Get more bats," he said.

"Someone can have mine," Raylene said. She put the bat down and picked up Felix Fox's axe instead.

Nobody thought to try and take it from her.

When they were all armed, they climbed across the steel spider web of the shelving and into the

262

gift shop. It was a wreck, and not just because of Felix Fox. The display window was shattered. Every shelf and clothing rack was smashed, and the contents were scattered from one end of the store to the other.

And there was blood. Lots and lots of blood. The floor was covered in puddles of it. So many that there was no way to reach the doors without stepping in it.

So roll your pants up, Aaron told himself. *You're getting Tess out of here. Nothing else matters.*

"It's a straight shot?" he asked. He knew that it was but he wanted something to distract them all, himself included, from trying to calculate how many people had to die before a store could be as positively drenched in blood as this one was.

Raylene nodded. "Right across the street. We climb a flight of stairs to the platform, and it will be right there."

"OK," Aaron said. "The second we're out the door, we just run. Whatever's out there doesn't matter. Just get to the platform as fast as you can."

"But we stay together," Tess said.

"Together," Aaron agreed. *But if it comes down to me having to stay and you getting out, that's what happens.* He had actually hoped that Raylene would have said that the controls of the monorail were complicated and that she was the only one that could drive it. He had no doubt that Raylene could be trusted to drive off no matter who was still on the platform. An order was forming in his mind. *Raylene, Tess, Erin... and then me. That's how I'd like to see us get on.*

But that might not be necessary. Despite all of the changes the park had undergone, the lights had never gone out. Main Street was as brightly lit as ever. Aaron looked through the smashed windows and saw no one. He heard nothing but the whistling of the wind and *The Turtle March* playing over the speakers.

They weren't running yet. They would once they made it to the street, but there was too much debris scattered across the floor of the store to run now. A twisted ankle would be a death sentence here.

And, of course, there was the wetness of the floor to worry about- the slippery, red wetness. There was nothing to do but walk through it. Walk through the blood of the dead and hear their shoes squelch in it. Raylene's heels whispered a different mantra now.

Slaughter.

Slaughter.

OH JESUS WHAT'S ON ME!?

Something poured over Raylene's shoulders from behind. Something with the temperature and consistency of hot fudge. It clung to her exposed skin and made her clothes feel heavy and soiled. Raylene shrieked in revulsion. She couldn't see what she'd been drenched with. She had no idea what had happened to her. All she knew was heat and damp and a feeling of complete and total disgust. She stumbled forward, desperately trying to recoil away from whatever was spilling over her.

264

The substance pulled her back. Pulled her so hard she nearly fell off her feet.

"SOMETHING'S ON ME!" she screamed.

Erin turned around first. She was the first to see what was happening. She was the first to fling herself back in the face of one more horror.

Tess and Aaron saw it soon enough. Raylene, screaming and thrashing and coated from neck to waist in what looked like black, rubbery slime.

"Get it off, get it off, GET IT OFF!"

Raylene twisted and writhed, but the sludge was connected to her by a long, putrid strand that moved with her wherever she went. Tess followed it from Raylene all the way back to its source.

When they had pulled the head off of the Felix Fox suit, they had assumed that the dark recesses inside of it were empty.

They were wrong. Whatever black power had animated the empty suit, it had geysered out from the back of the costume and splattered all over Raylene. And it did not drip down, but *up*. The substance was creeping up over Raylene's shoulders and towards her mouth.

Working its way inside her.

"HELP ME!" she screamed. And there was not a shred of the Evil Queen Bitch to be heard in it.

Erin hesitated. The noxious filth crawling over Raylene was *moving*. What if it moved towards her?

Tess didn't even blink. She grabbed Raylene's outstretched wrists and pulled for all she was worth. The sludge pulled back and its strength was undeniable. Tess' feet slid along the blood-greased

265

floor.

Raylene had dropped the axe in her panic. Aaron picked it up and went after the tether of sludge connecting Raylene to the suit. He swung with frantic strength but the black tar was too elastic. The axe blade couldn't bite into the grime. It could only strum the muck as if it were guitar strings producing toxic notes.

"Grab her!" Tess screamed and galvanized Erin into action. She assumed Tess wanted help trying to pull her free; but, the second Erin anchored Raylene, Tess let go.

"Tess!" Erin screamed. *She left me! Why did she leave me?!*

Tess ran to the door leading to the store room and slammed it shut as hard as she could. Raylene was barely through the doorway. If Tess could close it, she could cut off the bulk of whatever was oozing from the suit. The door smashed into the filthy fiber, pinning it in the door jam, but the material was too malleable to be severed. It was still connected to Raylene and it was still creeping towards her mouth and nostrils.

Tess pushed more desperately against the door. She kicked at it and threw her shoulder into it until her skin was mottled black and blue.

The sludge could not be cut.

"Help me!" Tess cried.

Erin let go of Raylene's wrists. She went to the door and they threw themselves at it together. Tess felt the strand of sludge vibrate through the metal of the door. She hoped that it was the only way for the mouthless thing to express pain and pushed

266

harder into it.

Raylene had her teeth clenched shut. The noxious, black sludge was at her mouth now. The turpentine scent of it burned her nose and lips. *Oh, God. God. God. God.*

Aaron changed tactics with the axe. He went to where Erin and Tess were straining to close the door and swung at the ooze there. The axe ground the ebony sludge against the metal and, with the frame to brace itself against, the axe found purchase. The rope of slime vibrated harder when the axe hit it there. Aaron hit it again and again. The door vibrated so hard that it rattled in its hinges. There was a high, whining sound in the air that made Tess' fillings ache.

Aaron hit it again and held nothing back. The axe blade struck the metal and the reverberations rattled his bones.

But the axe had done its work. The strand was severed completely. Raylene staggered forward, suddenly released by a hundred-pound weight, and spat furiously. Black slime diluted to gray by saliva spattered the ground.

"Euhhh, EUHHH," she panted. It was out of her mouth, but Raylene felt the thick layer of black grime still clinging to her back. She even felt it, thick and clotted, in her hair. She knew that she would always feel it there. No matter if she shaved her head and let all new hair grow back. No matter how many showers she took or how many spas she went to. That feeling of being unclean would always stick to her now. Hyperventilating, she ripped off her thousand dollar blazer and flung it to the ground.

It didn't make any difference, but she didn't have long to dwell on it. Two sets of hands, she had no idea whose, grabbed her by the arms and hauled her up.

Then they were running.

The group of four burst out onto the street and there was no order to their exodus. There was only terror and revulsion and the dim knowledge that they needed to climb a staircase somewhere.

There were characters waiting for them.

They stood just a little ways down the avenue. There was Graham, the master chef who was also a bear and the terror turned savior of a struggling mountain lodge. The bear was seven feet tall, eight feet if you counted his chef's hat, and the only thing sharper than his teeth was the butcher knife he had clamped in one paw.

Beside Graham was Giuseppe, the young orphan boy with a heart of gold who was actually the amnesiac, hidden prince of a fairy kingdom. In the movie, Giuseppe's "inside self," was a tall, shining figure of gold that was supposed to teach kids to never doubt their true value. Here, he was a hunched figure of tarnished bronze. His heavy knuckles dragged along the stone with an ugly sound that echoed through the streets.

Winding her way through their legs was a white cat with distinctive black marks like bruises around her eyes. Aaron knew she was female because this was Ketchup, the extremely grumpy rival candidate from *Kitty-zen Sugar Caine*.

Except Ketchup didn't look grouchy, even from

268

this distance. The cat's voice was elated as her emerald green eyes focused on them.

"New eyes!" she screamed. "New eyes for the master!"

They ran. Behind them, they heard Graham bellow and the pace of bronze knuckles scraping over stone quickened like a jackhammer revving up.

The cat made no noise, but Tess knew it was sprinting right there along with them.

Aaron, Erin, Raylene, and Tess ran. They ran away from Turtleshell Mountain faster than they'd ever ran towards it in happier times.

The elevated monorail station loomed over them. This stop was Timmy Turtle themed, and the smiling, chubby-cheeked reptile beamed at them from every surface as they took the steps in threes and fours.

Tess was wheezing and the blood pounded painfully in her aching muscles. It had nothing to do with fear. Tess was coming off a year-long battle with cancer. A battle that she had very nearly lost. The others hurt but they had been able to catch their breath between the hotel, the tunnels, and this. Tess felt like a phone on the brink of dying that kept being left to charge for just a few minutes at a time. She kept going, acting like she could function normally while feeling like at any moment she would simply run out of life.

This marathon stairwell was going to be too much. The others were pulling ahead of her, and she heard the characters getting closer behind her. She could smell the warm, raw meat huff of the

Bear's breath at her back.

Tess wasn't quitting. She had sworn to herself a year ago that she would not die a quitter; but, she didn't lie to herself either, and she knew the old joke about not having to outrun a bear and she knew that she was part of the punchline.

But I won't cry out, she swore as she watched her friends pulling farther ahead of her. *Nobody else is going to die for me. Especially not Aaron.*

Fingers wrapped around her wrist. They were so cold and hard they could only belong to Giuseppe, Boy of Gold.

Except they didn't. They belonged to Raylene, Bitch of Ice, but the Bitch of Ice was hauling on Tess' arm as hard as she could. Dragging her up and supporting her as they kept running.

"Move!" Raylene bellowed in her ear as they ran together. "You've got two legs, you lame cunt! Make them both work!"

They reached the platform and, like a third-act miracle, the monorail was there waiting for them. The doors were closed but Aaron still had the axe. He swung vertically into the seam between the sliding door panels and levered it open with all of his weight. He shoved his shoulder into the gap and pushed until the resisting doors swung completely open.

"COME ON!" he bellowed. Erin made it through first. Raylene and Tess came next.

Graham, Giuseppe, and Ketchup were right behind them. Aaron let the doors slide closed again the second they were through.

"Open it!" Ketchup screamed. "BRING THEIR

EYES TO THE MASTER!"

Aaron measured the thickness of the door against the thickness of the incoming Grizzly Bear and the Metal Boy. They would rip through it like a ticket taker through a day pass.

Aaron turned on the cockpit door with the axe. At the crisis moment, a dozen obstacles he had never even considered suddenly flared up in his mind. If the door was metal, he wouldn't be able to chop through it. How long did it take the monorail to start moving? With the monsters of Turtleshell Mountain right behind them, any one of those things would be a death sentence.

Then Aaron saw the door and slowly let the axe fall to his side.

The door to the monorail controls had been ripped off its hinges. There were blood splatters all over the conductor's cabin, including the windshield, and a splotchy trail of it led out back through the door they'd just come through.

Raylene pushed him aside without even bothering to look at the blood. "Get out of my way," she ordered.

She took over at the controls. Aaron wheeled back towards the door just in time to see that Graham had gone down on all fours. The bear's chef hat had fallen off, and his head was lowered like a battering ram.

But Aaron felt the ground vibrating beneath their feet. The monorail was powering up.

Graham was still coming. The bear roared so loudly it made the windows shake in their panes.

Graham struck the door. It crumpled inwards.

271

Tess and Erin screamed. They both grabbed at Aaron.

Running alongside the slowly moving monorail, the bear's claws worked their way into the gap between the doors. The monorail was picking up speed, but not fast enough. The bear pushed at the door. The metal didn't slide apart completely, but the frames bent enough for Graham to force his head and shoulders into the car. Jogging alongside the train on his back legs, the bear pushed hard at the doors with his front legs.

Aaron took his chance. While the bear was still tied up in the door, he lunged for it with the axe held high over his head. He swung, but Graham saw it coming and batted the axe aside effortlessly with one massive paw.

Aaron staggered beneath the swipe, but managed to hold onto the axe. He could have tried to swing it again, but at what? He looked for a weak point, but all he saw was fangs, and claws, and muscle. Graham was primal fury and hunger. In the face of it, Aaron's axe didn't even feel like a weapon.

The Bear saw the fear bulging in the human's eye and relished it like the delicious seasoning it was. He bellowed down at them and pushed harder. The monorail doors were almost forced open wide enough for him to get the whole of his bulk inside. His mouthful of fangs was already watering.

Maybe five hundred pounds of meat between them, Graham estimated. *Flank steaks, rib meat, shoulder cuts. We'll eat for days.*

The skinny one stepped forward. She was stringy, probably no good for anything but stew.

The male, easily the main course, roasted whole with an apple in his mouth, tried to stay between them.

"Get away, Tess!" he shouted.

The stew ignored him. She stepped up to Graham, completely unarmed, offering herself up first like an obedient little appetizer.

Still needs more fear flavor, the chef decided. Graham leaned in and roared right into her face, rustling her hair and buffeting her face with his raw-flesh breath. He put all his animal fury into it, trying to work a little more terror rub into her meat.

The girl's hands went up to her head. She grabbed two fistfuls of hair, obviously mad with fear.

But then her hair was actually completely off of her head. Graham saw the blonde rag of it clutched in her hands. The bear's brow furrowed. For a moment, he was once again the loveable, harmless lug that had inspired one theatrical sequel and two direct to video follow ups.

Quickly, before he could turn back into something else, Tess threw her wig over his eyes.

Graham bellowed in fury and confusion. He was blind and still trying to keep pace with the accelerating monorail. He pawed at the hair hanging over his eyes. He swatted it aside just in time to see the roast coming at him with the axe again.

Aaron didn't hesitate, even when the bear's wild stare met his own gaze. He'd wound up his swing while Graham was still fumbling with the wig over his eyes. Aaron kept that comical image in mind while he brought the axe around. The blade hit Graham in the snout and took his bottom jaw off in a single neat, intact section.

Graham collapsed, maybe still alive even as blood gushed from the ugly wound where his jaw once was. Either way, his body was still lodged in the doorway of the monorail so Aaron kept after it. He chopped into Graham's head and shoulders again and again, spraying blood everywhere in wide fans.

Get out! Get out!

The corpse finally came loose, but not because of Aaron. Giuseppe grabbed Graham's body by the leg and pulled the dead bulk free from the door. The better for Giuseppe to get closer to the monorail. Running alongside them, he wound up with one telephone pole arm and punched through a Plexiglas window. Erin screamed as shards littered her hair. She leapt back, just narrowly avoiding Giuseppe's metal fingers as they clawed for her.

"Hurry!" she screamed.

"It's as fast as we can go!" Raylene screamed back.

But still Giuseppe kept up with them. One hand gripped at the window frame. His other arm found purchase in the smashed doorway, and Giuseppe hopped up and wedged himself in the doorway.

Aaron hit Giuseppe with the axe. The blade

came down square between Giuseppe's eyes and bounced back. The boy with the heart of tarnished bronze just laughed. The only evidence of the blade he'd taken to the face was a scuff mark on his forehead. "That better buff out," Giuseppe laughed. "I'm very vain about my looks, you know."

He bent the door open further. A little wider and Giuseppe would be all aboard.

Tess laughed with him. "The scuff'll come out. It's this next dent that you ought to be worried about."

Giuseppe pushed, crunching the monorail doors further apart. He bared his mouthful of brass teeth. "You going to ring my bell next, girlie?"

Tess wanted to smile back at him but found that she couldn't. She shook her head. "The quipping's not as much fun when it's real."

"When what's real?" Giuseppe asked.

The only answer was a sound like a hammer hitting a bell. Giuseppe was the bell. The hammer was the safety rail at the edge of the platform. It hit Giuseppe in the hip and peeled him off the side of the train like a scab.

And then the train was out of the station, racing away and leaving Graham and Giuseppe sprawled out behind them. Ketchup stood on the railing and watched them go. The cat's disappointment was clear even as she faded into something the size of a souvenir toy.

Aaron still held onto the axe, and none of them would sit down. They'd been in fear for too long to believe they might actually be safe. There still had to be some terror left. Something waiting for them to relax so it could come through the floor or the window and grab them.

And then Tess sat down beside the window Giuseppe had smashed out. Her eyes rolled back in her head. She was bleach white from her chin to the top of her bald head.

"Tess!" Aaron was immediately beside her.

"You ever get tired of shouting for me?" she said weakly. She waved Aaron off. "I'm ok."

She sat there with her head between her knees, sucking in breath until her head no longer felt like it was full of exhaust fumes. Finally, she raised her head and Aaron was relieved to see no color in her eyes except vivid blue.

"Thank you."

Aaron almost answered just on instinct. But Tess was not looking at him.

She was looking at Raylene.

Standing at the controls because there was too much blood on the conductor's seat, Raylene didn't turn around. Her ink-stained shoulders rose in a shrug. "I told you I could drive it."

"Not what I meant," Tess said.

"It is what I meant," Raylene said.

Aaron looked between Tess' face and Raylene's back and decided that he didn't want to know. Not with Tess looking as grateful as she did. What he could already infer was enough to run ice slush down his spine.

"We really are okay," Erin said. "We're okay." She giggled in a way that didn't sound okay at all. It quickly turned into almost a sob.

"Come here," Tess said.

Erin didn't need to be told twice. She sat beside Tess and acquiesced easily into the comfort of her friend's arms.

Aaron let the axe slip from his hands. It fell to the floor of the bullet capsule shooting them past the confines of this warped, bastard version of a place that had once been a sign that all could be right with the world.

Aaron looked out the window beside him. They were speeding over the Wild Jungle section of the park. The nine-foot torches that illuminated the pathways there burned brightly enough for Aaron to see the monkeys from *Jungle Tails* swinging through the deliberately overgrown trees that lined the streets.

He could even see the dull pink of the vines they swung from and realized that they weren't vines at all. The red sheen said they could only be one thing.

Human intestines.

"What is it?" Tess asked from where Erin was buried in the crook of her arm.

Aaron shook his head. "Just making sure nothing grabbed onto the monorail."

He doubted she believed him, but he was grateful she didn't push it.

He silently prayed that the Monorail could go faster.

34

At first, Ed assumed that he was in hell. He awoke to sweltering heat, dim light through clouds of smoke, and a pounding in his head that he took to be guilt personified.

But it's not smoke, part of him realized. *It's steam.* And then there were the labels. Ed doubted that there was pipework in hell funneling steam towards "Pirates of Tripoli" or "Space Tower." He also didn't think that Satan was so big on putting up signage warning his demons to wear safety goggles.

No, Ed was in a worse place than hell.

He was still in Turtleshell Mountain.

And something had dragged him down here. Fear clutched at Ed for a moment before he remembered the course of events that had brought him to this point.

And why he was without his children.

Ed shut his eyes again. Obviously, something had brought him down here because it liked playing with its food. Tabbytha the Cat, maybe.

You keep thinking in terms of the good guys, a voice whispered in his head. *All of these movies had villains too. If the heroes are throwing kids off of roller coasters, then you may have been taken by something even worse.*

No such thing. If he'd been brought down here by the Dungeon Master from *The Adventures of*

Princess Pashmina, then there was going to be one severely disappointed torturer. Ed didn't value his own life enough to scream for it. He would lie there and silently absorb whatever punishment there was to absorb until his captor finally grew bored and did Ed the favor of ripping whatever was left of his heart out of his chest. He had no fear of shattered kneecaps or screws through his eyes. It would all be no worse than he deserved.

There was a gentle click against stone. It sounded like a cane tip. Perhaps Godfrey, the genteel but sadistic suitor of the independent-minded Victoria Elizabeth, was to be his executioner. The dagger kept in his cane handle would do the job as well as anything else. Ed spun around, but he did not see the silhouette of a figure in a top hat and tails slinking through the steam.

All he saw was a cafeteria tray. There was a turkey leg there and a carton of milk. Ed saw that there was even a straw.

"The meat's cold," a voice said. It sounded apologetic. "The power's still on, but nobody's thinking about the food too much."

Ed tried to see the speaker, but the acoustics made it seem like the voice was coming from all around him, and the dim light couldn't pierce the haze of steam leaking from the boilers and pipes. He couldn't see more than a few feet in any direction.

"You're in the steam room," the voice said. "That is to say, the steam generator room. None of... *them* are really bothering with it since it's so separate from the rest of the park. They don't think

279

anyone could find their way down here. Not to mention how uncomfortable it is."

There was a pause. Then a chuckle like that of a nervous host who hasn't had time to get ready for company.

"Personally, I like it just fine."

Ed didn't. His shirt was sticking to his back, his soaking hair clung in front of his eyes, and everything reeked of mildew. None of it made him feel much better about still being alive.

"Either way, you'll be safe here is what I'm saying."

Ed was still crumpled on the floor. He got his knees underneath himself and winced as he did it. However long he'd been unconscious, it was long enough for the soreness to settle in from his long and ultimately futile climb up the roller coaster.

"You should have left me where you found me," he muttered. He forced himself to stand against the aches in his joints and the pounding in his head.

"What are you doing?" the voice asked.

"I can't stay," Ed said.

"You can't leave is what you can't do! The park isn't a safe place."

"So then you'd better stay here. Enjoy your Sauna."

"You don't have to be afraid of me," the voice pleaded from somewhere in the steam. "Is it because I attacked you?" The voice was actually the one that sounded afraid. Afraid and desperate. "I'm sorry! You were just so exposed. You were right there in the middle of Main Street, and I didn't want to risk anyone else finding you while we..." the voice hesitated. "While I convinced you it was ok to come with me," it finally settled on.

Fuck it, Ed decided. He picked a direction and started walking through the haze of steam, keeping his hands in front of him so he could feel for a door.

"BE CAREFUL!"

Hands grabbed Ed. Pulled him roughly to the side.

"You almost burned yourself on a boiler."

Ed swung blindly into the steam and hit nothing. "Stop trying to save me!" he screamed into the haze.

"You can't leave!" The voice screamed. It was hard to tell, but it seemed closer. "You can't! It's not right!"

"Nothing's right! And it's not going get better because of a turkey leg," Ed snarled.

"You don't despair in Turtleshell Mountain!" The voice was hyperventilating. High. Squeaking. "You don't cry! You don't feel bad! And you don't kill! You, them, everything, it's just NOT RIGHT!"

The voice felt so earnest about this that it reached out from the steam and grasped Ed by the arm.

The hand was wearing a white glove. It had four fingers and the wrist attached to it was green and pebbled with scales.

Ed's "savior" had finally come close enough that the steam parted around him. He looked through the haze and into the wide, earnest, deeply unhappy eyes of Timmy Turtle.

35

"What will we tell people?"

That was Erin's question. The first thing any of them had said since the monorail had hit cruising speed. Apparently, at least one of them had stopped waiting for the Dragon from *The Slumbering Beauty* to rise up and cook them with a blast of fire. They were all shaken, traumatized, and seemingly incapable of feeling joy ever again, but they were beginning to accept that they had a future outside of Turtleshell Mountain to think about.

"I mean, how can we explain any of this to someone who wasn't... here?"

We say nothing, was Aaron's instinctive answer. *We say it was all masked psychos with hatchets and let SWAT work out the differences for themselves. I didn't survive this asylum just to spend the rest of my life in another one.*

None of that made it past his lips, though. He wasn't a street cop but he was still police. You didn't let your own walk into an ambush with no warning like that.

Tess squeezed Erin's hand. "We'll think of something. What matters is we'll make sure they know to be careful."

"You can just tell them that Charles Tuttle's investors are finally getting their money's worth," Raylene muttered.

"What does that mean?" Tess asked. "What investors?"

Raylene considered denying she'd said anything. In the end, she didn't see the point. The company was probably sunk anyway. There was no way to recover a family friendly brand that had this much blood splattered all over it.

"You know the rumors about Charles Tuttle, right? One of you has to."

Erin spoke up hesitantly. "I mean, I know some people said he was anti-Semitic."

"And a racist," Raylene supplied. "And more than a little bit bisexual. That's all small beans, burnt crust underneath Apple Pie America stuff. We let all of that that go because we'd rather have people think that's all there is to dig up. There are other things about Mr. Turtleshell Mountain that we keep secret. I mean so secret that you get fired for even hinting at them. That's not an exaggeration. When I was starting in the mailroom, there was this ditzy cunt who delivered a package to the head of the Tuttle Charity Fund. She made a joke about overnight deliveries and human hearts, and they put her on the bus back to Bumble Fuck before lunch."

"Human hearts?" Aaron asked. He felt his stomach contract at the image. He'd seen too many actual human hearts to find that funny.

"Charles Tuttle was a demon worshipper," Raylene said bluntly. "Real nine-horned, goat-headed, drink-the-blood-of-infants Demons."

"Come on," Aaron said. But he already knew that his skepticism was a lie. He wasn't skeptical of anything anymore, and Raylene didn't even waste a breath on his objections. She went on with her story like he hadn't even spoken.

"When he died, he didn't have any kids or next of kin. Everything was left to the Board of Directors. They toured his mansion, and they found a locked room in the basement with books made of human skin and Dark Age shit drawn on the floor in blood."

An image rose suddenly in Tess' mind. The coloring was grainy and the film was scratchy, but it was far too detailed nonetheless.

The Charles Tuttle every child grew up knowing about. The skinny, balding man with the pencil mustache and bad teeth, hard at work on a drawing of Timmy Turtle on his sketching table. He looks over his shoulder, sees the camera recording him at work. He smiles and waves to all the little boys and girls at home.

There's a Bella Badger mug on a stool beside him. Charles picks it up to take a sip.

And the mug is filled with blood. *Charles Tuttle smiles again, and his teeth are sticky and red with it in grainy 1960s Technicolor.*

"You saw it?" Erin asked. "I mean, you saw this yourself?"

"Yeah," Raylene drawled. "I'm a real well-preserved ninety." She rolled her eyes. "For 99.9% of employees, talking about Charles Tuttle's religious freedom gets you fired. For the last tenth of a percent, it's a rite of passage. It means you've got what it takes to be a lifer, and they're going to pay you enough to make sure you stay one. It means you know everything." Even now, a touch of pride entered her voice. She remembered that dinner party at Bob Morgan's house. No spouses, only the ruling council of the Turtleshell Empire gathered around a table that had cost more than the house Raylene had grown up in. And Raylene had not grown up poor.

She was not the only woman there, but she was by far the youngest person in that group sitting atop the tallest peak of Turtleshell Mountain. She still remembered that they were into dessert, raspberry sorbet, when Bob decided it was time for Raylene to be told the darkest secret Turtleshell had to offer.

She didn't know it yet but, on that day, the Evil Queen Bitch received her crown.

"They didn't just stumble on the room, either," she said. "Tuttle had it right there in his will along with his final instructions for the company. He told the other Directors that the runaway success of Turtleshell Productions and Turtleshell Mountain was all a gift from his "Sovereigns of Spiders" and whoever took over the company after him was supposed to make sure that favor was still shown to his benefactors. Tuttle insisted that the prosperity of everything depended on it."

"What did they do?" Despite herself, Tess was on the edge of her seat, sucked in by the final fairy tale of Turtleshell Mountain.

"They didn't keep butchering virgins, that's for sure. They burned Charles Tuttle's will, forged a new one without any provisions about a never-ending midnight, and demolished the mansion with

286

all of that sick crap still inside it."

"But that wasn't everything," Tess guessed.

Raylene shook her head. "He talked about something in the park. 'The Funnel.' That was the final instruction in his will. 'Fill the Funnel and the Darkness will smile.' He said that was the agreement he made with...well, with his own fucked-up head."

"You can't fill a funnel," Aaron said. "It's got a hole in the bottom. Whatever you put into it runs right back out."

"Nobody cared what he meant. They were all just terrified that there was an altar to Dread Lord Cthulhu hidden behind a toilet somewhere just waiting for some guest to find it. After Tuttle died, there were major 'renovations' at the park that were really just a million-dollar excuse to rip this place apart and find whatever the hell he'd left here."

"But you didn't," Aaron said. Looking out the window, he could see the fence that marked the final border of Turtleshell Mountain. They were almost out.

"Not so much as an upside down crucifix. The company finally decided that, whatever Charles Tuttle had hidden here, it was buried so deep that nobody was going to find it. The company just moved past it and, of course, no ruination ever came to the house that Timmy Turtle built."

"Until now," Tess said quietly.

"Yeah," Raylene said, not telling stories anymore. "Until now."

"Maybe this is what happens when the funnel

empties out," Tess said. "This is what happens once whatever Charles Tuttle made his deal with finally gets tired of being ignored."

They all turned that idea over in silence. Aaron was still looking out the window. They sped past blurring lights and, try as he might, Aaron didn't believe it was DWP electricity running those lights. No, it was liquid fire pumped from the veins of a Black God that illuminated Turtleshell Mountain now. Just one of the many favors bestowed on a man who was willing to pay for smiles with screams.

Until the payments stopped. Almost sixty years to us but maybe just a blink of an eye to something as old as forever. It's patient. It waits for someone to honor a bargain it made in good faith. Finally, it decides that the deal's off and it's going to take back what belongs to it.

"That doesn't have to be it," Tess said into the quiet. She cast her eyes down. "Maybe a radioactive comet flew too close to the Earth or..."

Aaron shook his head and turned around in his seat so he was looking at the others.

"No. Whatever was supposed to go into the funnel, this is the consequence for not keeping it full." He gestured out the window. "This is the punishment for Turtleshell Mountain not paying what it owes."

"Maybe," Raylene said from the control room. The fence was just ahead of them. In moments all of this would be, literally, behind them. "Or maybe this is what happens when the funnel is finally filled."

288

The horizontal track suddenly tilted into a steep dive then. Aaron, Erin, and Tess were thrown violently from their seats. Aaron bit his lip and tasted blood. Tess and Erin collided skull-to-skull. Their vision swam.

The track rattled and groaned as the monorail became a roller coaster. The three of them were thrown around the car like dice in a cup. Aaron tried to reach for Tess and couldn't get a hold of her. Erin was screaming.

And somewhere, Raylene was laughing.

36

Ed threw himself backwards so quickly that he overbalanced and fell on his ass. He scrambled away from Timmy Turtle on all fours until his questing hand hit the edge of the plastic tray the… *thing* had left for him. Ed grabbed the turkey leg and flung it at Timmy as hard as he could. "Stay away from me, you fucking monster!" he screamed.

Timmy ducked his head into his shell. The turkey leg that would have struck him on the nose flew by harmlessly instead. In a cartoon, it would have been hilarious. Ed only grabbed the can of soda and threw it even harder. The can hit the Turtle's chest, ricocheted off, and burst against a boiler. Carbonated, crystal liquid sprayed everywhere.

"You shouldn't be so loud," was all Timmy said. "All of these pipes and vents go upstairs. Something might hear you."

"FUCK YOU!" Ed shrieked like a dying hawk. He charged at Timmy and threw his shoulder into the turtle's stomach. He hit it like a linebacker hitting a tackling dummy, and Timmy was just as leathery and unyielding.

"Fuck! You! Fuck you! FUCK YOU!"

This was not in the plan. Ed had expected to just roll over and die for the first Turtleshell creature he encountered. But seeing Timmy Turtle, the emblem of every joyful memory turned black and gangrenous, had pinched a nerve of rage deep inside of him. He threw punches with bent wrists and was too blinded by tears of fury to see where they landed. He didn't care. He only wanted to give this lying, false-faced monster even a fraction of the pain his children must have felt.

Timmy's arms went around him. Ed's aching hands were pinned against his chest as the Turtle's grip tightened around him. *Good, let it crush me.* Ed felt better knowing he'd played the game right to the end. He'd not gone like a lamb to the slaughter. He'd fought.

Then he realized what was happening.

Timmy was hugging him.

Ed snapped a head-butt into its chest. He threw it with all the force he could muster and only succeeded in triggering an earthquake of agony in his own head. His knees wobbled. His vision greyed.

Timmy Turtle held him up.

"Easy," the Turtle crooned. "Easy."

Ed's dazed eyes sharpened. He ripped himself from the Turtle's embrace, lost his balance, and fell. He didn't get back up.

"Monsters," he moaned. "You're all monsters. My kids... my poor kids. Why did you do this to them?"

"No!" Timmy reached out with a gloved hand, like Ed's pardon was a physical thing he could grasp. "Not me, I didn't do this! I didn't start it, I didn't know it was coming, and I didn't want it!"

The turtle's big, balloon eyes blinked and

shimmered with tears. "Please, I swear. All the days I sat up there on my Father's shoulders, I never knew that this would happen" he said.

The statue. Timmy Turtle on Charles Tuttle's shoulders.

"I loved it up there," Timmy went on. "I watched them all come in, and I watched them all run beneath me. They ran because they couldn't wait to get inside. I could see it all- the laughter, the joy, and so, so many happy endings."

The Turtle sucked in a shaky breath. Ed watched its wrinkly neck tremble with the effort of it. "And then I was pushed. We were all pushed. We fell and we cracked, and what came out was... awful."

Timmy toppled forward without warning. If Ed had not scrambled out of the way, he would have been crushed. Timmy dropped like a fallen tree and retracted his arms, legs, and head. Limbless and headless, his shell loomed like an abandoned, haunted house.

"But I'm not awful!" Timmy's voice wailed out from the shell like a shrieking ghost. "I'm not a monster. I'm Timmy Turtle! I'm not what the voice wants me to be!"

From the floor, Ed peered into the cavern of the shell. Twin eyes stared back at him from the darkness. They should have been like cartoon eyes- twin, pure white ovals with ink drop centers; but, the anguish inside of them was too real for that. They were eyes that were drowning in despair.

"I tried to make them understand that! If they

would just… but nobody trusts me. Before I saw you, I saw a family that was looking for a place to hide. The boy was still wearing a turtle shell hat. I tried to call them quietly. I whispered that I knew a place where I could keep them safe. They screamed when they saw me. They screamed and they wouldn't stop, no matter how much I begged them to be quiet." The shell rocked back and forth with the force of the Turtle's distress. "…The Dingo Sisters heard their screams. And they… they…" Timmy Turtle wailed. "I want to be better but I can't be! I couldn't even help *you* without hurting you!"

Timmy couldn't say anymore. He could only sob. He could not even bring himself to talk about how he felt after he hit Ed. When the man was down, Timmy had looked at the reverend's unconscious body and a voice, a voice made out of a thousand different voices, had whispered in his head. *Finish him. Step on his skull. Shatter it like a lollipop.*

Timmy couldn't tell him this. Even if he wasn't so ashamed of himself, he had no words left. He only had sobs. Sobs that said, *It's all gone wrong. It's all gone wrong.*

Ed's hands were on the turtle's shell before he even realized what he was doing. He slowed the stormy pitches of the shell and slowed it down to a gentle, regulated rocking.

"It's all right," he whispered into the dark chasm where Timmy's self-loathing eyes resided. "It's going to be all right."

"I remember the love," a small voice whispered

from the darkness. "I remember every hand that waved at me from the monorail. I can still feel every hug a Timmy Turtle costumeer ever got and every kiss on a stuffed Timmy Turtle's nose." A shuddering sigh echoed from the shell. "I'll never know that again. It's all... gone."

Ed let his forehead rest against the shell. He closed his eyes against his own ghosts of long-gone hugs and smiles and continued to rock Timmy in a steady, lulling rhythm. "It's not easy to lose everything that you care about; but, it doesn't mean you lost who you always were. Not if you don't want it to."

Listen to you talk, a voice sneered. Minister Ed ignored it.

"You spoke about voices leading you to wickedness. Tell me, was there anyone telling you to try and take me in? Did a voice compel you to carry me out of harm's way?"

Silence from inside the turtle's shell.

"You did that on your own, Timmy. You didn't let your loss or the voice of anger decide who you were going to be! Despite everything that's happened to you, you listened to your own soul."

More silence. Then, timidly, with hope that barely dared to breathe, "I have a soul?"

"You do," Ed promised. "And you stayed true to it, even when you had every reason not to."

And the cartoon character did a much better job of it than you did.

But maybe not. For all of Ed's own despair and anger since the Coney Island Coaster, as sincerely as he'd tried to throw his own life away, he realized

294

that all he needed was the first hint of an opportunity to reach out and salve the suffering of another soul.

"Come on out," Ed coaxed. "We can make it all right."

Timmy didn't want to. It was safer inside the dark of his shell.

Because voices were still with him.

Hunt.

Kill.

Ruin.

But if he listened carefully, there was another voice speaking beneath that one. It was low, oh, so low, but perhaps that voice had always been there, going all the way back to 1938.

Care.

Shelter.

Save.

That voice had its say as well. And it wouldn't let him just hide away while everything fell apart around him.

Slowly, Ed watched Timmy Turtle's head poke tentatively out of its, *no, out of his*, shell. He looked at Ed with such sincere hope that Ed began to realize how much of a fool he'd been for thinking that there was no longer a place in the world where he could do good.

"Can you get people out, Timmy?" Ed held his hand out, waiting for Timmy's arm to extend from his shell and take it. "We can approach them together. It's not too late. Not if there's even one life we can save."

Slowly, hesitantly, Timmy's white fingertips

ventured out from his shell. Then the slightest hint of a green wrist.

Ed kept his hand right where it was. *Come on, Timmy,* he prayed. Prayed for both of them. *If you can do this, I can do this.*

And then the air around them was alive with thunder. The ground started to shake.

Ed was a California transplant. He had never experienced an earthquake before but this was a hell of an introduction to the concept. The ground started rattling more violently. The steam around them swirled and thrashed into nightmarish shapes.

The ground shook harder still. Ed tried to stand and fell down just as quickly. The ground wasn't even solid anymore. It rose and fell in hills and valleys before his very eyes. Ed gave up on trying to run. He merely clutched Timmy's shell and waited for the ground to stop waving and start shattering,

But it was not the floor, but the ceiling that exploded in a rain of sheetrock and piping. Steam blew out of control from ruptured pipes, raising the already sweltering temperature to unbearable levels. Then, just as quickly, relief as the heat escaped upwards but more debris thundered downwards. Rocks and twisted chunks of metal flew everywhere. Ed simultaneously tried to shield his face and yet keep his eyes open to see just what impossibility had reared its head now. The lights had been destroyed. It was impossible to see for sure what it was in the darkness, but Ed swore that, before all light was lost, he could see a pair of giant eyes and a toothy grin dropping down on them.

The giant bullet kept going. It smashed through the floor. More stone shrapnel flew. A piece struck Ed in the head. He tried to shield his face better, and a whizzing safety valve broke his pinky. A piece of metal shrapnel ripped through his forearm.

Ed's prayers for death were about to be answered, whether he was still asking or not.

And then a shadow fell over him. A round shape mounted on two stout trunks. Almost lost in the thunder of the collapse, Ed heard a hollow rattling like rain against a tin roof.

Timmy Turtle. Head and arms tucked away safely, but standing on his legs and letting his shell serve as a shield for Minister Ed.

Care.

Shelter.

Save.

Ed lowered his hand. There was no danger now and there was so much amazement to see. The world was not as dark as he'd thought. With the ceiling gone, light filtered in from Turtleshell Mountain above them. Between Timmy's legs, he saw the falling object better. It was a long cylinder of Plexiglas and steel, still sinking deeper into the earth.

Inside of it, Ed could see people flying about like limp, lifeless rags in a dryer cycle.

The Monorail, Ed had time to think. And then, *I think those people inside it are already dead*.

That was his last thought before the floor collapsed underneath them and, protective shield or not, he fell.

They all fell.
Into the heart of the funnel.

37

1947

"This is amazing," Nathan says. His words echo off the marble floors and the gleaming golden dome of the ceiling. The boy does a full spin, his large eyes taking in everything they can. His mouth is wide open as well, as if there were a third eye in there that could help shoulder the load. "It's huge! You could fit my whole school in here! Is this going to be your house?"

Charles Tuttle chuckles. It, too, echoes inside the giant chamber. "It's a little big just for me. I built this so I could have a place to meet with my friends. I guess you could call it a conference room."

No. Nathan's gone to work with his dad and seen a conference room. It's a big table in a little room where people just talk and talk and never seem to do anything. This place, THIS, is something else. Nathan can only look up and whistle. "They must be some really good friends," he says.

"The best," Charles says. "They were actually the ones who helped me build Turtleshell Mountain."

"THEY DID!?" Nathan turns his gaze away from the dome. He's never heard this before. He thinks, maybe, that *no one* has ever heard this before. He is a young boy. His hair is still fresh yellow, not yet tarnished by maturity and impurity, and his face is equally untouched. He is as Charles Tuttle thinks everyone, young and old, should be-continuously amazed by the wondrous world around him. But, for Nathan, this goes beyond wonder. This, to be a confidant of Charles Tuttle, is simply unbelievable.

Charles Tuttle nods. "They helped me build everything, actually. The cartoons. The movies. The studio. Everything."

"What do you mean?"

"I mean that Timmy, Bella, and the others wouldn't be much good if nobody ever got to see them, would they?"

Nathan is too scandalized by the thought to even speak. His entire universe revolves around the Turtleshell Gang. The idea of a world without Timmy Turtle is as absurd of a suggestion as a world without Christmas. "That could never happen," he protests.

"It could happen if you're a twenty-year-old kid from some no-name town in England and the only job you can get is as a janitor in a movie theatre. When you're mopping floors with nothing but a bent notepad full of drawings in your back pocket, it's pretty easy to think that nobody's ever going to look in that notepad and the only thing you'll ever draw for an audience is an "Out of Order" sign on the outside of a bathroom."

"But you're brilliant!" Nathan tries to imagine that not being enough and can't. His mind stalls out on the concept like a weak engine trying to climb

300

too steep of an incline.

"That doesn't take you as far as you think. Every day, plenty of brilliant people die in tiny apartments without anyone ever knowing they even existed. You need to be more than brilliant to succeed. You need to have people who are able to make the inroads that you need. You need to be able to make the people with the money pay attention."

"So these friends, they were, like, your agents?" Nathan is taking careful notes in his head. He wants nothing more than to be a cartoonist himself one day. Great, or almost as great, as his hero Charles Tuttle. He even has a drawing folded in his own back pocket. A character named Molly Macaw that he's waiting for just the right moment to take out.

"That's close," Charles says, "but it doesn't go far enough. They did more than just make introductions. They forced connections. Agreeing to work with them didn't just offer me opportunities. They gave me guarantees. Thanks to them, my dreams make people happy all over the world. That's a good thing, isn't it?"

Charles' voice rises. It bangs in the golden dome like a bell. "I've made the world a better place, haven't I?! Because of them, I've built something that transcends nations and generations. Grandchildren will share it with grandparents. Children in Britain share it with children in America!" He slams his fist into one of the walls. "Does it really matter what I had to do to make it a reality?"

"Did you work hard?" Nathan asks honestly.

Shoulders heaving, Charles Tuttle turns and stuffs his bloody knuckles into his pocket. "Yes," he says. His voice is returning to a normal pitch. "I've worked incredibly hard."

Nathan shrugs. This open, trusting boy who didn't think that anything was remotely amiss when a strange man lured him away from the tour of Turtleshell Studios.

"Then you deserve everything you have. That's what my dad says."

"He sounds like a wise man, your father. And you, son? Can you work hard?"

"Can I?!" The excitement burns even more wildly in his eyes than when *THE* Charles Tuttle offered him an exclusive look inside of the soon to be unveiled Turtleshell Mountain. "Mr. Tuttle, I can work harder than a mule and faster than a robot!" Inwardly, he winces. What a stupid thing to say.

Mr. Tuttle doesn't seem to think it's stupid. He kneels down so he and Nathan are eye to eye.

"That's good, Nathan. Because, my Backers? They're hiring."

"For a cartoonist!?" The ambition, blatant and stupid, comes out before he can rein it in.

Charles Tuttle's kind smile stays in place. "Not a cartoonist. Not yet. But..." he strokes his chin. "In the future, who can say? But right now, what we're looking for is more like... a house detective."

A detective! Thoughts of Dick Tracy and Sam Spade cluster in Nathan's head. Not a cartoonist, of course, but he's still young. He can work his way up.

"We'll need you to watch over the park," Charles says. "Every foot of it."

"Every inch!" Nathan promises. "I won't let anything of yours get stolen. I'll protect everything here like it was my own."

"It will be," Charles assures him. "But that's not the kind of detective we need. Your job will be to watch the guests. We need someone who can find every frown. Every angry brow. Every sourpuss. Find them and store them all away. Can you do that, Nathan?"

"Absolutely!" Nathan gushes.

"Good."

Charles cuts the boy open from hip to hip and Nathan's intestines pour from the slit like an avalanche. The child's knees buckle. Nathan pitches forward, but Charles pushes him backward so the child lands spread eagle on his back. The reflection of the golden dome overhead shines in his lifeless eyes. An obscene parody of the excitement those eyes once held.

Charles Tuttle kneels beside the body. The dagger he holds is double-sided. One end is razor sharp and smooth as melted butter. That was the edge he used to slice out Nathan's guts.

The other side of the blade is jagged and saw-toothed.

Crocodile Villain, Charles thinks as he looks at the teeth of the blade. *Start thinking of names that start with a C.*

He uses the cutting teeth to saw through Nathan's rib cage. When he's done, he cuts out

303

Nathan's heart, lungs, kidney, pancreas, and liver. He doesn't stop cutting and carving until the boy's torso is completely empty. Just like his Backers requested that it be.

Charles keeps the warm, inviting smile on his face until the work is done. Only when he lets the knife slip from his fingers does he start to shake.

He staggers back against the wall, fighting to contain the sobs that buck against his insides. The Backers hate it when he cries.

He fumbles into his pocket and comes out with a palm-sized, tin metal cast of Timmy Turtle. Charles clings to it as if it were an oak tree.

Next month we're releasing Lily White and the Eight Gnomes. They'll come out of that one singing the Cleaning Chorus for DECADES. And next summer, the park opens. The Turner Brothers couldn't support a million-dollar theme park with their characters. Nobody else could. There's nothing in the whole world that people love as much as the characters I made. Not the President. Not Betty Grable. Not Jesus.

But he can't think about the park without a part of him thinking about what it's eventually going to become. He clings tighter to the toy turtle and ignores that part. That won't be for decades. Maybe it won't ever even happen.

None of them understand. They think it's the money I care about, or the attention. They don't understand the love I have for these children. Love like that is too pure for them to wrap their filthy minds around. He thinks about that Irish pedophile Mickey. That drunk who sees Charles looking at

304

the children and makes sick jokes about the priesthood. If Mickey could see him now, would he finally understand why Charles had to look so closely at the children on every tour? Of course not. No one would understand. They'd think he was doing it for himself. Like this... *this* was something that he enjoyed.

It was for the children. Everything he did was for the children, damnit!

I'll build a statue, he decides. *Something with me and Timmy right by the gate. Me and Timmy, but I'll make it so there's no doubt that Timmy is the one who's more important. I'll make it so everyone can see it and have no doubt that everything I've done is just so I can bring some happiness into their lives.*

The blunt points of Timmy's hands and head have dug into Charles' palms. His blood is flowing.

"It's worth it," Charles says inside the empty dome lying underneath Turtleshell Mountain. He repeats it again. "It's worth it."

"Of course it is," Nathan's empty corpse responds.

"It's for Turtleshell Mountain."

<u>38</u>

Aaron woke up and everything was upside down. Upside down and dark.

Then memories hit him, fittingly, like a runaway train.

The monorail.

The crash.

"Tess!" he called out. "Erin!" He tried to see them but his head was full of static and he couldn't make sense of anything. He couldn't even tell if he was standing up or lying down. He tried to move but one leg wasn't cooperating. Even as the other kicked wildly in the-

(air?)

His trapped leg was at least something he could use to orient himself. He found his knee and followed it down-

(That's wrong. You're following it up. Not down.)

That was too much for Aaron's short-circuiting head to focus on. He could circle back to that later. Right now, he was just following his knee to his shin...

To his foot that was twisted almost entirely around and wedged between a seat and an arm rest. And with awareness came agony. His leg was scalding pain from hip to toe.

Aaron bit his lip against the pain. *Focus. Get ahold of yourself. You don't even know where you*

are yet. You can't just sit here and scream.

That argument meant nothing. He could barely even hear it over his body's well-reasoned counter argument: *My leg. Oh, God, my fucking leg!*

Aaron closed his eyes.

Tess, he repeated to himself. *Tess. Tess. Tess.*

When Aaron opened his eyes, the pain was still there but he was able to think through it clearly. He could see clearly too. He was upside down, hanging by his trapped foot, and the entire monorail cart was standing on its nose. That was why everything looked like a picture that was standing on the wrong end.

He tried looking for Tess and Erin again. He could see more clearly in his mind, but the rest of the monorail was only vague shapes in the darkness. Dark humps of what could be seatbacks, but nothing that resembled Erin or Tess.

"Tess! Erin! Is anyone there!?"

Nothing. Maybe they'd left to get help.

Maybe they're right below your upside down head and they're never going to leave again. Maybe this last ride was such a doozy that they're never going to get off.

No. He wasn't going to think of that. He was going to get his leg free, and he was going to find them. Then he was going to get all of them out of here.

He tried to reach up to get his foot free. He could not get his hand past his knee. He stretched more anyway, until his abs and back groaned like overtaxed engine parts. His hand made it to his shin.

307

Nearly... there...

Something in his knee separated with a pop that was almost discreet. Aaron dropped and swung in screaming agony. He couldn't stop the screams from coming, but he could at least try to make them productive.

"TESS!"

"ERIN!"

He howled their names as loud as his agonizing body could manage. He twisted his head back and forth, desperate to pick their shapes out of the gloom.

"That's three times you've ignored me now."

Aaron twisted his head all the way back. There was a silhouette down there, all the way below him where the nose of the monorail had smashed into the ground. There was a silhouette of a person there that hadn't been there before.

"Raylene?"

"I can let once go. I can even make my peace with twice."

His eyes were starting to adjust to the gloom. Raylene was standing in the doorway to what had been the cockpit. He could make out the outlines of her head and shoulders and of her hands resting against the doorframe. He still could not see her features.

"But I'm a baseball girl. Three strikes and I'll smash you in the head with a fucking baseball bat."

He saw with a lurch that there was also a bundle of angles nestled in the corner of the monorail cart. Twin sets of arms, legs, and splayed out hands.

Erin and Tess.

"Raylene, are they breathing!"

Raylene did not move to their aid. She only took a step forward, which couldn't have been right because, in the vertical monorail cart, forward was really *up*.

"That was four, Aaron. I'm honestly not even sure what to say about being ignored four times."

"Raylene-"

"As you might imagine from the whole bat thing, no one's ever got past three before."

"I'm sorry, Raylene. It wasn't..." He greyed out as another wave of pain rolled through his head. When he came back to, Raylene was taking another step

(up)

forward.

"It would be better if it was really both of them that you were worried about. Except it's really just *her*." She kicked Tess' foot out of her path.

"If you're pretending to care about the skank, is it so hard to tack me on too?"

"Jesus Christ, Raylene, it wasn't on purpose!" Aaron finally snapped at her, hanging upside down after a goddamn Monorail crash. "Will you just tell me if they're all right!?"

Raylene was suddenly right in front of him, clearing ten vertical feet without seeming to move at all. Even this close, her face was still wreathed in shadows, but he could clearly see the hand reaching out for his neck. It had long, curved nails painted as black as oil on a moonless road. The

309

fingers were long and delicate, but they wrapped around his throat and pulled his twisted leg free with brutal ease.

"They're not all right," she hissed. "None of you are going to be all right." She held him up in the air, her fingers so tight around his throat he could barely breathe.

"Raylene-" Aaron choked out.

She squeezed his throat tighter.

"You will call me 'Your Majesty,'" the Evil Queen Bitch growled. "Or you're going to find out just how bad 'not all right' can really get." She yanked him closer to her, finally letting Aaron see past the curtain of shadows and revealing a face he didn't recognize.

The woman of indiscriminate, well-preserved middle age that had weathered onslaught after onslaught with them was gone. In her place was a creature with thin lips of black cherry and skin the same shade of faded purple as an old wine stain. She was beautiful, but it was a beauty meant only for terror and subjugation.

Aaron barely noticed any of that.

Her eyes. Jesus, HER EYES!

Raylene's eyes were pure black. The same black as the slime that had poured out from the Felix Fox suit.

The Evil Queen Bitch let Aaron go. Whatever power allowed her to stand on the vertical floor was not granted to Aaron. He fell. His back smashed against the end of a row of chairs before he plummeted to the bottom of the car, inflicting more bruises and internal injuries on a body

310

already riddled with them.

But what mattered was that he had landed near Tess. He could get to her, not to make sure that she was alive, but to make sure that she was already dead.

He could not save her. He didn't understand exactly what had happened, but he had looked into Raylene's eyes and seen nothing but unending cruelty.

I can't save her. He had finally accepted that, but he could hope that Tess had at least died in the crash- quickly and so disoriented by sound and shaking that she didn't know what was happening as the end came.

Please. Please let her have had that much.

But he couldn't know for sure until he got closer to her. And no matter what he did, he couldn't make his body crawl in her direction. His arms worked, but his legs were nothing but sprawled out dead weight behind him.

What's wrong? It wasn't the fall. I'm not hurt any worse than I was before. I can't even...

He couldn't even feel his legs.

"No," Aaron whispered. "No!"

"Yes." Raylene, or Your Majesty, or whatever she had become, was coming closer. She walked effortlessly down the vertical expanse of the monorail car. Even the long, thick cable of her shiny, black hair stayed perfectly in place.

"I can hear it, you know," she said. "I hear your legs weeping. They know that they'll never work again." The Evil Queen Bitch closed her eyes, savoring a symphony that only she could hear. "It's

311

amazing, all of those terrible movies were right. Everything is alive. Everything has a voice." She smiled. "And so much of it is suffering."

A knocking sound brought her back to reality. Raylene turned her gaze to the side. Aaron tried to follow it, but his neck couldn't tilt that far back and the rest of his body could no longer turn to make up the difference.

"They're over here," Raylene called out. Aaron heard the doors open. So did Tess. She stirred and moaned at the sound.

Alive. Bitter tears clouded his eyes. *Alive just to die like this.* More than the massacre. More than all of the characters turned into monsters. This cruelty, that there could be no mercy even now, was the final perversion of everything Turtleshell Mountain was supposed to be.

The monorail doors were forced further open with a protesting scream of metal. Lantern light flooded the car. Aaron saw Tess, Erin, and what Raylene had become with far more clarity than he wanted to.

And he saw shadows. Eight of them, long and dancing in the flickering firelight as they scaled the inverted seats and worked their way down to the bottom of the car. They were led by a creature with a gruesome, curved horn protruding from the top of its head.

Aaron lay flat on his belly. He tried to make himself sit up. He sucked in fast, trembling breaths and tried to roll over so he could see more clearly see what was coming.

He might as well have been shouting orders

312

into a dead phone.

He needn't have bothered. They were already in front of him. Aaron was rolled over by short, stubby hands, and he realized that there was one trick left in Turtleshell Mountain.

Under it. Not in it. Under it.

It had only been a trick of the lanterns that had made Aaron think that they were giants. The creatures were actually stout, two-foot-tall things in heavy boots. And their leader didn't have a horn. The lantern light simply caught the pick axe slung over his shoulder.

Aaron remembered something...*she* had said back in the tunnels. Even if he hadn't, he'd seen the movie enough times to know what he was looking at.

Gnomes.

Popular as the film was, the *Lily White and the Eight Gnomes* ride had been shuttered a decade ago to make room for something newer, and these cast-off animatronics showed it. Their beards were coated with cobwebs, and clotted grease seeped from their joints. A thick layer of dust covered dull, marble eyes that didn't blink.

"Take them," the Evil Queen Bitch ordered.

Three sets of grimy hands reached for Aaron. He could only feel the two pairs that grabbed at his arms.

Aaron twisted away. He waved his arms back and forth and held them high, away from the gnome's stunted reach.

The lead gnome, *Gleeful*, Aaron remembered, *His name was Gleeful*, stepped up. He slammed

313

the blunt crossbar of the pickaxe into Aaron's nose. Aaron's head snapped back. Blood gushed from his nostrils.

By the time Aaron came back from the haze of pain, he was being excavated from the floor and carried out by his shoulders and knees. From the edge of his vision, he saw Grouchy, Snoozy, Dummy, Sniffly, and Frank hauling Erin and Tess up.

Tess was even more aware now. She was looking around, trying to place their surroundings.

Go back to sleep, Aaron pleaded. *You don't want to wake up.*

Tess wouldn't. "Where are we?" she asked. "Did we make it out?"

Erin was coming back around too. She was still half-unconscious, but she groaned and rubbed at her own face. "I'm not going running with you, Jack. Stop asking and let me sleep." she murmured.

The gnomes carried Aaron out on his back. He twisted his head around until he finally caught the Evil Queen Bitch's regal gaze.

"WHY!?" he demanded. "Just kill us! What else do you want?!"

"It's not what I want," the Evil Queen Bitch said. "You've been requested to the King's chamber."

And she would say no more. She only watched as the gnomes worked together to hoist first Tess and Erin and then Aaron out of the monorail cart.

Blood from his smashed nose clogged Aaron's throat. He screamed just to clear it so he could keep breathing.

And then Aaron discovered he was unable to stop screaming.

39

The space they were carried through was old but not ancient. Drifting along on his back, Aaron had little to do but stare at the ceiling and hack out his own blood to keep from choking.

And it was a true ceiling. A golden dome lit by amber lights housed in coves of swirling silver. Wherever they were, it was made by man.

Occasionally, he saw Raylene, or what Raylene had become, from the corner of his vision. Every time he did, she was more *become* than the last time Aaron had seen her.

First time.

Raylene's conservative but expensive suit had turned into a gown of swirling black. It looked like she had clothed herself in spider webs dipped in shadows.

Second time.

Her black hair had become a thick braid of tightly woven thorn branches. He looked desperately for some trace of the woman who might recognize him. The one who had gone through the lobby and the tunnels with them and had risked herself to save Tess.

Third time.

She was looking right at him with her jet black eyes. She winked. It sent vibrations of fear through Aaron's whole body, even the half that was dead.

"You're wrong," she said, letting him know that

even his thoughts weren't safe. "It wasn't Raylene that pulled Tess up," the Evil Queen Bitch said. "It was me."

"Why?" Aaron asked.

"Because I was told to."

"By who!?"

"Wait and see for yourself," the Evil Queen Bitch said. "Hold here!"

She was not speaking to Aaron. The gnomes came to a halt. They dropped Erin, Aaron, and Tess on the ground.

Erin and Tess were left on their hands and knees, both of them trembling and fully aware that they had not escaped Turtleshell Mountain. Both of their unblinking, terrified gazes were fixed on something directly in front of them.

Aaron, of course, could not kneel. The Gnomes left him sprawled out on his back, staring up at the stately dome above them.

"What is it?" he asked Tess. "What are you looking at?"

Tess didn't answer. Her eyes were welling with tears, and she was shaking her head in muted denial against something. Her jaw hung open but no sound came out.

"Moron!"

Aaron heard the savage sound of flesh against fiberglass, and one of the gnomes staggered forward.

"Do you think he's lounging at the pool!?" the Evil Queen Bitch screeched. "Make him KNEEL."

Four sets of hands scrambled over Aaron in their haste to satisfy the Queen. As they lifted and posed him, Aaron was able to see more of where they were. He saw the full scope of the depression era theatre they were in. There was the ornate dome above them, and there were thick, red walls around them and polished, green marble under their feet.

He saw the monorail, rising up like a ruined tower not too far away from them. He saw the pile of debris even closer, and he saw the hole in the center of the golden dome that they'd fallen through.

And then he was propped up on his dead knees and left to support his weight on his arms.

And he saw Tess.

Not the Tess he'd arrived with that morning when the sun was a perfect seventy-eight degrees and just enough of a breeze came down from the mountains and the day seemed untouchable.

Not the Tess he'd battled Lavender and Leyland and the Old Man with.

Not the Tess he'd ached, bled, and survived a monorail crash with.

This Tess looked even closer to death. She was bone white, except for the thin worms of blue veins running across her face and arms. Her skin was so filmy that Aaron could see the angles of her bones like an outline beneath tracing paper. Her eyes were sunken deep enough in their sockets to cast them into permanent shadows.

Yet, the shadows around her eyes were not so dark that Aaron could not see the morbid joy blazing inside of this dying Tess' eyes.

"Honored Guests," this Tess boomed. She

318

bowed and didn't care as her wig fell off, exposing more flimsy skin and blue veins. "Welcome. It is such an honor to have you in my home."

"No," Tess' voice, but it didn't come from the Tess standing in front of him. Aaron looked to his left. Another Tess was there. His Tess.

"No," she said again. She shut her eyes but this image of herself, this herself that had come so close to being real as she waited in hospital waiting rooms, was inside of her mind too.

"I'm in remission," she swore to herself. "I got better. You didn't happen. You didn't take me!"

The Single Rider looked down and saw the form that he'd taken. He made his Tess' face smile. "Oh," he said shamefacedly. "Forgive me, I didn't realize how I was dressed."

The true Tess opened her eyes, and the death's head reflection was gone. In its place was a tall man with thinning hair and a warm smile that they all recognized.

"You're Charles Tuttle," Aaron gasped.

The Single Rider waved Aaron off like an exaggerating admirer.

"No, just wearing him. But it's fitting, isn't it?" His voice was 1947 American Assurance personified. "None of this would have been here without Mr. Tuttle's imagination."

He beamed at Erin, Aaron, and Tess before striding past them to the Evil Queen Bitch. "And these three would not be here if it weren't for you." He gently cradled the Evil Queen Bitch's hand. "Thank you, Your Majesty, for bringing them to me." He kissed her nightshade-tinted knuckles, and

319

she returned the gesture with a regal nod. One sovereign to another.

This, of course, was all theatre. The Evil Queen Bitch belonged to the Single Rider as much as anything else that crawled or hunted in Turtleshell Mountain. She had been his ever since the black sludge inside of the Felix Fox suit had poured over Raylene's back. Her companions had stopped it from reaching her mouth, but skin contact was still enough. It just meant he had to wait a little longer for the ooze to soak inside of her. Now, he was in her head the same way he was in every...

The Single Rider listened. Could it be?

It was.

Turtleshell Mountain was quiet. His hundred fingers had sought and slaughtered every last huddled, frightened refuge of life inside the confines of the park. He heard nothing. Nothing except the heartbeats in front of him and...

Oh, what's this now?

"One moment," he told his guests. The Single Rider walked past them, towards the rubble brought down in the wake of the falling monorail.

<u>40</u>

In the beginning, darkness.
Darkness and pain.
Then, cracking sounds. The plates of the earth shifting. The rock rolling away from the tomb.
And then there was light.

The Single Rider shifted aside the last of the rubble and looked at what there was to see.

He saw the preacher man first but nothing special there. He was just another dead man. Very little rubble had actually fallen on him, so he wasn't even disfigured enough to be interesting to look at. There was nothing other than the white collar to make him stand out from all the other corpses the Single Rider had seen that night.

No, the Single Rider was much more interested in the green arms wrapped around the man's chest.

"Timmy! Timmy Turtle! I knew you were out there somewhere!"

The dead preacher was clutched tight to Timmy's chest. The Single Rider bent to pry him out from between them but then, surprise of surprises, the dead man groaned.

Still alive, the Single Rider marveled. Timmy's work, of course. The turtle had grabbed the preacher, even with everything falling apart around them, and had managed to hold him close and then turn them so his shell would take the brunt of the fall.

Such selflessness. It was almost a shame that the man was dying anyway.

Timmy had protected his precious egg from the fall, true, but not from the strip of rebar that was protruding from the preacher's torso just above the hip. The Single Rider didn't need to turn him over to know that the yolk was broken on the other side too.

The Single Rider tossed the holey holy man aside like the nothing that he was and knelt beside the overturned shell. Timmy's head and legs were retracted into the shell, but the Single Rider knew he was in there. Not just because he could see Timmy's arms and knew that he wasn't running around someplace in boxer shorts covered with little hearts. He knew because-

"I could feel you this whole time, you know," the Single Rider said. "All night you've been stuck in my head like feedback from a bad speaker. And it's going to be such a relief to turn you off."

He flipped Timmy onto his stomach. Chunks of the turtle's fractured shell fell like broken roofing shingles. The Single Rider grabbed Timmy's shell by the rim of his head hole and pulled him out of the mountain of rubble. Timmy's head didn't come out, but the Single Rider heard a whimper from inside of the shell.

Good.

"Come out," the Single Rider said.

He waited.

Nothing.

"You've been fighting my commands since I took over. It's impressive, actually; but until now you've only heard me whispering." The Single Rider knelt down right beside the hole where Timmy's head was recessed. "I could shout in your mind right now and have you out in an instant. I could make you juggle and ride a unicycle. I haven't because if you were under my control I wouldn't be able to feel your fear. And I want your fear, Timmy. I want it very much. So, please, be an obliging little goody-good and poke your head out where I can crush it." He drummed on the broken shell of Timmy's back. "Be brave, Timmy!" He bellowed. "Be bbbrrrraaavvveeeee!"

He waited without any real expectations. He was resigned to having to march Timmy out by his puppet strings.

"Stop this, Nathan," a small voice said from inside of the shell.

The Single Rider grew very still. The good humor was gone from his face like the first buds of spring swept away by a late frost.

"What did you say to me?" he asked.

Timmy still wouldn't come out of his shell, but the Single Rider heard every word from that tiny, mewling voice just fine.

"Turtleshell Mountain is my place too," Timmy said. "I know everything, Nathan. I know what Father did to you. I know you're hearing voices of your own. But you don't have to listen to them. Turtleshell Mountain is scarred but it's not destroyed yet. Please, stop this now and maybe we can save it."

The Single Rider laughed. There was nothing frightening about it. That laugh was a laugh of genuine joy. It was not taunting or cruel. It radiated sincerity from every note.

"Destroy Turtleshell Mountain? Timmy, hurting Turtleshell Mountain is the last thing I would ever do."

The Single Rider reached into Timmy's shell.

"I love this place."

The Single Rider reached with his hand, not with his mind. He reached and twisted and burrowed until he got ahold of something thick and leathery. The Single Rider didn't care what it was. He grabbed on tight and pulled.

Timmy Turtle's head came out of his shell with the Single Rider's hand wrapped around his neck.

The Single Rider kept pulling. He pulled until Timmy's wrinkly neck was stretched smooth.

And then he kept pulling.

"Nathan," Timmy croaked out. It was his last word before the Single Rider's grip cinched even tighter, like a seat belt just before the ride was about to take off, and cut off all of the turtle's breath.

But strangulation was not the Single Rider's goal. His goal was not clear until the first rift of split skin opened at the base of Timmy Turtle's neck.

"It was never yours," the Single Rider snarled. He was losing control of his shape. He was Charles Tuttle with the long, kinky hair of a black woman. He was a young Asian boy with the furious, round eyes of a Caucasian. Then he became a geriatric Hispanic man with the freckles, red hair, and deep blush of a raging Irishman.

The one thing that never changed was the powerful, masculine hand applying steady pressure to Timmy Turtle's neck and the widening chasm of bleeding, open flesh.

"They built this place on my BONES," the Single Rider snarled. He forced Timmy's head up so the turtle could see his eyes. Blue, green, brown, or black, there was no questioning who they belonged to. "I can taste the cement of the foundation in my teeth! Your face on the lollipops and t-shirts means NOTHING!"

The Single Rider pulled harder still. He cinched his fingers tighter around the throat that dared to call him "Nathan." He was not Nathan. He was the Single Rider. He was the true son of Turtleshell Mountain, and he had given everything he had for its greater good. It was time for Timmy Turtle to do the same. He squeezed until the whole of Timmy's throat fit in one clenched hand. He squeezed until Timmy Turtle had no more breath to plead with.

Of course, Charles Tuttle would have told him that it wasn't the turtle's breath that mattered.

It was all in the eyes.

If an art student could have been among the witnesses, she would have wept at the beautiful craftsmanship behind Timmy Turtle's eyes. As the Single Rider squeezed tighter, Timmy's eyes bulged with terror and desperation; but, the truly masterful touch was the plea for reconsideration that swelled in those eyes. Timmy's eyes were an entreaty to end all of this. Not just his own suffering, but all of the ruin that had fallen on the

House of Turtleshell Mountain. Inside Timmy Turtle's eyes was the long dead Charles Tuttle's final masterpiece. A perfectly crafted plea to peace, compassion, and mercy.

The Single Rider was not an art student. He ripped Timmy Turtle's neck and head from his body in a final, titanic surge of strength. He did not feel a single ounce of regret as the blood gushed from the recesses of Timmy Turtle's shell and his legs beat their death spasms against the interior of the shell.

All the Single Rider felt was satisfaction.

And, still, he didn't even feel enough of that.

He dropped Timmy Turtle's head and dug back in to see what else he could find.

Before Aaron, Erin, and Tess' horrified eyes, the Single Rider ripped out Timmy's heart.

He pulled out the turtle's lungs.

He yanked out stomach and liver and ropes of intestines like they were handkerchiefs from a magician's sleeve.

He ripped and yanked and spread Timmy's viscera as far afield as he could.

And still, the Single Rider's fury was not sated.

When there was nothing left to rip from Timmy's shell, the Single Rider filled his hand with Timmy's neck. Holding it like the handle of a flail, he swung Timmy's head against the turtle's own shell.

"It's mine," he said as he took the false face that had kindled joy in a million hearts and smashed it against its own carcass.

"Mine!" he repeated. "MINE!" He swung

326

Timmy Turtle's head against his own shell over and over again, leaving bloody splotches all over it and producing a sound that started like a coconut hitting a rock and then gradually degraded to sound more and more like a wet sponge slapping a wall.

"MINE! MINE! MINE!"

"STOP IT!" Tess screamed. She was not an art student either, but she was a student of people and, for all the horrors they'd seen at Turtleshell Mountain, she knew exactly what she saw in Timmy Turtle's eyes before the Single Rider had killed him.

She saw innocence.

"It's enough!" She wept. "Just stop it!"

The Single Rider turned. As he did, his form solidified. It became a young woman whose beauty was partially, but not completely, obscured by her patched, threadbare dress and the smudges of dust on her face.

"You're wrong there," The Single Rider said through the mouth of Dustimona. "It could never be enough." He let Timmy's head drop. "But you do have a point." The Single Rider changed shape again as he walked back towards them. His face remained the same, but the dust blew away and his hair coiled into an elegant bun. The rag of a dress turned into an exquisite gown of blue periwinkles and he stood a few inches taller as glass high heels sprung up beneath his feet. Princess Dustimona, fresh from the Fairy Godmother Salon.

"I got so distracted making sure my wicked stepbrother got the ending he deserved that I completely forgot I still have my own happy ending to attend to."

The Single Rider reached for Tess. "As a thank you for reminding me, I'll try to make this quick."

Aaron threw his dead weight forward. He flopped into Tess' lap and rolled over so he was lying on his back.

"Stay away from her," Aaron warned.

"Really?" the Single Rider taunted. "Because you said so? It doesn't seem like you have much of a standing army."

The Evil Queen Bitch grabbed Aaron by the ankle. He didn't even realize it until she pulled and Tess' legs began to slide out from under him.

"No!" Aaron screamed. "No!" He clung to Tess' thighs to keep from being pulled away. "Get away from her!"

Her Wicked Majesty was not to be denied. She dragged Aaron away and brought him to heel at her feet. Even then, Aaron struggled as well as he could with no legs and The Evil Queen Bitch's stiletto heel firmly between his shoulders.

"Get off of me! Stop! STOP!"

The Single Rider tuned all of this out. Threats, screams, anger, terror. He hated to admit it, but it was starting to get repetitive.

But the girl, the girl was going to be different. She struggled as he loomed over her, but the gnomes did an admirable job of keeping her in place. The Single Rider reached for her eyes.

"Take me," Aaron pleaded. "Whatever you want, you can have it. Just take it from me."

The Single Rider stopped then. He stopped with

Tess' eyelashes brushing the tips of his lacquered nails.

Are you sure she's the one? He asked himself. He looked at the others. Erin, curled up and squinting at the Single Rider from between her hands like a child playing peek-a-boo. Aaron, braced up on his arms with his hackles raised and his dead legs sprawled uselessly behind him. The three of them had been in close proximity this whole time. It was possible it could be one of the other two.

But, no. He wasn't making educated guesses based only on what he could sense from the sludge burrowing into Raylene's mind now. He had them all right in front of him. He was listening with his own ears and seeing with his own eyes. Most of all, he was *feeling* them with his own internal antennae, and there was no mistaking the readings he was getting.

"No," he said to Aaron. "I understand where you're coming from; but I'm afraid it can't be you."

"Well, it's not her!" He screamed. He tried to lunge forward, but the Evil Queen Bitch had her nails in his shirt neck like a dog reined in by the collar. Aaron lunged and frothed at the mouth with equal vigor. "She's done nothing!" he raged.

"Nothing?" The Single Rider said. He chuckled. "Dear boy, she's the CAUSE of all this."

Erin gaped at Tess. Loathing himself for it, so did Aaron. Tess looked back in utter bewilderment. "You were with me!" It was the only thing she could think of to say. "I didn't know about any of this! I don't have any idea what he's talking about!"

"That's true enough," the Single Rider allowed. "No one accused you of acting maliciously." He turned to the Evil Queen Bitch.

"Your Majesty," he said to the Evil Queen Bitch. "You and I weren't as... close then. What exactly did you tell them of the arrangement Charles Tuttle had entered into?"

"I told them of what was in the will. The funnel and the instruction to fill it."

"The funnel. Is that what he called it?" The Single Rider sighed and smiled fondly. "He had such a way with words, that man."

The Single Rider bowed low so his head was level with theirs. "The funnel," he said. "At your service." He opened his mouth wide for them. Aaron, Tess, and Erin looked inside and saw nothing behind his teeth. No tongue, no uvula, only a darkness that moaned like midnight wind blowing past an empty cavern.

Then the darkness inside of the Single Rider's mouth *rippled*. It was no further back than the top of his throat.

Not empty, Aaron realized. *Full. Full dark. Practically flooding out of him.*

"Filled with wishes that didn't come true," the Single Rider said. "That's what I was put here to do- collect every tear, disappointment, and bad feeling in this wonderful place. Slow work to be sure, a favorite ride closed here, an argument between spouses there. But I was fastidious and, drop by drop, the funnel filled. For what purpose?

330

Maybe Charles Tuttle knew, but I did not. I didn't know anything until *you* came along."

The Single Rider pointed at her. On cue, the lights dimmed and a spotlight flared up somewhere, putting the focus entirely on Tess.

"*You!* A brave, kind young woman who grew up without her father and lost her mother at seventeen. Worked through school. Built a career. Fell in love! Got cancer! Wins the Susan Komen lottery and beats it! Naturally, she wants to go to her favorite place in the world to share the news with the people she loves best. Finally, she thinks that everything is exactly the way it's supposed to be… and then the man she cares about most of all rejects her."

The Single Rider licked his lips, as if the taste of Tess' suffering was still there. "You have no idea, the sheer AGONY she felt when you told her that you didn't love her-"

"But I do love her!" Aaron burst out. "I do!"

He looked into Tess' eyes. This time, he said it only for her. "I love you more than anything."

If they expected the Single Rider to wail and shriek as he shrank to nothing, they were disappointed.

"Yes," the Single Rider said mildly. "I'm sure she's relieved. Believe me, I know what I'm talking about. Her grief at the thought of losing you washed over me like a flood. But the tide's already gone through and it doesn't matter if it pulls back now. The funnel is filled. The group of you came to Turtleshell Mountain and you brought the final ration of unhappiness to this happy place.

Thanks to you, the deal is done as it was always eventually going to be done. Charles Tuttle mortgaged his dream to Nightmares. They helped him spread his creations all over the world, and he agreed to tuck a little heart of darkness into each one. And we held to our bargain. We let him have his time in the sun." The Single Rider spread his arms wide. "But now it's time for everything to come back to the shadows where they belong."

"Not everything," Tess whispered. She was looking at the cracked arch of Timmy Turtle's shell, like the dome of a majestic mosque gone to ruin.

The Single Rider sighed. Exasperation this time instead of admiration. "No, not everything. But the Turtle was always an exception. He was Charles Tuttle's first creation, and he always had a bit more… fluff in him than the rest of us." He brightened. "That's all over with now. The others have all fallen in to serve their true owners. Besides, what good story doesn't have a few obstacles on the road to its happy ending?"

"Certainly not any story that wants to be on the Turtleshell Pictures' distribution schedule," the Evil Queen Bitch said. "We made sure every producer had the mandatory story structure framed in their office. Start idyllic. Then, introduce a conflict. Then, suffering. Some more suffering. A little bit of hope. Then complications. More complications. Make it so all seems lost… and then fix everything wrong and tie it all up in a nice little package."

"And here we are to slap a bow on it," the

Single Rider said. "Not that there isn't room for a little more suffering before we wrap everything up."

"As you like it," the Evil Queen Bitch granted. "We have the characters here, we can arrange them however we want." She ran her fingers through Aaron's hair like scorpions through his scalp. "Shall we torture the heroic prince first?"

She turned to Tess. "Or should we be traditional and mangle the damsel in distress?" She had no hair to brush, so the Evil Queen Bitch tenderly stroked her cheek instead.

Tess spat in her face. The wad of saliva landed perfectly on the Queen's cheek and ran down towards her jaw. The Evil Queen Bitch stared at Tess. She didn't say a word, but her full lips thinned into a tight line, and the speckle of spit froze solid on her face and hung there like a cluster of spider eggs.

She nearly smited Tess right there. It would have been so easy. She was strong now- one flick of her wrist and she could have taken that defiant, self-righteous sneer and turned into so much red hamburger meat splattered across her beloved's face.

But that's not how you hurt someone who's already prepared to die, the Single Rider whispered in her mind. *You can do better than that.*

Tess refused to drop her defiant stare. The Evil Queen Bitch saw that the Single Rider was right. She wanted it.

He was right about something else too. The Evil Queen Bitch could do much worse.

Without saying a word, Raylene brushed the chip of ice from her cheek. She turned away from Tess.

She turned towards Erin.

"You," she said. "You don't really fit anywhere in the Turtleshell character mold. We're a family company. There's no spot here for slutty best friends."

"LEAVE HER ALONE!" Tess screamed.

Raylene just stalked closer. "But I know another genre that does. Let's see how you fit there."

"She didn't do anything!" Tess cried.

"You did."

Erin tried to recoil back from the Evil Queen Bitch. "Get away!" she shrieked. Erin kicked at the questing hand. She scrambled backwards, not caring where she was going. Just trying to get away.

Gleeful the Gnome brought the pick-axe down on Erin's hand. The paint-chipped point was blunt, but not so blunt that it couldn't puncture Erin's palm and pin her to the ground.

Erin didn't need to look to know what happened. The pain hit her first, huge and instantaneous, but the scream was close behind. It started inside her hand and raced up her skewered arm. It surged up towards her already open mouth-

And the Queen's lips clamped over Erin's mouth before the scream could escape.

Obeying a silent order, Gleeful yanked loose the pick-axe pinning Erin down. The Evil Queen Bitch lifted her up, keeping their lips pressed together all the while. She didn't break the kiss until both of them were standing. The Evil Queen Bitch pulled away then and looked deep into Erin's terrified eyes.

"Remember, we've got an audience," she whispered. "So make sure this looks good." The Evil Queen Bitch kissed her again. Long and deep and excruciating.

Erin didn't disappoint. She thrashed and shuddered and filled the dome with screams muffled by the seal of the Evil Queen's lips. She tried to push away, but the Queen's talons kept their faces tight together. Her tongue, strong and supple, forced Erin's lips open and slipped inside. A taste like nail polish remover came with it and Erin retched. That tongue, painting her mouth with its acrid tang, was more than she could take. Erin vomited.

And it went on anyway. Even after Erin threw up, The Evil Queen Bitch kept the kiss going. The vomit running down their chins and passing back and forth between their mouths didn't deter her. It just made her lips curl into a smile.

Tess tried to help her. She pushed and shoved at the gnomes holding her and lashed out with her teeth from side to side.

Snoozey and Grouchy kept her where she was. Hot tears ran down her face. Grief, rage, and guilt.

I'm sorry, Erin. I wish you'd never met me.

Aaron stuck his hand out and nothing tried to stop him. He didn't reach towards Erin. Even if he had been close enough, there was nothing he could do to help her. Or himself. Or Tess. What he could do, if he stretched as far as his dead weight legs would allow, was take Tess' hand. He intertwined his fingers with hers and held on as tight as he could.

They watched together, pathetic and helpless. Aaron waited for it to be over. He waited to see Erin catch fire or shrivel and wither as the life was sucked out of her or maybe even simply fall down dead without a mark to be seen.

Instead, Erin's skin began to lose color. It started at their connected lips, as if the Evil Queen was sucking out the hue from her flesh, and then it spread over Erin's cheeks and neck, tinting her skin the same uniform shade of lifeless grey.

Erin had no idea that her skin tone was fading and becoming monochromatic. All she knew was the taste. The burning, suffocating, raw alcohol taste that overpowered even the vomit coating her mouth. And then she wasn't burning, but cold. There was a wet chill clinging to her whole body. And it was spreading.

It's her lips, Erin realized. If Erin could only break the kiss, she could break whatever spell was being cast on her. She cocked her fist back and threw blindly, hoping for the Evil Queen Bitch's chin.

The punch never landed. The greyness spread to Erin's hand and stopped her hand mid-punch. Her arm hung perfectly still in the air.

The Evil Queen Bitch broke the kiss and stepped back.

Erin stayed exactly where she was. Her mouth was pinned in place. Her eyes were stuck wide in perpetual terror. Her clenched fist remained unmoving.

Her skin was a uniform sheen of grey.

Raylene wiped the ring of vomit from around her lips. She eyed Erin's frozen form skeptically, still posed in its final, revolted kiss.

"Personally, I don't see what all the fuss was about."

No one answered her. They all stared silently. The Single Rider in admiration. Tess and Aaron in horror.

She turned her into stone. That was Aaron's first thought. Yet, some small part of his mind that refused the comfort of insanity insisted on pointing out that her skin was still smooth, and the lifelike quality of Erin's terror was too well preserved. The grey of her skin also had a dull shine to it when the light hit it right.

Tess squeezed his hand tighter. "They made her a picture," she moaned.

That's what it is. Not a statue. A black-and-white picture. Cracks appeared in his final refuge of sanity. *Smile. It lasts a lifetime.*

Erin was not smiling. All that was on her face was terror, pain, and misery.

It was really all in the eyes.

Aaron was still trying to comprehend this final monstrosity when those black nails plunged into his hair again. This time, they grabbed Aaron and hauled him up to his useless feet.

"Your turn, handsome. If you've got a pose, pick it now and pucker up."

<u>41</u>

There's always something you can do.

Ed was not dead. Dying, yes. But, not so far removed from the world that he didn't understand what was happening around him. Not far enough gone that he didn't understand what was at stake when the Creature With Many Faces spoke about spreading shadows.

He remembered something from seminary. A joke with a philosophical lesson.

An old woman living by a river sees a flood warning on TV. It's urging everyone to evacuate as fast as they can. Now, this old woman considers herself a devout Christian. She's got bibles on every shelf in her home, framed photos of Jesus in every room, and a completed jigsaw puzzle of the Last Supper that's been on her dining room table for twenty years. Now, she can't just pack all of that up. So she decides she's going to stay right where she is, sing "Amazing Grace," pray her very hardest, and God's going to divert the flood away from her home.

So she stays right where she is as the flood gets worse. And worse. A concerned neighbor stops by and offers to take her away along with his family. She politely declines and says, "God will protect me." So the guy leaves and the water keeps rising. Pretty soon, bye-bye, first floor.

The woman takes refuge on the second floor of

*her house. Ok, so God decided that her bibles,
pictures, and jigsaw were a wash. Literally. That's
fine. Surely, the pious woman herself will be
spared. And then along comes a man in a boat. He
motors right up to her second-story window and
offers to ferry her away.*

*Again, she refuses. "God will protect me," she
says.*

*The water's even higher now. This lady's sitting
on her roof, soaked to the bone, but she still
believes that God's going to save her at the last
second, Abraham and Issac style.*

*And then down comes a helicopter, shining a
literal light down from the sky, and it wants to take
her away to safety. But no, "I will not deprive the
Glory of God," she says.*

*So the helicopter moves on to find someone else
to rescue.*

*Finally, the water rises once again and, what
do you know, the old biddy drowns.*

*And she goes to Heaven, primed to give God a
divine ass chewing* (Much like I was, Ed realized.)
*"Why didn't you save me!?" she demands. "I
prayed and I prayed and you let me drown." And
she says it again- "Why didn't you save me?"*

*And what does God have to say for himself?
God throws his hands up in the air, rolls his eyes,
and says. "I sent you a car, a boat, and a
helicopter. Maybe you should have been listening
instead of speaking."*

God has his reasons. That was a sermon
Edward Harrison had given a hundred thousand
years ago. It sounded insightful when he said it

from his spotless pulpit. It sounded like absolute bullshit when he said it over the broken bodies of children he'd loved as his own.

What had the old woman wondered as the water clogged her lungs and she died slowly and painfully?

Stupid. Ed didn't have to wonder. It was the first word out of her mouth as the joke wound down to its punchline.

Why?

God had not given Ed a car, a boat, or a helicopter. God had taken his children from him and left him to wander among serpents.

Why?

Lying there, the strip of rebar in his torso grating painfully with every weak breath he took, Ed was finally listening.

Why?

Because there was God's work to be done here.

God's work that Ed might not have been willing or able to do with his children still under his protection.

There were still other ways You could have asked, Minister Ed thought.

Nevertheless, there was still God's work to be done.

Slowly, stealthily, Ed eased the strip of rebar from his own torso.

42

The Evil Queen Bitch chuckled as Aaron pursed his lips together like an infant refusing food it didn't like.

"Oh, sweetie. My camp counselor tried that trick when I was fourteen." She licked her lips, letting Aaron see a green tongue that ended in a twitching fork. "He didn't hold out very long either."

Raylene released Aaron's hair and caught him under the chin before his legs could collapse. She squeezed until his jawbone creaked and his cheeks scrunched and lips puckered forward.

"That's more like it." Holding him with one hand like he weighed nothing, she lifted Aaron towards her black lips. Her corrosive kiss was almost on his mouth when the Evil Queen paused. She shifted Aaron's head to the side so she could better see the look on Tess' face.

"Is he a good kisser?" she taunted. "Do you know, or did he never get up the nerve?"

Tess met the jeer with nothing but a cold stare. She did not plead. She did not whimper.

"I'm not doing this," she said.

The barest flicker of surprise tugged at the Evil Queen Bitch's eyebrows. Tess' face stayed just the way it was. This was a face very few people saw, but it was always hiding behind her smile. It was there when she was a teenager gently cajoling the bus driver to let her on when there was no money for bus fare. It was there when she still smiled even when she'd been told her tumor had grown again. This stern face that could never be intimidated was the steel that buttressed her veneer of good humor.

But every other veneer at Turtleshell Mountain had been cast aside. Why should she keep hers?

"I had a thought," Tess said. She stood up and none of the gnomes made an attempt to stop her. "A daring, novel, groundbreaking paradigm shift." Tess spun on her heels, away from the Evil Queen Bitch, and looked directly at the Single Rider.

"It occurred to me that the Bad Guy might be lying to me."

The Evil Queen Bitch huffed behind her. Tess didn't care. Her focus was only on the one who was orchestrating all of this. "I don't see anyone else getting brought in alive," she said. Her eyes burned more powerfully without a frame of hair to take away from them. "You still need me for something. And whatever Lavender Twist's 'party favor' is, I promise you that you won't get a goddamn thing from me if anything happens to Aaron. Tell that bitch to put him down."

Aaron tried to protest and could only get out a garbled murmur. His lips were still pinched together.

"You want something from me? Ask me yourself," the Evil Queen Bitch challenged.

Tess still wouldn't look at her. "I know a bitch on a leash when I see one. If I need something, I'll talk to your owner."

342

The Evil Queen Bitch was a part of the Single Rider's web. She had been ever since the sludge had leapt from the Felix Fox suit and seeped into her soul. She was also different than the other creatures the Single Rider had wrought. She still had an ego and, right now, that ego was compelling her to crush this pathetic wretch's skull and rub Tess' bald head in the mess. That would show her who the real bitch was.

"Do what she says," the Single Rider said.

The Evil Queen Bitch hissed.

"Do what I said," the Single Rider ordered.

Seething, the Evil Queen Bitch let Aaron drop. He crumpled into a wasted heap. Blood leaked from inside of his mouth.

"Tess," he croaked through a mouth of loose teeth.

"It's my turn, Aaron," she said. That was the truth. No matter what he said about not owing her, it was her turn now.

"Turn?" The Single Rider asked. His hand shot out with baffling speed. It palmed Tess' head like a basketball and held her tight. "There's plenty of room on this ride for two."

Tess squealed in pain and shock. Each fingertip on her head was a dime-sized circle of searing heat. "That was a bold move," the Single Rider complimented her. "But there's one thing you didn't consider." The Single Rider yanked her closer. She was so close to him now, she could smell his breath. Blood and cotton candy.

"What if... the only thing I need from you is your blood on my hands?"

With that, Tess' buttress of inner steel collapsed. All that was left among the rubble was uncontrollable terror. She barely even understood the rest of what he said to her.

"That was why I had them looking for you in the park. I knew it was your pain that finally gave me the strength to open the doors. I wanted to kill you myself just to make sure that there wasn't any more suffering I could squeeze out of your pulped innards."

He spun Tess around so she was looking back at Aaron.

"Your Highness!"

The Evil Queen Bitch needed no further prompting. She straddled the collapsed pile that was Aaron. One long, curved nail went to the top of his throat.

"The last thing you'll see will be his face when he dies," The Single Rider said. "And I'll be right here to lick up that final agony from your soul before I kill you."

The nail pressed harder against Aaron's throat, already drawing blood, but the Evil Queen Bitch held off on making the final cut. Tess knew why she was waiting. Hating herself for doing it, knowing it was exactly what the Single Rider wanted, Tess took that time to savor every line of Aaron's face. If they were going to die, she wanted to die remembering as much of him as she could.

But she barely even got to look into Aaron's eyes before the five pressure points around Tess' head squeezed even tighter. The pain was overwhelming.

He lied again, she thought,

The Single Rider was not waiting. He was going to kill Tess at the same time. Not with any more theatricality or iconic characters brought to life.

He was simply going to crush her skull.

43

Tess was wrong. The Single Rider wasn't trying to crush her skull at all. His grip on her head had only tightened as an involuntary reaction to the strip of rebar stabbing between his shoulder blades.

Minister Ed had had to crawl, leaving a thick trail of blood behind him as he did. Twice his heart almost stopped, but he kept it going by sheer force of will.

Perhaps it was even God's will.

He used the rebar as a crutch first, an aid to get back to his feet.

Then, he drove the metal bar into the Single Rider's back.

Whatever else the creature was, his flesh was only flesh and the iron punched through it with ease. Vivid red blood gushed from the puncture wound.

The Single Rider roared like a dying lion. Ed pushed harder on the rebar strip. *This is for my kids!* He wanted to shout. *Do you understand that, you son of a bitch!? This is for taking my children away!* He wanted to scream all of their names while he twisted the rod back and forth in the monster's wound.

He couldn't. He'd taken all of his energy, even the little bit it would take to yell, even what it took to keep his heart beating, and put it towards driving the strip of rebar through this joyful

346

bastard until the tip erupted out the other side of his body and Ed's clenched fists touched the hot stain spreading across the back of the Single Rider's gown.

And Ed was rewarded with more than blood. The Single Rider's howls of agony were more beautiful than any hymn in his ears. He could have listened to the naked, blatant agony forever.

Thank you, God.

Ed collapsed. Dark clouds had begun to cloud at the edges of his vision, but he tried to keep them at bay just a little longer. *Please God, one more favor out of the eighteen you owe me and I'll call it square. Please, just let me see him fall.*

Miraculously, his prayers were answered. The darkness rushing to claim him held where it was. Ed was cold all over but his heart burned with joy. He would see it. He would see the monster die.

The Single Rider was reeling back and forth on his glass heels. He'd let Tess drop to the floor. Ed saw the blood dribble from the sides of his mouth and his hair fall from Dustimona's bun in haggard strains. He heard the Single Rider's breath whistle from between gritted teeth. He saw him sway, a condemned house in a high wind, ready to collapse on itself.

He saw the Single Rider get his hands around the tip of the rebar strip poking out in front of him and start to slowly work it out from his body.

He was not falling.

No, Ed thought. *No. No. No. You bastard, NO!*

Minister Ed was still screaming in his head when the darkness claimed him and only him.

44

The Single Rider needed both hands to wrench the rebar out of his chest. When the strip of metal was free, the Single Rider held it like a bat and whirled around. The form of Dustimona was gone and in its place was a red-nosed, big-bellied slab of an abusive father. The Single Rider choked up on the rebar with both hands, fully intending to beat the minister to death with it.

"Where is he!?"

When he saw the Minister already dead, the Single Rider beat him anyway. He broke the bones of Ed's corpse. "Get up!" he screamed at the corpse. *"Get up and let me kill you!"* He pulverized the body, mashed it until its features were completely unrecognizable and sluggish blood oozed from a dozen fresh ruptures. When the rebar was so badly warped that it could no longer be useful as a club, the Single Rider spat on him. He spat his own blood on Ed's remains until his spittle finally ran clear again, and then he started kicking the body.

"How dare you get off!?" He drove his heavy work boot into Ed's ribs, too furious to take any satisfaction from the sound of cracking bones. "You don't lay a hand on me and then die before I can make you pay. You don't DARE!"

The fury kept building inside of him, no matter how much he vented on the Minister's carcass. The wound in his chest was closing, but the memory of it was still there. The memory of the first physical pain he'd suffered since that day in 1947 when Charles Tuttle had cut him open.

No! he raged. *Not me! Nathan. NATHAN.* Nathan was weak and delusional. The Single Rider was the Dark Prince of Turtleshell Mountain. He was the favored son of the Aristocracy of Arachnids. The world would be ripped asunder, and it would be at the hands of the beasts that *HE* let loose. He was not human. He was not Nathan. He was the Single Rider.

Yet, no matter how many times he repeated it to himself, the ghosts of pain and fear said otherwise. *It hurt more last time*, they whispered. *When he cut into you with that knife again and again and you were so, so scared. At least this time you didn't wet yourself, NATHAN.* The Single Rider stomped on Ed's testicles until he heard a pair of minute *pops*, but the sound was nowhere near loud enough to drown out those voices.

It was no good. The happiness and satisfaction of a job well done that he'd carried around with him all night was gone. *Gone* because of that bastard Timmy Turtle and this fat preacher and that smart-mouth bald girl and her love-struck cripple.

Defying him.

Making him feel small.

Like a child.

He stepped on Minister Ed's crotch two more times before the solution, staggering in its simplicity, occurred to him. He felt upset? He needed to be cheered up?

He was at Turtleshell Mountain.

The Single Rider stopped desecrating the Minister's body. He turned to the Evil Queen Bitch with a smile on his face. And, thank the Spiders, it was a *good* smile. An easy smile.

He bowed, took the hand that wasn't poised to cut Aaron's throat, and deliberately freed the Queen from his control.

"Your Highness, would you care to tour the park with me?"

The Evil Queen Bitch still had her nail to Aaron's jugular. "Don't you think we have our hands full here?"

The Single Rider smiled at her words. The black sludge had let him take control of Raylene's mind and warp her appearance.

Her black heart had been inside of her all along.

"We'll take care of it," he assured her. "But, do you know that I've spent decades preparing for this night? I don't want it to be work. I don't want to spend it fuming and furious. I want to enjoy it." He kissed her nightshade hand and relished the taste of poison on his lips. He felt better already.

"We'll kill them later. Perhaps tomorrow even. Look at them. One of them doesn't even have a leg to stand on. The other…" To prove a point, he kicked Tess in the ribs. She moaned in pain. The Single Rider kicked her again. Tess didn't even have the strength to cringe away from the repeated blows.

"See? They're done. Lavender and Leyland trapped in a jar. We can take them anytime we please." He laughed wildly. "I've conquered

Turtleshell Mountain. We can do *anything* anytime we please." He sniffed the dank air of the auditorium. "Right now, what would please me is some fresh air. Fresh air and the height to see my kingdom."

"Everything the moonlight touches," The Queen mused.

"What was that?"

She shook her head. "Something from another life," The Evil Queen Bitch said. Her fingers closed around the Single Rider's. Her flesh absorbed the still wet blood on his hands like soil drinking up water.

"The only one I really wanted to kill was the other mouthy cunt. These two can wait."

The Single Rider gallantly helped her over Tess' curled, groaning form. He led her back towards the crevice in the ceiling where the monorail had crashed down. The gnomes scurried ahead of them, clearing debris from the royal couple's path.

"Will we fly?" The Evil Queen Bitch asked as they drew closer to the ruined train and the gaping hole above it.

The Single Rider laughed. "There's another, more leisurely path from this chamber than the direct route. Didn't we say that we would take the time to enjoy ourselves?"

"Yes, so we did."

They detoured around the wreckage of the monorail. The Single Rider regaled the Evil Queen Bitch with the tale of how Charles Tuttle himself had first taken him down this very path.

They looked for all the world just like any other

blissfully carefree couple about to embark on a well-earned vacation.

<u>45</u>

Tess had been crumpled on the floor like this before. She knew this feeling well from back when she had been sick. Sprawled out. Unable to move. Insides aching. All she needed now was a toilet to hug and it would be just like old times.

Back then, Aaron had always come to her. He would help her back to bed if she was able. If she wasn't, he would crouch there on the floor beside her until she had the strength to get up.

But, obviously, Aaron wasn't going to be coming to her now.

So Tess went to him.

She had to crawl. Her aching head threatened nausea if she tried to stand. Even moving on all fours provoked a thousand excruciating pains all at once.

She didn't care.

Tess had heard what that... *thing* had said. They had lost. Erin was dead. Timmy Turtle was dead. The priest, whoever he was, had sacrificed himself on a play better than anything Aaron or Tess were capable of, and it had all been for nothing.

The story was over. These were the end credits. All that was left now was to wait for the fade to black.

But neither of them would wait alone. She would make sure of that.

Aaron was sprawled on his side with his back

to her. Tess touched his shoulder. He shirked away from her as well as he could without a working lower body.

Tess touched him again.

This time, Aaron let the gentle weight stay where it was.

"I'm sorry," he whispered into the silence.

"Shut up," Tess groused.

Aaron rolled on his back so he could look at her. His legs jutted at grotesque, unnatural angles, but his smirk somehow unfolded perfectly.

"Shut up? That's what you said when I mentioned maybe we could all go someplace a little more relaxing than Turtleshell Mountain. You didn't listen to me then and look what happened." Aaron said.

"Next year you can pick where we go, smartass. Maybe a nice hike."

"Oh, so racism is bad but making fun of the disabled is hilarious?"

"Jed and Lulubelle would have thought so."

"Who cares what they think? Those two idiots didn't even know they were in love."

Silence fell across the chamber then. It was not the silence of despair or terror. It was not the grim wait of the executioner's chamber. This was the quiet two people might take to savor a moment they've been waiting a very long time for.

Tess lifted Aaron's upper body into her lap. She brushed filthy, bloodstained hair away from his face.

Aaron's hand went to the side of her face. There was no hair to stroke. He just wanted to feel her skin. He wanted to feel her cheek to confirm the reality of it as her face moved closer to his.

"I wouldn't want to be them either," Tess whispered. Her mouth was so close to his. He felt the breath of her every word, and it made him burn all the way down to his numb toes.

This time, there was nothing to stop them.

Aaron and Tess kissed.

Their hands stayed chastely at each other's necks and waists, but that was all they needed. The simple movement of their lips opening and closing, fitting perfectly together at every angle, generated enough heat, light, and electricity to provide power for the entire planet. The love that passed with every breath they took from each other's mouth was more intoxicating than anything they'd ever known.

Tess had kept Aaron at arm's length after her diagnosis precisely because of what was exploding between them now. She knew that it would be this utterly perfect between them, and she believed it would be unconscionable to give that to him and then take it away.

But there was no reason to hold back now. It was not just Tess that was dying. It was both of them. So they kissed with everything they had. They kissed to make up for the wedding they would never have. They kissed for the children they would never know. They kissed for the marriage bed they would never share.

It was both not enough and more than they could have ever hoped for. None of that mattered to Aaron. All that existed in the entire world was

Tess' body wrapped around his. Her lips on his. The sensation building between them was so powerful, flashes of bright light were exploding behind his closed eyelids. It was shaking the ground beneath their feet.

No, that was wrong.

The explosions were not taking place behind his eyelids.

And the ground really was shaking underneath them.

Aaron opened his eyes. So did Tess.

They realized the light was not just coming from between them.

It was coming from in front of them.

46

The Single Rider had taken the Evil Queen Bitch on the Whole Wide World ride. They sat in a gondola all by themselves while the Single Rider showed her the sights.

They passed through Japan where a wood figurine Samurai sat in meditation, perfectly balanced atop a woman's severed head.

"Turtleshell Tokyo," the Single Rider whispered in her ear. "I can already feel them starting to wake up."

The Evil Queen Bitch's smile widened and the Single Rider matched it easily. It was much easier to be happy here, outside of the dome and away from the troubling bit players.

But why are they troubling you?

It didn't matter. All that mattered was that he felt much better.

He felt stronger.

"Try it," he prompted her.

The Evil Queen Bitch turned a darker shade of purple. She shook her head.

"You can do it," he insisted. They were floating downriver into France now. Porcelain figures in berets were working as a team to hoist a toddler's corpse up to hang atop the Eiffel Tower. "Just close your eyes," he said.

Still flushed all the way to her thorn hair, the Evil Queen Bitch closed her eyes.

"Listen for Paris," he told her.

"How do I-"

Something rippled through her. Made her gasp.

"I'm inside Tina Turtle's Beauty Salon," she said. "It's the part of the ride where you get a pretend haircut." Her eyes were still closed. Every word she spoke rode out on a small moan of pleasure. She may very well have been smelling the liberal perfume sprayed throughout the ride.

"The scissors are right behind a little girl's neck. She's with her mother and they're both smiling. They have absolutely no idea how close I am. I could just..."

The Single Rider listened but he also looked. The Evil Queen Bitch had arched her back in her seat. It made the swell of her breasts strain against her bodice and made the Single Rider consider a possibility he had never thought of before: the idea that there were some rides that weren't at Turtleshell Mountain but might still be very much worth going on.

The boat suddenly pitched forward, rocking the Evil Queen Bitch and the Single Rider from their respective revelries. There was no more Paris or heaving bosom. There was only the violent rocking of the Gondola. The Single Rider grabbed the sides of the boat to steady it, but it wasn't just the Gondola that was shaking.

It was everything around them.

47

The light was coming from inside Timmy Turtle's shell. A spotlight of burning gold blazed from the gore-ringed hole where the Single Rider had ripped Timmy's head off. Aaron and Tess weren't even directly in front of it, and it was still so powerful that they had to squint against its glare.

"What is it doing?" Tess asked.

The only answer was the ground buckling beneath them. The earth was no longer just trembling, it was rising up and down in violently peaking waves.

The light blazed through the cracks in Timmy Turtle's shell. It drew jagged, lightning patterns against the roof of the dome.

It had become warmer in the underground cavern. They were sweating.

Aaron pushed himself out of Tess' lap.

"Go!" he shouted at her from the ground.

Tess shook her head. "No."

A fresh crack opened in Timmy's shell. The temperature rose with it.

"GO!"

"You going to walk me out?"

"STOP JOKING AND GET OUT OF HERE, TESS! FIND THE STAIRS!"

It was getting impossible to keep their eyes open against the sun that was being born inside of the chamber. Aaron did it anyway because he wasn't going to be able to force Tess away with words.

This is what I want, his eyes said to her. *Whatever's happening here, if it's any kind of chance for you to get away, I want you to take it. It's my choice, Tess.*

Even with her eyes burning, Tess looked right back at him.

I'm not going anywhere, Aaron. Not if I can't go with you. That's my choice.

"Tess."

The world exploded before he could say anything else.

Tess couldn't see. Golden light enveloped everything. She reached out blindly.

Her hand found his.

48

The bewildered Queen Bitch clung to the sides
of the gondola. Water splashed up over the sides
and soaked their feet. The tranquil waterway
around them had become a roiling storm worse
than the typhoon created by the Sea Witch at the
end of *The Mariner's Maiden Voyage*. A monster
wave lifted the gondola out of the water and sent it
careening into a display. Figures in Arabian
headdresses fled for their lives as the boat cut
through the sand and smashed into one of the
pyramids.

"What's happening?" The Evil Queen Bitch
cried.

She would have been better off asking the
Sphinx. The Single Rider had no idea. In his
confusion, he'd taken on the form of a fat child
with a puckered, spoiled mouth and blank,
sightless white eyes. He tried to look through
another character's eyes to see what was
happening. But in every set of eyes he chose, all he
could see was blinding golden light.

Then only darkness.

They're dying. But how? HOW!?

And then the light exploded into the Whole
Wide World ride, and the Single Rider knew what
was coming for them. The golden light didn't break
down the walls. It burned through them like they
were made of gauze. And they may as well have

been. What the light was made out of, when it was strong enough, could get through anything.

But it was impossible. It was absolutely, utterly, entirely impossible. He'd killed everyone in the entire park except for the cripple and the bitch, and they were BEATEN. There could not be a single happy thought between them as they lay there dying. There was no way, NO POSSIBLE WAY, that the two of them alone could generate this kind of power. Even if there was, Nathan had been hollowed out and left to collect gloom and woe for decades. Aaron and Tess didn't have the time or the will. Even if they did, they had no receptacle. There was no hollowed out sacrifice to catch whatever spark they could make.

And yet, here it was, wiping out everything that the Single Rider had claimed as his own. Overwhelming the accumulated anger and sorrow it had taken him decades to accumulate and refilling the park with everything the Single Rider had banished.

Love.

Life.

Hope.

"NO!"

Yes, the voice of Timmy Turtle whispered from all around him.

The light hit the Evil Queen Bitch first. The Single Rider heard her scream and saw her boil. The thorn branches of her hair turned brittle, and her eyes shriveled, and then she was flying apart like so many ripped up park tickets.

The Single Rider threw his hands up as the

light came for him. Not in defense, but offense. He wanted to grab the light and banish it like he had before. Turtleshell Mountain did not belong to the light. It belonged to him.

But the Light could not be touched. It could not be ripped or torn or banished or driven back.

The wall of gold struck the Single Rider. Its warmth surrounded him.

The Single Rider raged against it. He threw all of the blackness in his empty soul against the light. He called to The Investors.

I opened the door to you! Help me, you cowards! Stand and fight!

Nothing answered him. The Single Rider roared in his void of light.

It wasn't fair. He'd won.

He'd won!

HE'D WON!

...He was gone.

49

2023

The candy blocks were falling faster now. And the obvious combinations were coming fewer and farther in between, but that was okay. Aaron was in the zone. He lined up blues and pinks and circles and spirals, and it was like he had a sixth sense. Even if it was five or six pieces later, every move he made set him up for a big combination down the road.

It helped that the new phone was so precise. Every piece went exactly where he wanted to. Now, to get a new top score, all he needed he was just one green square, one more yellow tear drop-

"DADDY!"

-And two more minutes before his cannonball of a daughter reached the front of the line.

Ellie threw herself into his lap. His legs didn't feel it, but her head struck him square in the stomach and punched the air from his lungs.

"Hey, Lollipop." He choked out the pet name without letting on that he could barely breathe because that was how love worked.

Her brother flung himself into the empty space on his other thigh. More considerate than his twin sister, Jason only smashed his skull into his father' already numb hip.

"Hey, Sourpop."

Ellie pulled her head out of his stomach and beamed at him. Her grin was so wide he could see the missing teeth at the corner of her mouth.

"Hi, Daddy."

"Long wait?"

She rolled her eyes theatrically, so much like her mother. "Ugh. FOREVER!"

The ride attendant appeared beside them. "I take it this is the rest of your party?" he asked.

"What gave them away?" Aaron asked dryly.

The attendant smiled. It was Ogreland policy to smile at every joke a guest made. "Right this way, sir," he said.

Aaron swung the wheelchair around with the twins still balanced on his thighs. He followed the ride attendant to the front of the Ogre Express roller coaster. "You know," he said to the kids. "You guys were on that line for so long, I think they actually changed the height requirement for this ride. I think you're going to be too short."

Jason, already a gymnast in the making, stood up and balanced perfectly on Aaron's leg as they rolled forward. "That's not true!" he yelled in Aaron's face.

A gymnast or a lawyer. Aaron pulled the little boy into a hug. "It is true," Aaron assured him. "Good thing it looks like you guys were also waiting long enough to grow an inch or two. I think we're all set."

The attendant was waiting for them by the roller coaster's four-person car. The restraint bars were up and awaiting passengers.

"Single Rider here!" he called out. "Any Single

Riders in the line!?"

Aaron stopped with his hands on the wheels of his chair. He was suddenly cold, and the warmth of his children could not touch it.

"Hang on!"

He wheeled around. It didn't matter that he knew she was coming. Aaron needed to see her.

Heavier than after the cancer. Lighter than when she was swollen with the twins. Just as beautiful as always.

Her hair was almost waist length now. But, pretty soon, she would make her Locks of Love donation, and then she would be back to the chin-length bob that drove him crazy.

"Sorry," Tess panted. "Had to tie my shoe." She planted a kiss on Aaron's lips and then one apiece for Ellie and Jason's foreheads. She straightened her ogre-ears and favored the kids with a big, excited grin.

"Everybody ready!?"

"YEAH!" the twins shouted back.

Technically, as a handicapped person Aaron and his party were allowed to cut to the front of the line. Tess always vetoed the idea. She insisted that the wait made the ride all the more enjoyable. The twins complained sometimes; but, Aaron thought back to the two years he spent chasing Tess and the year of chaos after what the media called "The Death of Magic," and knew that she was right.

The wait did make everything better.

The twins got the two front seats. Tess took the far chair, ready to help the attendant load Aaron into his seat.

Before he was lifted out of his chair, Aaron stole a glance at the cell phone that Ellie had nearly embedded in his pancreas.

"Game Over" stared back at him from the screen.

Whatever, he tucked the phone into his pocket and allowed the attendant and Tess to get him settled into the roller coaster.

"Precious Cargo," he shouted. "Very fragile, handle with care!"

"You're just lucky I lost the receipt," Tess said.

The twins giggled. "Return Daddy!" Ellie shouted.

There were bound to be questions after he and Tess were found, the only two people alive in a park with 60,735 confirmed guests for the day along with a staff of 816. But Aaron and Tess' injuries were severe enough that they could both plead ignorance without fear of suspicion.

Truthfully, no one even looked at them that closely. They were the sole survivors of an atrocity that left a scar on the psyche of the entire planet. It engendered an odd protection in people.

The Turtleshell brand died anyway. Not all at once, but slowly as more and more people found that they couldn't laugh at Timmy Turtle or any of the others without feeling like they were laughing over the graves of thousands.

Tess had insisted that other parks would fill the void, and she was not wrong. There was Uncovered Dreams Studios, with their stable of Misunderstood Trolls, talking lamp posts, and misfit cab drivers. And there was Ogreland from

Fairytale Films. Wonder World from Faraway Fantasies Studios. The list went on.

Tess insisted they go to all of them.

"I don't care what happened to us," she said. "We're not going to stay afraid, Aaron. We're not raising our kids that way. Joy and love, that's what always comes back if you let it. That's why more parks got built in the first place. I don't care what else our kids may have trouble learning, that's something they're going to know from the second they're born."

Aaron, of course, always assumed that she was right. But he knew it for sure as he saw Ellie and Jason grip the lap bar in anticipation of the moment the roller coaster would pull them up into the sky, so high that they could look around and see the Whole Wide World around them. It didn't matter that they'd been on this ride three times already today. All the twins were chasing was the feeling of excitement and wonder that came with knowing you were happy, healthy, and that everything was going to come out perfectly.

Aaron heard another call for a Single Rider in the car behind them and he didn't even turn around.

Everything was perfect.

The ride began. Aaron heard a low chuckle behind them as the roller coaster began its ascent.

"Here we go," a voice said.

THE END

Don't Leave The Park Just Yet. Read On For A Preview of:

Rock and Roll Death Wish.

Coming In Fall 2016.

They stopped for dinner at a diner somewhere north of Bakersfield. The signage outside hadn't been replaced since the 1970s. In LA, it would have been called vintage. Out here, it was just practical.

Inside, there was no wait to sit and no wait to order. Jack had a steak sandwich. Luke had a burger. Then a pot pie. Then another burger. Jack watched his friend dig into his third helping and tried to hide his amusement. "Not bad, huh?" he asked.

"The obesity epidemic in this country makes a lot more sense now." He washed down the last of his chili cheese fries with a gulp of Sprite. "You ever been here before?"

Jack shook his head. "Not this place, but a dozen like it. Back when I was young and free I'd go out like this all the time." He waved a hand out the diner window, out to the rocks and darkness beyond the glass. "Pick a direction and go," he said. "See what you didn't know was there. Half of what I know about music, I learned from guys playing on their off days in nowhere towns just like this" He sighed, lost in memories of bars that didn't bother to card and forty-year-old truck drivers and ranch workers who didn't care about anything but just getting a chance to fucking *play*.

Jack picked up his Coke but didn't drink. He stared into it like there were answers to be found in the dark well. "Sometime after you picked me up I stopped getting out here," he shook his head ruefully. "Too busy with press tours and launch parties to find the time for the things that made me *me* in the first place."

"Yeah, yeah," Luke drawled. "Let me wipe away my tears with a hundred dollar bill." He took another bite from his burger. "But while we're on memory lane, let me ask-" he gestured to the food spread out in front of them, "Was this always a happy meal?"

"What do you mean?"

"I mean, did your urge to become a rambling man kick up a notch every time some blue-eyed rancher's daughter gave your heart a kick in the nuts?"

Jack shrugged. His eyes stayed focused on his cup. "Maybe once or twice. Driving helps me sort things out."

"Sorted yet?"

Jack looked up from the Coke then. "Don't rush me, Luke," he warned.

Luke held his hands up. "Not rushing, just trying to get an idea of our estimated flight time. We've been on the road seven hours and we're up four hundred and twelve miles on the odometer. Just tell me who the record holder is."

Jack considered. "Becky Lambert, I guess. Summer after high school. Must have been fourteen hundred miles over three days."

Luke whistled. "Think we're going to beat that?"

Jack was silent, calculating imaginary maps across America and across his heart. Finally, he nodded. "Probably."

Then it was Luke's turn to consider. His mind, not an artist's, worked differently. It was a calculator- crunching numbers and running algorithms. Finally, it came to a conclusion.

"Hm," he said.

"'Hm,' what?"

"I'm going to assume that means it was Tracy that called it off on you and not the other way around."

"Don't start," Jack warned.

"Hey, if you don't want to tell me, then I'm stuck trying to figure it out for myself."

"She's done with me. That's all you need to know."

Luke leaned across the table. "No, not all I need to know. That girl was nuts for you, Jack. If she ended it that means there's a hell of a thing wrong with you that I don't know about. It's my job to take care of you, Jack. I can't do that if you're hiding things from me."

"It's your job to do whatever I tell you to do," Jack said. "And I'm telling you if you bring this up again then you can find yourself a ride back to LA."

In the silence that followed, Luke saw his real client for the first time since this whole mess with Tracy started. Jack was not really a fan of the type of music he created. There was no Rob Zombie, Black Sabbath, or Misfits on any of his personal playlists. He could pitch as many acoustic, stripped down albums as he wanted, but the truth was that Jackie Galindo's sound always was and always would be nothing but electric thunder set against a voice like a blender on high.

And this face right here was why. It didn't

matter what you liked to hear in your own ears, great music came from the gut and Jackie Galindo's guts were filled with nothing but fire and molten iron. You always saw it when he played, but Luke saw it now too. That fire and liquid metal poured out of him and you either got out of its way or you got burned alive.

So Luke got out of the way.

"Ok," he said. "Whatever you say, boss." He waved for the check. Their waitress brought it over, a fifty year old woman who looked like she'd never worked anywhere else in her life and didn't particularly seem to mind. She brought the check over on a dented, faded plastic tray that had probably been there longer than she had. Luke slapped down a hundred dollar bill without even looking at the bill. He stood up and slipped on his blazer.

"Come on, Jackie. Let's chase some telephone poles."

Jack didn't laugh. They left the diner in silence, the only sound between them was the phantom simmering of whatever Luke had stirred up.

Luke felt bad. Not because he was worried about getting fired, but because he was supposed to be along to make things better, not worse.

Well, your big mouth broke it, you're going to have to fix it.

"Hey!" he blurted out. "Let me drive a little, yeah? I want to double back to that last fork before we hit the diner. I got a feeling there's something worth checking out down the left hand pass or whatever. Maybe even a strip joint, and I swear to

God I didn't already look that up."

Jack cracked a grin and threw Luke the keys. "You're starting to get the hang of this."

"Not bad for a spoiled city boy."

They got into the car and turned left out of the lot.

A moment after they faded into the distance, four other cars pulled into the lot. A Porsche, an old Mustang, an Escalade, and a Ram Truck. All four vehicles as dark and sheenless as the fur of a black wolf, and their engines grumbled just as ferociously.

- - -

Jack and Luke's waitress' name was Anna. Contrary to what Luke thought, she actually had lived elsewhere. Back in 1984, she and two friends had thrown everything they owned into a Toyota Camry and went out to Los Angeles in search of fame and fortune. In eight months, they got exactly one gig- a hundred bucks each to be bikini girls in a Motley Crue video. Her friends had a blast and vowed to never leave. Anna got puked by Vince Neil, went back home to work in her father's diner, and never once questioned if she made the right decision.

She was manager and part owner these days. She could spend every shift sitting in the small office next to the walk-in cooler if she wanted to, but she still liked to occasionally come out and spend an hour manning the tables.

First were those two boys, LA boys if she'd ever seen two. And now here was a family of three.

374

Young parents and a four-year-old. Anna smiled to herself. A first born obviously, he had that swagger about him and his mother and father were scurrying about, clearly seeking his favor.

"Look, buddy! Check out all of those old pictures on the wall!"

"See the burger that girl had, Joey? Doesn't that look good?!"

Not that Anna was judging the child. Oh, she could and she had before but, little prince or not, the boy was smiling and holding his parents hands. Not kicking or throwing food everywhere, and that went a long way in Anna McCarthy's book. She went up to their table with her order pad in hand. "You folks coming or going?" she asked.

The father smiled proudly. Anna's picture of him in her head got a little clearer. Big promotion or a big new job about a year ago. This trip, wherever it was, was a victory lap of sorts.

"Coming back," he said. "Just made it out to the Grand Canyon."

Anna's eyes got wide, stretching out a little of that marginal acting talent she never put to use in LA. "Just? You don't *just* go out to the Grand Canyon! You say 'Oh my God! We came *all the way back* from the GRAND CANYON!" She fixed her attention on the little boy. "You must be starving! I hope you at least had some snacks in the car."

The boy, not such a little tyrant after all, grinned bashfully and couldn't look her in the eye. "Cookies," he mumbled.

"Cookies?!" she exclaimed. "You can't expect

a growing boy to make it all the way back from the Grand Canyon on just *cookies!* You look to me like you could use a milkshake. Does that sound about right?"

The boy looked to his mother first. "Go ahead, Eric," she said.

Permission granted, he beamed at Anna and held up two fingers. "Two, please!" he shouted.

"Coming right up," Anna said. "What else can I get you folks?" She took their orders and then went back into the kitchen, still smiling and shaking her head.

The smell hit her even before she made it through the swinging door, tantalizing hints of it riding the breeze out from under the door. Rodrigo had said he was going to experiment with some new barbecue sauces but God, something smelled fantastic.

"Roddy, whatever that is, save me a plate!"

Anna pushed the swinging door open and the full scent of Rodrigo's latest experiment filled her nostrils. She was reminded that she had once again neglected to take a meal break between lunch shift and dinner shift. She grabbed a biscuit from the bread station and went to the grill, hoping for at least a little extra sauce, just to get a taste.

She needn't have worried. There was plenty to spare.

Rodrigo lay face down on his own grill top. The flames were cranked all the way up, licking at the sizzling juices running down his bubbling, charred face. This close, the succulent scent of his roasted flesh was not just strong, it was the only

376

thing Anna could smell.

But not the only thing she could hear. There was another sound coming from behind her. A dull thumping like a heartbeat, and then a pattering like rain. Rain on an arid desert night.

It was the industrial dishwasher. The machine was running, even though it was half open. There was supposedly a switch that prevented it from starting when the steel box wasn't fully closed, but it had broken back in '95 and they'd never bothered to get it repaired. Normally, it wasn't a problem; but, every time they hired a new dish washer they could count on him running it partway open at least once. When that happened, water would overflow and come flooding over the edge of the countertop. Just like it was doing now.

But the water had never run pink before. Then again, the dishwashing machine had never run with the body of the dish washer crammed *inside of it* before. Luis' throat was ripped open. Clear water mixed with the red blood from the gaping wound, and the pink waterfall continued to pool on the linoleum floor.

Luis' twisted hand protruded from the dishwasher.

Not reaching out for me. Not really. He's dead.

Anna backed up anyway. She looked another twenty years older than her fifty-eight years. The layers of foundation were powerless to stop her from going pale as winter. The workings of terror made every line in her face stand out like dead riverbeds. She wanted to scream. Her hands, warped into claws of their own, pulled at her bottom jaw, opening it wider. The better to scream her head off with.

But she couldn't. She'd forgotten how. The only sounds in her memory now were the pumping of the dishwasher and the crackling of Rodrigo's burning hair.

It was coming though. *I have no memory, but I must scream.* Must scream because the terror and revulsion was too much to be denied. It was chipping away at the block in her throat. She could feel it. Any second now she would scream.

The drops fell into her open mouth. Maybe half a shot glass worth of hot copper.

Blood.

Anna looked up and Tony was there. The other waiter who'd gone to take a smoke break. He was pinned to the ceiling. Held there by butcher knives through his shoulders and knees.

Skewered. Bleeding. And worst of all, not dead. His hands were not impaled, and he reached towards her, even as more droplets of blood sprinkled her face.

"Run," he croaked.

Run. Not *Help me.* Just *Run.*

Anna staggered back towards the door, helpless eyes still fixated on Tony. She still couldn't scream, but her feet still worked. She was going to get the hell out of there.

She hit something solid and cold. *The cooler. You're going the wrong way! Focus, Anna!* Yes. Focus. She needed to stop looking at what had already happened. She needed to pay attention to where she was.

But then she turned around and what commanded her attention instead was the realization that she had not walked into the freezer.

She had walked into the lead figure in a pack of four. She'd run into the largest of four... *things* that had somehow moved in to take up half of her kitchen without her even knowing it.

Anna stared. She knew in a split-second flare of instinct that these... *things* had massacred her staff, but the terror that struck her at the sight of *them* was different than the horror of witnessing their handiwork. This fear was simpler and far more primal. It was the fear of being prey in a trap.

Quick as she knew this. She knew she was too late to do anything.

Too late, even to scream.

ABOUT THE AUTHOR

Sean McDonough lives in New York with his wonderful wife, beautiful daughter, and a room full of books. He has been a reality TV writer and writer for hire of low-budget horror movies that never get made. His first novel, *Beverly Kills*, is available at Amazon.com, Barnesandnoble.com, and the iTunes bookstore.

Get news about upcoming works at:

https://www.facebook.com/houseoftheboogeyman